"To hell with fireworks!

"I'll settle for companionship. Fireworks screwed up my life once before. But now my life's back on track and I'm not about to jeopardize it for . . . for a tawdry affair."

Mac took a deep breath and leaned back. "Holly, I'm not thinking of a tawdry affair. I'm thinking that you and I might really have something—something fantastic and unbelievable, something precious. I'm thinking of marriage, Holly, of children, of us growing old together. I'm asking you, Holly—I'm begging you—to just give us a chance. Oh, Holly, I don't want to spend the rest of my life wondering, what if?"

Holly looked down, avoiding Mac's gaze. But he still held her hands in his and his words still rang in her ears. And she had to admit the truth. She was already emotionally involved with Mac. If she didn't give her and Mac a chance, then she, too, might spend the rest of her life wondering, what if?

ABOUT THE AUTHOR

Like her heroine in *Prize Passage*, Dawn
Stewardson was born and raised in Winnipeg,
Manitoba, where forty below is a fact of
winter life. That made the idea of sending her
heroine to the Caribbean for a Christmas
cruise particularly appealing. "But the best
part about writing this book," she told us,
"was doing the research—I went on my first
Caribbean cruise. The worst part came after
we got home and I had to lose the five pounds
I gained at the midnight buffets."

Books by Dawn Stewardson

HARLEQUIN SUPERROMANCE
329–VANISHING ACT
355–DEEP SECRETS
383–BLUE MOON

HARLEQUIN INTRIGUE
80–PERIL IN PARADISE
90–NO RHYME OR REASON

Prize Passage

DAWN STEWARDSON

Harlequin Books

TORONTO • NEW YORK • LONDON
AMSTERDAM • PARIS • SYDNEY • HAMBURG
STOCKHOLM • ATHENS • TOKYO • MILAN

Published May 1990

ISBN 0-373-70405-4

To D'Arcy Lynn,
who reminded me how delicious
dry brownie mix tastes.

And to my fellow passengers
on the MTS *Odysseus*,
with thanks for sharing their experiences and ideas—
Marsha, Joy, Marion and Stanley.

And to John, always.

CHAPTER ONE

HOLLY GAZED at the glass-on-glass headquarters of the NBS network, fearful she was starting to hallucinate. The building was looking more like a giant ice cube by the second. A frosty, deliciously cold, ice cube.

She concentrated on breathing shallowly and keeping her lips pressed together. Seeing and smelling the infamous L.A. smog was bad enough, but tasting it? Until today the possibility of air being chewable had never occurred to her.

And the heat! This holding pen—this "exterior audience waiting area" as the girl who'd taken their tickets had called it—was an outdoor sauna.

Holly slid stickily along the wooden bench after her mother, making room for two new arrivals. The couple was so engrossed in discussing their game plan that they seemed oblivious to the crowd already waiting for the interviews to begin.

Interviews. The ticket taker's concept of an "interview" was a joke. According to her, the producer and his assistant would talk with every member of the audience before they entered the studio. Three hundred "interviews" in one hour. It didn't take a math whiz to calculate that meant barely ten seconds per person.

Well, Holly Russell would give them a break. She'd need scarcely any of her allotted seconds to tell them she had no interest in being a contestant on their game show.

Of course, *no interest* was a polite understatement. On her list of things to do in California, even being part of the studio audience for *Your Knowledge Is Your Ticket* ranked only marginally above experiencing an earthquake.

The show was targeted at morons, with a stage decked out like a giant map of the world. Watching three people racing around it, each trying to be first to locate places, was definitely not her idea of entertainment.

How could people in their right minds be eager for a chance to make complete fools of themselves in front of millions of viewers? And how could one of those eager people be her own mother?

Holly glanced surreptitiously at Kay. Nothing visibly hinted she'd become a game show fanatic. She looked... well, she looked like a normal, sensible person, like an older version of Holly. A small woman with delicate features and large brown eyes.

And at the moment, Holly forced herself to admit, her mother looked happy. Probably because she was anticipating the stupid game show! But she *did* look happy. And lifting Kay out of her doldrums had been the whole point of this trip.

Saying she'd made a poor adjustment to widowhood was a distinct understatement. Over the past three years she'd evolved from a vibrant, sociable doctor's wife to a reclusive, game show watching, couch potato.

A visit to Kay's sister in Santa Barbara had seemed the perfect way to jolt her out of her boring daily routine. And once they'd decided to trek all the way from

Canada to California, this stop in Los Angeles—with extra days spent at Disneyland and Universal Studios—had been a natural wrap-up to their vacation.

But Holly hadn't counted on her mother writing to *Your Knowledge Is Your Ticket*...hadn't imagined finding herself dragged along to a taping of the show.

She looked around, wondering if any of the eager-faced people surrounding her could possibly want to be a contestant as desperately as her mother did. Some personality quirk had made Kay obsessed with winning "a dream vacation."

She'd been studying geography for weeks, preparing for today as if she were facing finals. Since those darned tickets had appeared in Kay's mailbox, Holly had spent endless evenings with an atlas on her lap, quizzing her mother about locations of countries, cities, mountains and rivers.

Kay could probably win if she was picked to appear on stage. But her odds on that were three out of three hundred. Well, not quite three hundred, Holly silently amended. There was at least one member of the audience who wasn't in the running for contestant status.

"May I have your attention please?"

Three hundred pairs of eyes fixed gazes on a girl of nineteen or twenty—a typically gorgeous, leggy, Miss California type. She had the precise looks Holly had always envied. Tall and slim with straight corn-silk hair instead of ginger curls that frizzed at the first hint of humidity. And not even a sprinkling of freckles.

Holly absently rubbed the bridge of her nose. Her own freckles—the ones she'd been so happy to see fade away with the last of her teenage years—had mysteriously begun reappearing during these two weeks of endless sunshine.

"We'll be starting the interviews in just a few moments," Miss California announced. "Please ensure that you've signed the consent forms you were given when you arrived. And please have them ready for us, along with a piece of identification—driver's license if you've got one."

Two hundred and ninety-nine pairs of hands reached for identification.

"Holly?" Kay murmured, pulling her wallet from her purse.

"Mom, I've told you a hundred times. I don't mind sitting in the audience with you, but there's no way I'm taking a chance on hearing my name called out."

"I simply don't understand you, dear."

"Ditto," Holly muttered under her breath.

"I'd like you to follow along with me now," the blonde instructed, "and line up beside the studio. We won't keep you outside in this heat much longer."

The audience members rose with a collective sigh of relief and began shuffling into a ragged line. Eventually it started inching along the side of the NBS building.

Miss California had stationed herself near the back corner and was collecting consent forms and checking identification as the line straggled past. She'd been joined by a young man who rapidly printed a large name tag for each person.

When Holly and Kay reached them, the girl took Kay's form, glanced at her driver's license, then eyed Holly uncertainly. "You have to be at least eighteen to be allowed in the audience. It said that right on your ticket."

Holly drew herself up to her full five foot one. "I'm twenty-nine years old."

"Oh! I thought you were younger than me." The blonde smiled down an apology. "If you'd just show me some ID and give me your consent form, then?"

"Well, no, I don't want to consent to anything. I don't want to be a contestant. I'm just here to watch."

The girl's stare clearly said Holly was feeble-minded. "Everyone wants to be a contestant. That's why they come to the show."

"No, not everyone. I don't."

"Oh . . . well you can't be a member of the audience without filling out a form."

"But I don't want my name on your list."

"Sorry. Studio rules. If we don't have a form, you can't watch the taping."

"Holly," Kay said anxiously, "I don't want to go into the studio by myself."

"Just tell the producer you're not interested in being a contestant," the young man suggested, pressing a pen into Holly's hand and handing Kay her name tag.

Holly reluctantly pulled out the form she'd stuffed into her pocket. Name, address and a statement to sign, declaring she hadn't appeared on any television game show in the past two years.

Well . . . it seemed innocent enough. Aware of the growing restlessness behind her, she quickly filled in the blanks, handed over the paper, then dug into her purse for her driver's license. Ahead of them the line of people had turned the corner of the building. Holly produced her ID.

The young man slipped a name tag to her. He'd drawn a sprig of holly beside her name.

With an effort she managed not to grimace, wishing for the millionth time in twenty-nine years that her mother hadn't seen *Breakfast at Tiffany's* during her pregnancy, that she hadn't been enchanted by Audrey Hepburn as Holly Golightly.

Kay grabbed her daughter's arm and hustled her forward. They whirled around the corner and almost smacked into a table. On the far side of it sat a rotund, middle-aged man sporting a scraggly beard and a third-rate toupee. His eyes were almost hidden behind purple-tinted glasses.

A girl who smelled as if she'd bathed in cheap perfume was perched on one corner of the table. Her thin blouse was unbuttoned practically to her naval; her skirt covered her behind with a quarter inch to spare.

No one, Holly thought, could have come up with a more perfect-looking couple to produce *Your Knowledge Is Your Ticket.*

Pencil poised above a clipboard, the girl watched the man glance from Kay to Holly. "Where's your name tag?"

Holly flashed it at him. "I didn't put it on because I don't want to be a contestant. My mother does, though. And she'd be terrific. She's great at geography."

He eyed the tag. "Holly, eh? Cute name. Did you know we were taping for December today? For the Christmas week shows?"

"In August?"

"Yeah. Lead time. What do you do for a living, Holly?"

"I'm a child psychologist. But I definitely don't want to be a contestant. I'm only here to watch."

"Fine. Just put that tag on, though, would you, doll? Just in case the camera pans you during an audience shot." The man turned his attention from Holly.

She peeled the paper backing off the tag and stuck it onto her dress, praying no camera would pan her. If anyone she knew learned she'd come to this asinine show, she'd die! She certainly hoped Kay appreciated the way her only child catered to her whims.

"And you, Kay. What do you do?"

"I'm a housewife. A widowed housewife, that is. Holly and I are here on vacation from Winnipeg. Winnipeg, Manitoba. I love your show—watch it every afternoon."

"Watch it up in Canada, huh? Must be a lot of snow up there in December."

"Oh, there certainly is. Winnipeg usually has several feet of snow by Christmas."

"Several feet of snow. Cute. You said your daughter lives in Winnipeg, too?"

Kay nodded.

"Well thanks, ladies. Next, please."

An usher led them into the studio.

HOLLY SAT on the edge of her bed in the Pacifica Hotel, staring unseeingly out the window.

"Darling," Kay trilled, "I just don't understand why you aren't bubbling over with excitement. You were wonderful. I couldn't have done any better myself. That's even silly to say, isn't it? Of course I couldn't have done any better. You won, didn't you? And really, Holly, I'm not at all disappointed they picked you and not me. Watching you on that stage— you scampering around and finding places—was every bit as exciting as if it had been me. Just think. All those evenings you helped me bone up on geography were worth it after all.''

"Worth it? Good grief, Mother! Worth what? Knowing where to *scamper*? Making a damn fool of myself? I must have looked like the proverbial chicken with its head cut off!''

"Holly...you just won a two-week Christmas cruise in the Caribbean! Why are you having hysterics instead of dancing for joy?''

"Shock," Holly muttered. "I must have gone into shock when that lunatic announcer screamed out my name and the camera focused on me. Shock's the only possible explanation. Otherwise I'd have run for the door instead of letting them drag me onto that stage.''

"Well, the shock will soon wear off, dear. Then you'll start looking forward to the trip. Imagine! Spending Christmas sunbathing in the Caribbean instead of bundling up and fighting your way through snowdrifts.''

"Right! Sunbathing in the Caribbean and having nightmares about how many people back in Winnipeg are seeing me on that show. The tape's going to be aired during the Christmas break, Mom. Absolutely the worst possible time. All kinds of people will be at home who'd normally be at work or school. Some of my patients are bound to be watching. And their parents. Just what I need. Half the time they can't remember I'm an adult as it is. And now they're going to see me making a childish idiot of myself on television.''

"Holly, you didn't make an idiot of yourself. An idiot wouldn't have won.''

"Thanks. At least that's *some* consolation. At least I didn't come off as a complete dummy. But I must have looked ludicrous—running around on that stupid giant map!"

"Holly, for goodness sake, lighten up! Listening to you, anyone would think you'd been filmed robbing a convenience store."

Holly forced a smile, certain it looked as phony as it felt. "Sorry. I guess I'm making a bigger deal out of this than I should. It's just...well, you know how hard I've had to work at creating a professional image. And playing a stupid game on television sure isn't going to enhance it. I probably looked twelve years old."

"*Twelve* is definitely an exaggeration, Holly."

"Thirteen, then. Sometimes I wish I'd inherited Daddy's looks instead of yours."

"Your father," Kay said dryly, "had a big nose, a weight problem and went bald in his thirties."

Holly laughed despite herself. "I must admit I'd rather have thick hair than a bald spot. Or an awful toupee like the one that producer was wearing." She collapsed back onto the bed in a fit of giggles. "Oh, Mom, the moment I saw those two I realized why that show's so darn tasteless. He looked like a 'before' photo for a hair replacement advertisement, and she looked as if she'd just wandered in from a long night of walking the streets."

Kay grinned. "I'm glad to see your sense of humor's returned."

"Well...I guess it *was* stretching pretty thin, wasn't it? It's just that I try so hard not to get caught without my best adult foot forward. Then something like this happens."

"What do you mean, something like this? You mean being forced to spend two weeks on a cruise? That's going to be pretty hard to take, isn't it?"

"Mmm…well…maybe not incredibly hard. You're right, of course. I'm being silly. I should be looking on the bright side."

Holly closed her eyes for a moment, trying to picture herself and David on a cruise. It would be so restful…so romantic. Maybe it would be just what they needed to ignite more sparks between them. She smiled at her mother. "I guess I can always hope there'll be a power blackout the day my tape's aired."

"That's right, dear. Anything's possible. And even if Winnipeg Hydro doesn't cooperate, you'll be so relaxed by the time we get back that any teasing you might face won't bother you at all."

Holly stared at Kay, feeling her smile slipping, ordering her lips to remain curved. *We?* Had her mother said, "By the time *we* get back"?

Holly's mind raced. She'd simply assumed she'd take David on the cruise with her. After all, he was her fiancé.

"We've had so much fun on this trip, haven't we, dear?" Kay murmured wistfully. "You know, this is the first time I've really felt alive since your father died. I'll bet we'll have a marvelous cruise."

Holly eyed her mother's expectant expression. It clearly hadn't occurred to Kay that she might not be the one invited along. But why should it? After all, if she hadn't insisted on attending *Your Knowledge Is Your Ticket* there would be no cruise for anyone to go on.

But there was a cruise. And if Kay wasn't on it, if she was left alone at Christmas, she'd undoubtedly be depressed.

Being deserted over the holidays would likely undo all the good this vacation had done. Whereas another trip—a break from winter—would keep up the momentum this vacation had started, would help ensure Kay really began living again.

Holly carefully adjusted her smile, hoping David would understand. She'd have a lifetime to spend with him. She could give her mother another two weeks.

"You're right, Mom. We'll have a marvelous cruise."

DAVID LAWRENCE'S silver Mercedes crept along the icy pavement of Wellington Avenue, its headlights casting ghostly beams through the early-morning darkness. The car's interior was as warm as toast. But outside a strong wind whipped falling snow across the flat ribbon of road. The streetlights seemed to twinkle with each snowy gust that swirled around them.

Ahead, as the car passed the International Inn, the shoe box shape of Winnipeg's airport became visible. David switched his windshield wipers to a faster speed, then glanced into the back at Kay. "You two may not get away, after all."

The sudden roar of a plane overhead almost drowned out his voice. He shot Holly a rueful, side-long smile. "So much for my odds on getting to keep you here," he murmured, focusing on the road once more.

Holly looked across the front seat at David's even profile, wishing he hadn't insisted on driving them to the airport. His being so sweet was making her feel even more guilty about going on this cruise without him.

She'd explained the situation as soon as she'd arrived back from California. He hadn't been happy about the idea of her taking Kay instead of him, but he'd understood. And, by the time Kay had realized she'd been presumptuous, that Holly might have preferred her fiancé's company, the matter had been settled.

Settled. But not entirely to Holly's satisfaction. Much as she loved her mother, she didn't want to do a Siamese twins routine during the entire vacation. And even though Kay realized she'd grown far too dependent on her daughter over the past few years and had promised not to be a clinging vine on the cruise, promising and following through were two different things.

Holly gazed at David again, wishing for the thousandth time that he was the one going with her. They could do with two weeks alone together. They were so right for each other. All they needed was an opportunity to kindle a little passion in their relationship. That, she assured herself once more, might develop with time. But if it didn't, she could easily live without it.

She'd had passion. And despite it her short-lived first marriage had been a disaster. The compatibility she shared with David was far more important than the irrational, hormonal imbalance of passion.

Hormones clearly weren't to be trusted. At least not Holly Russell's.

Of course, five years ago at the ripe old age of twenty-four, she hadn't realized she'd been temporarily transformed into Holly Hormone, that insanity was the driving force behind her marriage to Brad Houghton. At the time he'd seemed perfect. In fact, her entire life had seemed perfect.

Within a few short months of her twenty-fourth birthday, she'd completed a master's degree, been accepted into the psychology department's Ph.D. program and became a bride. She'd thought she had the world by the tail. But she'd thought wrong.

After eighteen months of marriage, Brad had left her. Then, only a few weeks later, her father had died.

What a horrific time that had been. She'd battled her double dose of grief by immersing herself in work, tripling the hours she'd been devoting to her doctoral studies.

The time she hadn't spent with Kay, she'd worked on her research, then on honing her thesis to an acceptible quality. And that work had resulted in a Ph.D. As a bonus, her thesis research—about birth order and its ramifications for adult relationships—had enabled her to pinpoint what had caused the problems between herself and Brad.

He was the baby in his family, the youngest of five children. He'd grown up accustomed to being spoiled by everyone around him. And Holly was an only child, accustomed to spoiling no one.

If she and Brad had met later, after she'd learned about the importance of birth order, she'd have run for the hills the moment they were introduced. But way back then she hadn't known enough to run.

Now she knew better, knew she should marry an eldest sibling, knew that was the best possible mate for an only child. She needed an eldest son like David. *No, I need* David, her mind absently corrected itself, *not someone* like *David.*

Dr. David Lawrence was absolutely perfect for her. This time she'd even change her name. Well, she'd at least hyphenate it to Russell-Lawrence.

David pulled the Mercedes to a halt in front of the terminal and smiled across the front seat. "Here you are. Delivered safe and sound."

Holly laughed. "That sounds more like something an obstetrician would say than a cardiologist."

"Never mind what my specialty is. Just be careful to stay safe and sound until you get home." He glanced at her hands as she began pulling on her gloves. "You aren't wearing your diamond."

"No. The cruise book we read advised against taking good jewelry. The only thing I wore is my gold chain."

A frown flickered across David's face and he looked into the back. "I'm counting on you to watch out for her, Kay. I don't want any charming ship's officer putting a move on my fiancée."

"I'm sure you have nothing to worry about, David. But I promise to play the perfect chaperone. If nothing else, my guilt will make me. I still feel awkward taking this vacation when you're staying behind. I should have insisted that you go."

David shrugged as if the matter was insignificant. "Cardiac Care's a busy unit this time of year—all the excitement of the holidays and people overindulging. Mercy Hospital will be jumping for the next couple of weeks. It's just as well I'll be around."

"But, David, I still feel so—"

"It's all right, Kay. Really. Holly and I will have a lot of vacations together. You have a good time on this one."

Holly smiled to herself, silently thanking David for his kindness. This time she really did have the world by the tail.

CHAPTER TWO

MAC MCCLOY OPENED his eyes to the morning light and grabbed the motion sickness remedy beside his bed. The cabin was swaying like a gently rocking cradle. But the churning inside his stomach was a far cry from gentle rocking. He downed half of what was left in the bottle, silently cursing his stupidity.

Why hadn't it occurred to him that he might be prone to sea sickness? Even buying this one bottle of medicine had been a last-moment impulse. And he'd only picked it up in case his son had problems. Mac glanced across the cabin to where the boy was still sleeping peacefully.

Jason was clearly a born sailor. But Mac obviously wasn't. And he should have come better prepared. From what he'd seen last night, half the passengers had little patches stuck behind their ears—apparently infused with a time-release wonder drug that guaranteed smooth sailing.

Why hadn't he heard about the patches when all those other people had? They must be weekend sailors, he decided. That's what came of living in Colorado. It wasn't exactly the Great Lake State.

He gazed around, reacquainting himself with his surroundings, not wanting to get up until his nausea eased. The cabin was larger than he'd expected and more attractively decorated—gray carpeting, burgundy bedspreads, walls of rich wood paneling, a pair of gray armchairs on either side of the window. That window had surprised him. He'd expected a porthole.

All in all, for a last-minute booking, he'd done well. He looked over at Jason again, wondering once more why his ex-wife had suddenly offered to let them spend Christmas together. Over the past five years, since she'd taken their son east, Margaret had used her custody of him as a weapon.

Odds were, there was a hidden agenda behind her sudden generosity. And odds also were, whatever it was would come back to haunt Mac somewhere down the line. But he wasn't going to worry about that now. He and Jason would have a great time on this cruise.

From the moment they'd landed in Barbados yesterday, the boy had practically bubbled with excitement. And even Mac had felt a rush at sighting the *Taurus*, the flagship of the Greek Athena Line. It had been docked at the end of Bridgetown's main pier, its sparkling white hull towering from the water, its seven decks dwarfing the other vessels moored in the harbor.

And Jason had clearly considered their boarding an adventure in itself—the photographer snapping their picture on the steep metal gangway steps, the endless welcoming committee of white-uniformed crew members greeting them at the top, the room steward leading them to their cabin. Then—

"Dad?"

"Morning, son."

"What time is it, Dad?"

"Let's see...a little past seven."

The boy scrambled up. "We have to get going, then. Don't forget there's a lifeboat drill this morning. And we've got to eat breakfast first. You don't want to miss breakfast, do you?''

Mac grinned, relieved he hadn't heard any mention of breakfast before his stomach had settled. "Right. We don't want to miss breakfast." He climbed out of bed. With Jason as a traveling companion, there probably wasn't going to be much missing of anything.

"GOOD MORNING, ladies and gentlemen," a cheery female voice greeted them via the public address system. "International shipping regulations require all passengers to assemble at their muster stations for our nine o'clock lifeboat drill. Seven whistles will sound shortly, signaling commencement of this drill. The location of your station is posted on the back of your cabin door. Life vests are stored in your closet. Please bring them with you to your station."

Holly Russell headed across the cabin, pausing on her way past the dresser to smell the sweetheart roses that had been waiting for her when they'd boarded the *Taurus*. From David. With a card reading, "Save the next cruise for me."

She dug the orange Mae Wests out of the bottom of the closet, rechecked the posted letter of their muster station, then glanced at her watch. "It's not quite a quarter to nine, Mom. Let's have a quick look at that activities program."

Kay passed Holly their copy of *Taurus Today*. "You look, dear. My glasses are in my purse."

Holly flipped over the front page that boldly proclaimed December 23, at Sea, then scanned the list of events. There seemed to be enough going on to fill the entire two weeks, not merely the first day. Likely, she decided, that was because this was one of the few days they wouldn't be spending in a port.

"Here's something interesting," she noted, glancing hopefully at her mother. "Seniors Get-Acquainted Morning. In the Socrates Lounge immediately following the lifeboat drill. 'Share your midmorning coffee with new friends.'"

Kay made a face. "I'm only fifty-eight. That's hardly a *senior*."

"No, of course not. I guess they just mean people...I guess maybe they just mean *mature* people. That would be a better way of putting it. But this says, 'All passengers aged fifty-five and over are cordially invited. Come and learn about special events and shore tours organized with our senior passengers in mind.'"

"Holly, I don't want to go on shore tours with the geriatric set. I'll go on the ones you go on. I'm not exactly in a wheelchair."

"I wasn't implying you were. I was simply pointing out an obvious way to meet people you have something in common with."

"'Something in common' is people who like to play bridge or golf, dear. Not being fifty-five or over."

"I was only making a suggestion, Mother." Holly paused, forcing a smile and ordering the sharpness out of her voice. "Mom, we talked about not spending every minute of this two weeks together. You agreed with me about needing to get out and meet new people. You agreed you'd do that on this cruise. You know that since Daddy died you've been—"

"Holly, for goodness sake don't start analyzing me again!"

"I'm not analyzing you. Psychologists don't analyze. It's psychoanalysts who analyze."

"And don't lecture me on medical specialties. I was married to a doctor. I know who does what."

"I wasn't lecturing. I was merely reminding you that you agreed to make an effort to socialize on this cruise. You *do* remember that, don't you?"

"Of course I remember," Kay said testily. "I'm not becoming senile—despite the *Taurus* pronouncing me a *senior*. But we talked about socializing with people, not with categories."

"Mother, *senior* isn't a dirty word. The people at the get-together aren't going to be a bunch of old fogies any more than you are. The old fogies vacation in Florida. And you promised, Mother."

"Oh, all right. If it'll make you happy. But what are you going to do while I'm talking to people whose hearing aids probably don't work?"

Holly gazed down at *Taurus Today*, hiding her triumphant smile. "Oh, I don't know. I might just sit on deck and read...although I don't want to spend too much time in the sun the first day out.... Or, here's a note about a lecture in the library—on snorkeling."

She glanced at the Junior Cruisers Activities section of the page. "Oh. There's a screening of *E.T.* for the kids—in the Euripides Lounge at ten o'clock."

"*E.T.*? Holly, that movie's been around for years. How many times have you seen it?"

"Mmm...I think eight."

"And that's another fine example of putting your best adult foot forward, right?"

Holly laughed. "Well, maybe not. But it's one of the all-time great movies. Besides, talking about it is a good icebreaker with new patients. I haven't come across a child yet who hasn't seen *E. T.* Tell you what, Mom. You go to the get-acquainted morning and I'll watch *E. T.* Then we'll have lunch together. The movie notice says the Euripides Lounge is on the Plato Deck—the one with the pool.''

The ship's whistle erupted into a series of short blasts. Holly grabbed their two copies of the deck plan, scooped up the life vests and handed one of each to her mother. ''Why don't we meet by the pool?'' she shouted above the noise. ''Around noon? Deal?''

''Deal.'' Kay mouthed the word back with an unconcealed lack of enthusiasm.

The seventh blast ended as they left the cabin. Holly could hear her mother muttering but pretended not to notice as they headed along the passageway, following the signs for Muster Station C.

They were walking, she realized, like drunken sailors, listing from side to side, frequently clutching for support at the railing that ran along one wall between the cabin doors. The term *sea legs* popped into her mind as she lurched onto a staircase. She certainly hoped sea legs didn't take long to acquire.

MUSTER STATION C TURNED out to be the disco on the lifeboat deck. From there a ship's officer pointed Kay and Holly in the general direction of their assigned places outside. ''Any problem finding them, just ask a crew member. In a few minutes,'' he added, ''we'll be checking that everyone has their vests on properly and be running over basic safety information.''

Kay and Holly nodded and stepped outside onto the Zeno Deck. All the orange life vests made it look like a human pumpkin patch. It was impossible to catch even a glimpse of the sea through the crowd.

Holly noticed that some passengers were already wearing their life vests. Others were struggling into them. A few simply stood clutching them and looking lost, apparently awaiting explicit instructions. Irregular, shrill toots pierced the air as, one by one, people discovered the red plastic whistles attached to their Mae Wests.

"Surely this can't be difficult," she murmured, pausing to thrust her arms through the openings in her own vest. Kay continued heading across the deck, apparently confident she knew her destination.

"Rats!"

Holly glanced at the source of the exclamation. Beside her a little boy of nine or ten was wrestling with his vest.

He gazed up at her with huge blue eyes, then gave an exaggerated shrug that sent the vest slipping off his shoulders and down his skinny arms. "I've never worn one of these before."

Holly looked around. The child seemed to be alone. Mentally criticizing his parents, she knelt in front of him. "Let's see. I think if you just put your arms through here . . ." She held the opening.

The boy obediently thrust his arm through it. "But see?" he demanded. "It wraps around too far for my other arm to reach."

"You're absolutely right. The problem's not with you at all. The problem's with this silly vest. I'll bet they come in a smaller size. If you asked one of the crew . . ."

The lower portion of a naked male leg stepped into Holly's peripheral vision and stopped. A split second later it was joined by its mate.

Holly focused on them, her hands still on the boy's vest, her gaze drifting curiously upward, slowing at the bare knees, noting a long surgical scar down the inside of one of them. Just as she decided that letting her eyes wander any farther would be rude, the man dropped to his knees beside her, and she was staring at a thirty-something version of the little boy's face.

Clearly this was the child's father. The two had the same boyish good looks. And the same enormous blue eyes...eyes the exact midnight-blue of the man's Bermuda shorts and tank top...the man's tank top that, beneath his unfastened Mae West, was clinging to a muscular chest and exposing strong-looking arms...

But why on earth was she staring at this man's body? She ordered her gaze back to his face and was caught once more by his gorgeous eyes. She'd kill for long dark lashes like his.

"Hi. I'm Mac McCloy." He shot her a friendly grin...a friendly grin that ended in a crooked little tilt on the right-hand side.

"Hi. Holly Russell." She smiled back. Not to would have been impossible; Mac's grin was infectious.

He turned his attention to the child. "Problem, Jason?"

"Nope. No problem with me, Dad. The problem's with this silly vest. I'll bet they come in a smaller size. If you asked one of the crew..."

Holly almost laughed aloud. Jason was a veritable parrot.

"You're right, son. Give me that one and I'll go trade it in for you."

Holly bit back the unsolicited advice that leaped to the tip of her tongue. Jason was old enough to make the trade himself. His father should simply steer him in the right direction. But what Mac McCloy should do, she told herself firmly, was absolutely none of her business. Dr. Holly Russell, child psychologist, was officially on vacation. She glanced surreptitiously back at Mac as Jason shrugged out of the vest and handed it over.

The man's face was interesting—but merely in comparison to his son's, of course. The two had the same strong chin and straight nose. And, like Jason, Mac had a lock of dark hair falling onto his forehead.

Tucking Jason's vest under his arm, Mac rose. Holly found herself staring at his naked legs again and scrambled to her feet, looking everywhere but at him. The majority of men on deck, she realized, were wearing shorts. Why was she so aware of Mac's legs when she hadn't even noticed any others?

Because none of the others had practically walked into her face, she told herself, answering her own question. That was the only reason. She concentrated on looking straight ahead, which focused her eyes midpoint on Mac's chest.

"I'll just be a minute, son." He started away, then paused looking back. "Wait right there, Jason. Don't get lost again. Being a one-man search party is wearing me down."

"Okay, Dad. I won't."

Holly watched Mac stride off, wondering how keeping track of one small boy could present a grown man with problems. She sensed Jason watching her and turned.

He was eyeing her with a conspiratorial grin. "I haven't really been getting lost. My dad tends to over-react."

This time she did laugh out loud. "Tends to over-react? Where did you get a phrase like that?"

"My mom. She's always saying my dad tends to overreact. She's a psychologist."

"That's quite a coincidence. I'm a psychologist, too."

Jason stared at Holly for a long moment, his expression unreadable. "Anyway," he finally went on, apparently deciding to ignore the coincidence, "I haven't really been getting lost. I've just been checking out the ship and I got a little mixed up a few times."

Holly nodded her understanding. "How many times have you not really gotten lost so far?"

"Oh . . . five or six. But I've got everything figured out now."

"Good for you. I have a deck plan in my pocket. I guess I'm not as adventurous as you are."

"I had a deck plan, too. But it sort of blew away . . . out of my hands and right down into the water."

"I'll have to hold tight to mine, then. Even with a map I'm terrible at directions."

"Oh, I can tell you exactly where everything is. Where are you going from here?"

"Well, after the drill, I'm going to the Euripides Lounge. Do you know how to get there?"

"Sure! That's where I'm going, too. You just go down one flight of stairs and to the front . . . to the bow," Jason corrected himself with a grin. "It's called

the bow on the ship. But that's where they're showing
E.T. Why are you going there?''

"To watch the movie. You don't think anyone
would mind an adult sneaking in, do you?''

The boy shook his head.

"Good. Because *E.T.*'s still my favorite movie.''

"Really? It's still mine, too! What part do you like
best?''

"Oh . . . there are so many good scenes. But I always laugh the first time Elliot and E.T. are on Elliot's
bicycle and E.T. makes it fly.''

Jason nodded rapidly. "That's a good one. But I
like it better when all the boys are on their bikes and
they ride them over top of the police car. And my all-
time best part is when the kids set the frogs free in the
classroom.''

Holly smiled. It was easy to imagine Jason himself
gleefully letting a horde of frogs out of jars.

"How many times have you seen *E.T.*, Holly? Is it
all right for me to call you Holly?''

"Sure. It's fine. And I've seen *E.T.* eight times.''

"Really?''

"Really.''

"All right! I've seen it twelve. And my mom's seen
it four. But my dad says two is his absolute limit.''

"Your dad says two is his absolute limit for what?''
Mac's voice interrupted.

Jason grinned up at his father. "*E.T.*, Dad. Holly's seen *E.T.* eight times already. And she's going to
watch it again this morning.''

Mac shot Holly a quizzical look.

She shrugged. "Great movie.''

"I think I'd rather be in the fresh air," Mac said, holding out a junior-size life vest to Jason. "Let's have a shot at this one, son."

"Maybe I'll see you at the movie, Jason," Holly told him. "Right now, though, I have to catch up to my mother. Bye." She gave them a quick wave, fleetingly wondering where Jason's mother was, and hurried in the direction she'd last seen Kay.

Mac absently helped Jason fasten the vest, his gaze following Holly Russell until she disappeared into the crowd. That didn't take long. She was awfully tiny, not more than six or seven inches taller than Jason.

Darned pretty, though. Dancing dark eyes, long reddish-brown hair. And a thousand-watt smile that had grabbed two hundred percent of his attention each time she'd flashed it.

But she was probably even younger than he'd initially guessed. Years younger. That white cotton jumpsuit had fooled him. She looked cool and sophisticated in it. And her perfume. Selling that teasing perfume to minors should be illegal.

But Holly Russell had to be a minor—or not much beyond. No real adult would have sat through *E. T.* eight times. And she had to catch up to her mother. That was a pretty solid clue.

Mac shook his head. Thirty-five years old, a divorced man with a ten-year-old son, ogling a girl of...he didn't even want to think about how young she might be.

He'd never been a cradle robber and now was definitely not the time to start. He could just imagine the expression on his ex-wife's face if Jason even hinted that—

Mac tried to erase Margaret's image from his mind. For Jason's sake he wished he could manage to think of the woman without gritting his teeth. It certainly wasn't the boy's fault that she was his mother. That was entirely Mac's doing. He was the fool who'd married her.

Why hadn't he married a teacher or a nurse? Anything but a psychologist!

He'd never been able to decide whether studying psychology turned people into manipulative know-it-alls, or whether the profession simply attracted that type of person. But if his dealings with Margaret and her associates were a reliable indication, all the psychologists on earth must think they knew what was best for everyone they came into contact with. They were the most condescending, controlling, manipulative—

"Did you like Holly, Dad?"

"Ah ... yeah, sure, she seemed fine."

"Did you like her better than Judy?"

"Better than Judy?" Mac stared at Jason for a moment before the light clicked on inside his head.

"Jason, Judy and I are just friends. Seeing her has simply gotten to be a habit. You know that. Every time you ask, I tell you I have no intention of marrying her."

Jason shrugged. "Then how come she hangs around your apartment all the time?"

"She doesn't, Jason."

"When I visited you last summer, she was there almost every day, making me watch her dumb game shows when I wanted to watch baseball."

"Son, I know you don't like Judy. You've made that perfectly clear. But forget about her. She isn't 'hanging around' nearly as much anymore."

Jason merely gazed at Mac with an expression of apparent disbelief.

"Don't worry about Judy. Okay? I doubt she'll be around at all by next summer." In fact, Mac added silently, after the row they'd had about his taking Jason on this cruise instead of her, Judy probably wouldn't even be around in January.

Not that it mattered much. Their relationship certainly wasn't going—

"But did you like Holly better, Dad?"

"Jason, was *The Dating Game* one of the game shows Judy made you watch? Don't get any bright ideas. I barely met your friend Holly. And she looks about as old as your baby-sitter. She's far too young for me to *like* in the way I gather you mean."

"No, she's not. She said she's a . . ."

"A what?"

"Uh . . . I can't remember exactly. But it was something grown-up."

"Well, that's neither here nor there," Mac lied.

Something grown up, he repeated to himself. What a nice little phrase to hear when merely looking at Holly Russell had caused such a strong reaction within him. What a nice little phrase . . . assuming Jason was right, of course.

CHAPTER THREE

JASON EYED Holly closely on their way out of the lounge. "Makes you cry, huh?"

"Yeah. Silly, isn't it? Even though I know E.T. doesn't really die, that scene where they think he's dead gets me every time." Holly paused as they reached the promenade. "I have to meet my mother for lunch now, Jason. Did your parents tell you where to go after the movie?"

'It's just my dad. My mom's not with us. They're divorced. I'm spending Christmas with my dad."

"Oh…well, did your dad tell you where to go from here?"

"Yup. To the pool. He was going to sit in the sun and wait for me."

"The pool must be a popular meeting place. That's where I'm meeting my mother, too."

"Do you know which way to go, Holly?" Jason's grip clearly told her that he did and hoped she didn't.

"I'd certainly feel more secure if I had a guide."

The boy's grin broadened. "It's this way—toward the stern."

They walked along the promenade. On their left, beyond the ship's railing, the azure Caribbean stretched smoothly away until, eventually, it melted into blue sky. On their right, windows offered peeks into a bar, a casino, then the library before they reached the stern.

They stopped in front of the rows of candy-colored lounge chairs surrounding the postage-stamp pool. About half the chairs were occupied. Holly couldn't spot Kay, but Mac was impossible to miss. He was lying, eyes closed, on his back on one of the stretched-out chairs. He'd changed from Bermudas and a tank top to green bathing trunks and nothing.

Holly's gaze latched onto his torso. She couldn't seem to pull her eyes away from the clearly defined musculature of his shoulders and chest. Mac McCloy had to be into weights . . . a whole lot of weights.

There was no shade by the pool and Mac's skin, where it wasn't heavily dusted with dark hair, was already glowing with the first faint tint of a tan. If she got much sun on this cruise, she knew she'd turn red, freckle, then peel. Mac would obviously become a gorgeous shade of gold.

"There's my dad over there, Holly."

"Yes . . . I . . . I just noticed him."

"Is your mom here?"

"No. No, I don't think so. Not yet."

"Well, come on. You can wait with us." Jason started off, leaving Holly little choice but to follow. "We're here, Dad," he called out.

Mac opened his eyes, propped himself on one elbow and grinned lazily at them. "Hi, son. Hi, Holly. Sit down."

The crooked little tilt, Holly noted, was a regular feature of Mac's grin. "Hi. Sorry to interrupt," she offered, slipping into a chair. "I'm meeting my mother, but she's not here yet."

"You aren't interrupting. It's nice to see you again."

An imaginary neon sign began flashing the word *mistake* in front of Holly's face. Mac's eyes were lingering far too long on her. And his expression was one of distinct interest.

She shouldn't have sat down. But now that she had she could hardly leap right up again—any more than she could announce, completely out of context, that she had a fiancé. She absently rubbed her bare ring finger, wishing she hadn't left her diamond at home, wishing she had it to subtly wiggle.

There was something about Mac McCloy that unnerved her in a way she didn't want to be unnerved. Not by a virtual stranger. Not when she was engaged to a perfectly wonderful man.

But maybe she was misreading Mac entirely... although she certainly didn't think she was.

She forced her gaze away from the hypnotic blue depths of his eyes, but everywhere else she glanced seemed inappropriate. Firm pectorals, flat stomach, muscular thighs—it was difficult to decide where to look at a man who was practically naked.

Conversation. That was what was needed. She fixed on the scar that ran down the inside of Mac's right knee. "Football injury?"

"No. Skiing. Tore some cartilage."

"Oh. I guess you don't ski anymore, then."

"Sure I do. I wear a support on my knee. You just can't keep a good man down."

Holly swallowed uneasily. She'd already noticed that; Mac's green bathing trunks were hardly camouflage apparel. What she'd been reading as his distinct interest hadn't been limited to the look on his face. She'd been trying to ignore the rest but it was making her extremely uncomfortable.

"I was skiing outside Aspen when it happened," he went on. "While I was five feet in the air, a teenager who probably had a future with the Denver Broncos came flying off a mogul and blindsided me."

"A mogul?"

Mac laughed a warm and deep laugh. "I take it you don't ski, Holly."

"No. No, I've never even tried it. I was brought up on the prairies...in Winnipeg...Manitoba..."

Enough! a little voice shouted in Holly's ear. *If you add Canada to that, he's going to think you're a moron.*

"You should give skiing a shot sometime. You might like it. But you still live in Winnipeg?"

Holly nodded, trying to think of something even marginally intelligent to say, suspecting her current discomfort was causing a brain dysfunction.

"And you? Where do you live, Mac?" Good grief! How could that obvious question have been difficult to come up with?

"In Denver."

"My dad's the best architect in Denver!" Jason exclaimed. "Probably in all of Colorado."

Mac laughed again. "And Jason, whose opinion about that isn't the least bit biased, lives in Maine—with his mother."

"It's...it's nice that the two of you are getting to spend the holidays together."

"Yes. It's very nice. And you, Holly? What made you decide to spend them on a cruise?"

"Oh...well, actually I didn't decide. I won the cruise on a game show, *Your Knowledge Is Your Ticket*." Oh, no! She hadn't actually admitted that, had she?

"Really? A game show?"

Oh, no! She had!

"I have a friend who watches a lot of game shows," Mac went on, as if it was almost a normal pastime. "Jason sometimes watches them, too. Right, son?"

Holly glanced at Jason, hoping the deck would open beneath her.

The boy rolled his eyes. "I don't like them, though. I'd rather watch baseball."

"I'd rather watch baseball, too," she quickly assured him. "It's a long story, but the game show's why I'm here with my mother. She's a widow and..." Holly stopped speaking. She was sure she was sounding more like an idiot by the word. What on earth was wrong with her? She was reacting to a marginally awkward situation with all the aplomb of a fourteen-year-old.

"And what do you do," Mac prompted, "when you aren't winning cruises on game shows?"

"I'm a—"

"Dad! Dad! I forgot to tell you something!"

"Jason, you interrupted Holly."

"Sorry! Sorry, Holly. But this is real important, Dad. One of the other kids told me Santa Claus is going to come aboard ship on Christmas Day. I was wondering what—"

"Here I am, Holly," Kay called.

Holly had never been so glad to hear her mother.

"Sorry to be late, dear," Kay added, stopping in front of Holly's chair. "But I got talking and..." Kay paused, obviously waiting for Holly to forgive her.

"It's all right, Mom. I was busy talking myself. Mom, this is Mac McCloy...and his son, Jason. My mother, Kay Russell."

They all nodded appropriately.

"And this," Kay said, "is Sid Lambert."

Holly looked at the man standing beside her mother, suddenly realizing they were together. "Ahh... hello... Sid."

Sid greeted her with the gruffest voice she'd ever heard. It suited his appearance perfectly. Holly eyed him curiously as Kay introduced him to the others, wondering what her mother was doing in the company of this bald hulk of a man.

"I met Sid at the singles get-together, Holly."

"Oh."

Oh. Brilliant response. Her conversational skills were sinking farther down the drain by the moment.

"Sid's from the Bronx," Kay elaborated. "He retired last year, but until then he was a detective."

A detective. Somehow that wasn't a surprise. Give Sid a lollipop and he could double for Kojak.

"A detective like Magnum P.I.?" Jason demanded.

Sid shook his head. "Not a private investigator, Jason. I was with the NYPD. Homicide division."

"Homicide? All right!"

"I invited Sid to join us for lunch, Holly," Kay offered. "He's on the cruise alone."

"Hope that's okay with you, Holly," Sid added.

"Oh...oh, of course." Holly shoved herself up out of the chair and echoed the others' goodbyes to Mac and Jason.

"Holly?" Mac murmured and she started off.

She paused; Kay and Sid continued on their way, apparently oblivious to losing her company.

"Holly, you're welcome to have lunch with Jason and me. Although I think we'll skip the dining room and go for some of those hamburgers they're cooking on the far side of the pool.''

"Oh . . . thanks, but no."

Mac grinned. "I just thought you might be feeling a little like a third wheel."

"What? What do you mean?"

"Holly, don't you believe in love at first sight? They met at the *singles* get-together? Your mother's a widow? Sid's traveling alone? You can't have missed the stars in their eyes."

"I can't have? No. I mean, of course I didn't." Stars! Oh, Lord! Her mother and Kojak? Kay Russell and a man who would wear a rumpled Hawaiian print shirt? Mac had to be wrong! Didn't he?

"I . . . I'd better catch them. Bye for now."

She started after Kay and Sid, walking slowly, wanting a moment to think before she reached them. Possibly spending most of her time on this cruise with her mother wasn't such a bad idea after all . . . for either of them.

When she'd envisioned Kay making new friends she'd pictured other middle-aged women—certainly not a rough-looking, tough-sounding ex-cop from the Bronx. Sid looked as if he'd as soon kick butt as . . . well, as anything.

But her mother was undoubtedly just being kind— had merely invited Sid along to lunch because he was on his own. Yes. That was all it was. Mac had been imagining things. Or maybe he'd been teasing her. He seemed to have a good sense of humor.

She banished the image of Mac's grin from her mind. Yes. Either Mac had been teasing or her mother had simply . . . well, there couldn't possibly be anything to worry about as far as Sid Lambert was concerned.

But what about as far as Mac McCloy was concerned? Was there anything to worry about there?

No, she told herself firmly. She might not even run into him again. And, if she did, she'd simply make a point of mentioning David. If Mac had any ideas, that would end them.

So...there was nothing more to think about...unless she wanted to consider the ridiculous issue of her reaction to Mac. Well...maybe she'd better consider it briefly, because it certainly hadn't been the sort of reaction an engaged woman should have. Just for a moment she'd felt a tiny pull...felt a possibility that...but just for a moment.

No, damn it! There was nothing to be gained by lying to herself. It hadn't been just for a moment. And it hadn't been tiny. Mac had ignited an unexpected, uneasy, unwanted excitement inside her. Hell, his nearness had started her babbling like an idiot.

Of course, she knew precisely what had happened. The scientist in her recognized her response for what it was. She'd had a pure and simple hormonal reaction to Mac McCloy. There was no mistaking it.

And there was no doubt it was her cue to run for the hills—the way she should have run from Brad Houghton years ago. Maybe she hadn't run then, but this time she knew better. And this time she had David.

And, to answer one of Mac's questions—no, she didn't believe in love at first sight. And she didn't believe in letting physical urges overrule her brain. Hormones were nothing more than Mother Nature's agents for promoting mating, for ensuring procreation.

Well, she intended to procreate. But she intended to do it with David. She believed in the compatibility and trust between the two of them. She believed they were a perfect match. And she also believed—with every fiber of her being—that the smartest thing she could do for the duration of this cruise was to steer entirely clear of Mac McCloy.

She gazed out at the expansive blue sea, thinking the *Taurus* suddenly seemed much smaller than it had before... and thinking how difficult it might be to run for the hills when there wasn't a speck of land in sight.

SEVERAL SMALL BOYS, shrieking with laughter, bounced in and out of the tiny pool like live beach balls. With each cannonball dive, brilliant diamonds of water sprayed the deck for six feet in every direction.

"Hey, Jason!" one of the boys called. "You finished lunch yet?"

Jason shoved the final bite of his second burger into his mouth and jumped up. "I'm going to change into my bathing suit now, Dad. Okay?"

Mac nodded, fishing the cabin key from the pocket of his trunks and handing it over. "Just take it easy till your lunch settles, son."

He watched Jason race off, then put his own half-eaten burger down and took a slow, deep breath. It didn't help. The queasy feeling was building in his stomach again—still infinitesimal, but definitely growing. He'd finished off his final shot of medicine after the boat drill but surely, if he could just hang on a bit longer, his system would adjust to the ship's constant roll.

His stomach gave a worrisome burble. On second thought, maybe he'd better ask one of the crew if there was somewhere aboard ship he could—

He spotted Sid Lambert walking across the deck and waved him over, deciding that locating more medicine could wait a few minutes. "Enjoy lunch?" he asked as Sid lowered his solid frame onto an adjacent lounge chair.

"Enjoyed the company." Sid glanced at the remains of Mac's burger. "But I think, if I'm on board at lunchtime tomorrow, I'll try one of those. The dining room was serving Greek specialties—with Greek names. Whatever it was I ordered was swimming in oil. I think it was raw fish."

Mac's stomach roiled seriously.

"The buffet last night was okay," Sid went on. "I just avoided everything I couldn't identify. But apparently first night out is the only time there's an open buffet. Starting tonight we'll be into the organized sittings. Yeah," Sid added decisively, glancing at the burger remains again. "Lunch out here's a good idea. Eating dinners in that dining room is likely to be more than enough."

"Funny you should mention dinner, Sid. I wanted to ask you about that. Have you talked to the maître d' yet? Reserved a table?"

Sid suddenly looked uncomfortable. "Well...I told Kay I was traveling alone, but actually...well, I booked with a group tour. You know the kind of deal. We flew from La Guardia to Barbados together, shared the transport to the ship. Figured with a package deal I'd get to know a few people."

"So you're eating with them," Mac concluded.

"That was the plan. There are a couple of large tables reserved for us. But the group didn't turn out to be exactly what I was expecting." Sid glanced around, then continued in a gruff whisper. "This is a little embarrassing, Mac, but the group's called Swinging Seniors."

Mac nodded, managing not to grin.

Sid paused, clearing his throat. "I should have known to avoid it—just given that name—but the daughter was nagging me about taking a vacation. You know how kids are. Anyway, I finally gave in and called the travel agent who was advertising the package. But this group...well, for starters, the average age is about a 107. The only thing most of them are swinging is canes. And there are only two men. Course, I'm bunked in with the other guy, and he looks as if they dragged him out of a nursing home for the cruise. Last night I could hardly sleep. I kept listening for his breathing—didn't figure he'd make it till morning, let alone for the next two weeks. And the women! I think every last one of them is looking for a man. Some of them have come on to me already. Half the reason I hooked up with Kay this morning was for protection."

Mac couldn't contain his laughter any longer.

"It's not funny, Mac! Look at me. I'm sixty years old, twenty pounds overweight and as bald as a billiard ball. If they're desperate enough to consider me sexy, Lord knows what they might do."

Mac tried to stop laughing; it was almost impossible. "Sid, surely an ex-New York cop can handle a geriatric barracuda or two."

"Hell, no! Give me crooks or murderers anytime. Those old ladies are scaring the bejeezes out of me!"

"Well, look, Sid. I've got an idea you might like. Kay and Holly will obviously be eating dinner together. And there aren't any tables for two—most of them seem to be for six. So, as long as you wouldn't mind sitting with Jason—"

"Not at all. I like kids."

"Great. Then the worst that can happen is we'll get a dud as table partner number six. Did Kay mention whether they'd booked a sitting?"

"The second one."

"Fine. Why don't I see what the maître d' can do for us? I was just about to go poking around the ship, anyway. The motion's getting to me and I figure there have to be seasickness pills stashed someplace."

"There's a supply at the information desk, Mac. That's on the Zeus Deck. But those pills take a while to start working. So, after you get them, stop by a bar and ask for a stabilizer. That'll set you up for the short haul."

"Thanks. You must be a veteran cruiser, Sid."

"Nah. My first time. It's just being a cop for so many years. Picking up information's second nature."

Mac pushed himself off the lounger. "Would you mind waiting here for a couple of minutes, Sid? Keeping an eye out for Jason? He should be along soon. Just tell him I said he's to stay away from the pool until I get back."

"Sure. No problem."

Mac grabbed his tank top from under the lounger, tugged it on and started off. Sid settled into his chair, took a deep breath of sea air and closed his eyes for a moment, resting them from the glare of sunlight on the sea.

KAY PAUSED at the end of the promenade that led to the pool area, anxiously brushing at her new, above-the-knee, white eyelet cover-up. "Are you sure this is all right, Holly? I don't want people to think I'm an old lady who's trying to look twenty."

"It's fine, Mom. Lovely, in fact. And you're not an old lady. You just lectured me about that this morning."

"But it's been years since I wore a bathing suit, Holly. And in front of all these people?"

Holly took Kay's arm and drew her along. "If you look at 'all these people,' you'll see almost everyone has a bathing suit on. And your figure is far better than most of those women's."

"Well," Kay murmured uncertainly, "I guess... Oh, there's Sid! He's all alone. Why don't we sit with him?"

Holly's gaze followed her mother's gesture. It was no challenge to pick out Sid's Hawaiian shirt. The man was lying on a lounge chair on the far side of the pool, face lifted to the sun, hands folded across his paunch.

"He looks as if he's asleep, Mom. We probably shouldn't disturb him. Let's sit over there at one of those tables by the railing."

"Oh, but, Holly, if Sid's fallen asleep in that sun, he'll burn. I should at least go over and make sure he's awake."

Holly gently jerked Kay's arm as she started forward. "Mom, he's a grown man. He can take care of himself. You shouldn't be telling him what to do. You hardly know him." *And for goodness sake* she added silently, *let's keep it that way.*

Sid seemed nice enough, but definitely not for her mother. And the way he'd been looking at Kay over lunch had been disturbing. And the way Kay had been looking back had been downright upsetting.

"Oh...I guess you're right, dear. But if he lies there for long, I'll go over...just to be kind. You know what the cruise book said about the hot sun in the Caribbean."

Holly nodded, dragging Kay over to a table and plopping her into a padded wicker chair.

"There's little Jason," Kay said, pointing toward the pool as Holly peeled off the turquoise, thigh-length T-shirt she'd put on over her bikini. "See him, dear? In the red bathing suit? Just listen to those boys shrieking! I was always so glad I had a girl, Holly. Girls are much more civilized."

Holly sank into a chair, looked across the deck and picked Jason out of the group of boys racing around the pool. Given the way he was whooping, he could have been wearing a loincloth and war paint. Her mother was right about the difference between boys and girls. Those boys sounded like a band of small savages.

"That bikini's new, isn't it, dear? I don't recall you having a black one."

Holly nodded, trying to ignore the disapproval she heard in Kay's tone. She uneasily adjusted the bikini top—what little there was to adjust. It had seemed far less revealing in the dressing room at Daffodil's than it did at the moment. She gave the edge a final little tug, then glanced around the poolside lounge chairs, searching for Mac McCloy...only because she wanted to be sure someone was watching out for Jason, of course.

Mac didn't seem to be there.

She gazed about more slowly, checking each chair in turn. Mac definitely wasn't anywhere nearby. She looked back at the pool, mildly concerned. The deck area surrounding it was soaked. One of the children could so easily—

Suddenly it happened.

Jason's feet skittered out in front of him as he rounded the far corner of the pool. For a slow-motion instant he was airborne, then he crashed to the deck. The back of his head slammed soundly against its surface, jerked up a fraction at impact, then smacked solidly down once more. He lay motionless, a crumpled rag doll on the slick wood.

Holly leaped to her feet instinctively and was running across the deck before her mind consciously registered what had happened. She skittered to a stop beside the child before any of the adults sitting nearer to him were halfway out of their chairs.

She knelt beside his still body and spoke his name, then urgently repeated it. There was no response. She glanced frantically about, looking for a crew member, focusing on a waiter who'd paused uncertainly, drink tray aloft. "Call for the doctor! Right away!"

The man hurried off, and Holly searched for Jason's pulse, wishing she didn't feel so helpless, thinking that irresponsible parents should be hung by their thumbs.

CHAPTER FOUR

"A STABILIZER?" The bartender grinned at Mac. "Touch of *mal de mer*, huh? Well, you've come to the right place. A stabilizer'll fix you up like magic. I always do a good business with them the first couple of days out."

Mac nodded, lowering himself cautiously onto the stool, resting his elbows on the bar, silently imploring the other man to stop talking and start tending. He glanced out through the room's wall of windows and watched the horizon dip beneath the ship's railing, then slowly rise again. There was a frighteningly similar motion going on inside his stomach. He closed his eyes and swallowed hard.

His side trip to the dining room had taken longer than he'd expected and, by the time he'd reached the information desk, the remnants of lunch had already been churning in his stomach, threatening imminent upheaval.

The woman on the desk had confirmed Sid's statement about seasickness pills taking a while to begin working. And that meant he'd better save them for later because, right now, he didn't have a while.

Given the way he felt, his immediate well-being depended on the power of this stabilizer. If its magic wasn't both potent and fast-acting, he'd be facing a session of hanging over that railing.

"Here you go." The bartender slapped down a dark, menacing-looking concoction. "Just what the doctor ordered."

"Must be. It definitely looks like medicine." Mac took his time signing the tab, eyeing the stabilizer suspiciously and having second thoughts. "What's in it?"

"Half brandy. Half port. Works best if you down it in three gulps."

"I'm not much of a gulper.... I don't—" A nauseating wave washed up from his stomach into his throat, almost escaping his body entirely. He grabbed the glass and began gulping, trying not to smell the liquor, trying to ignore the way it burned, trying to get it all down before—

"So here you are! So this is what you've been doing!"

The woman's voice was fiercely accusing. Her words were accompanied by a finger that poked Mac sharply in the back, making him choke on the last of his drink.

He wheeled around on the stool, his insides lurching dangerously as he turned and stared down at the scowling little person for an instant before his mind clicked into gear. "Holly?"

"Very good, Mr. McCloy." She thrust her hands onto her hips and stood staring at him.

Mac sat carefully still, eyeing her uncertainly. All she was wearing was a turquoise T-shirt. No. That wasn't right. She had on something beneath it. The T-shirt was hugging her breasts, and he could see that there was a darker fabric over them. But the T-shirt scarcely covered her behind. And her legs were bare...and very shapely. He forced his eyes up and focused on her face.

Disgust was written all over it. She looked as if she wanted to hit him. Why? He'd done nothing. Could this woman he'd just tipped the maître d' to seat him with at dinner be deranged? "Holly, what the—"

She grabbed his arm, jerking him from the stool with surprising strength. He half doubled over, clutching his stomach.

"Can you even walk?" Her voice dripped sarcasm.

"Of course I can walk!" he snapped, still bent over, his face level with hers. "What in blazes—"

Holly dropped his arm and stepped back. "Don't talk into my face. Your breath smells like a brewery."

"Well, excuse me very much. But I wouldn't be talking to you at all if you hadn't come in here poking and grabbing." He straightened up and stared down at her. "And who the hell do you think you are, yelling at me? What do you want?"

"I want to tell you that your son is in my cabin—not that you likely care."

Mac took a deep breath, hoping it might both settle his nausea and clear his head. Either Holly wasn't making any sense or that stabilizer packed a terrific wallop. "Holly, would you calm down long enough to—"

"I'm perfectly calm. What you see is not lack of calm. What you see is anger. What kind of father are you?"

"I try to be a good one. But—"

"Good? Ha! I'd hate to hear your definition of bad! If you like to spend the afternoons drinking yourself senseless, that's up to you. But maybe you should remember you didn't come on this cruise alone. With you looking out for Jason—or *not* looking out for him, to be accurate—he's liable to fall overboard.

"What happened?" Mac demanded from between clenched teeth. "What's wrong?"

"Jason was running by the pool. He slipped and fell."

Mac suddenly ceased being aware of Holly's belligerent tone.

"He's all right," she added quickly, "He was knocked unconscious for a minute, though."

"Unconscious! Are you sure he's okay?"

"He seems to be fine. The doctor checked him over thoroughly."

He was *fine*. Mac heaved a sigh of relief. No. She'd said Jason *seemed* to be fine. Not precisely the same thing. "He's in your cabin?"

She nodded. "The doctor gave him a mild sedative, wants him to sleep for a few hours, and said someone should stay with him. When you weren't in your cabin we took him to mine. My mother and Sid are sitting with him."

"Let's go." Mac started off and was halfway down a flight of stairs before he realized he didn't know where Holly's cabin was. He paused and waited impatiently for her to catch up, barely mindful that she'd been running, unable to match his long strides.

She brushed past him and hurried ahead—down two more flights, along a passageway, finally stopping to open a cabin door. She stepped aside, allowing him to precede her in.

"Hi, Dad!" Jason sat up in the bed, shoving the blankets off his skinny chest and giving a sleepy-looking grin. "Wait till you see the bump on my head. The doctor said it's as big as a goose egg, but Mrs. Russell says it's more like an ostrich egg."

Relief flooded Mac. "As big as an ostrich egg?" He smiled over to where Kay and Sid were sitting by the window.

"Well, I'm not an egg identification expert, Mac," Kay told him, "but it's quite a bump."

Mac crossed to the bed and sat down beside Jason.

"It's right here," the boy offered, tentatively touching the back of his head and wincing.

Mac looked closely, glad to see there was no trace of blood. "I'll have to go with Mrs. Russell, son. That's definitely ostrich-sized."

"Mr. Lambert said he's seen smaller bumps on guys who got hit over the head with gun butts."

Sid cleared his throat. "Mac...I owe you and Jason an apology. Instead of passing on your message to him, darned if I didn't fall asleep before he showed up. Just closed my eyes for a second. But the next thing I knew, I heard Holly yelling for the doctor. Lucky thing she was by the pool...and I'm awfully sorry."

Mac shrugged, too relieved that Jason was in one piece to worry about a missed message. "Doesn't look as if any permanent damage was done. And Jason should have known better—even without you reminding him. There's a pool in my apartment building, and running anywhere near it is forbidden."

"But, Dad, all the kids were running. And I was really just sort of walking fast. I didn't even lose the key out of my pocket." Jason dug under the blankets, then handed Mac their cabin key, yawning as Mac put it away.

He reached for his son. "Come on. We'd better get you into your own bed. Arms around my neck."

"I'm ten, Dad."

"I know you are. But you look so sleepy you might nod off en route and fall again. One bump on the head per customer is enough, so let's see if I can still carry you."

"Can Holly come?" Jason asked as Mac lifted him.

"No. You're supposed to get some sleep. And Holly's undoubtedly had enough of you for the moment."

"I . . . I'd like to come along, Mac. Just for a minute. I'd like to explain about . . . about the bar."

Mac glanced back, realizing this was the first time Holly had said a word since they'd reached the cabin, since before they'd left the bar, in fact. Her voice had lost its stridency and was back to the warm, dulcet tones that had made him smile when she'd spoken to him this morning.

As he looked at her, every bit of his anger over her harangue dissipated. She was standing near the door, her big brown eyes silently saying she was sorry about her outburst, her face softly framed by that sexy tangle of reddish hair . . . her body, under the T-shirt, assuring him she was no minor.

And this gorgeous, half-naked woman wanted to come to his cabin to apologize.

It certainly wasn't necessary. He'd calmed down enough to realize what had happened. She'd been upset about Jason's accident, then had jumped to the wrong conclusions when she found his father guzzling the stabilizer.

Well, he could see that being a natural mistake. So no apology was necessary at all. But the expression on her face was saying she'd cry if he didn't let her come along. And he certainly didn't want to make her cry.

He smiled reassuringly at her. "Sure. Why not? You can help me tuck Jason in."

Holly managed to smile back. Mac's friendly grin made her feel immensely better. She'd acted like an absolute shrew. And she'd been wrong about Mac.

Maybe he wasn't the best father in the world but, from what she'd seen in the past five minutes, she could tell he did try. And, given what Sid had just said, she'd been way off base about Mac being irresponsible. And he clearly hadn't had anywhere near as much to drink as she'd first imagined.

She felt like two cents. But at least, once she'd apologized, she'd be able to look him in the eye if she happened to run into him again.

She moved a step closer to the door. "Shall we get going, Mac? Jason looks as if he's about to fall asleep on your shoulder."

"Will you be long, Holly?" Kay asked.

"Only a few minutes."

Kay shifted in her chair, tugging her cover-up down a little. "I'm just going to put some clothes on. Then Sid and I are off to the Aesop Lounge."

Holly eyed the two of them, feeling her sense of *better* slipping away.

"There are horse races in the lounge—films of races, I mean," Kay explained. "We thought we'd go and bet on them. Would you like to meet us there, dear?"

"I..." Her mother betting on horse races? Her mother didn't gamble. She wouldn't even play bridge for money. Holly focused worriedly on Sid.

He and her mother had nothing in common. A doctor's widow from Winnipeg and an ex-cop from the Bronx? Absolutely nothing in common. So why was Sid hanging around? And why did Kay seem so pleased by that? And those looks between the two of them at lunch! Holly hadn't liked those at all. Her mother might be fifty-eight years old, but she'd led an incredibly sheltered life. The less time she spent alone with this man the better.

"Yes. Horse races sound like fun, Mom. I'll catch up with you in a bit."

"Fine, dear. Then, after the races are over, the casino will be opening and Sid's going to teach me to play..." Kay paused, reaching across the space between their chairs and touching Sid's arm. "What is it you're going to teach me to play, Sid?"

Holly caught the adoring gaze her mother was giving Sid and stifled a moan. Surely Kay wasn't seriously considering... Surely Sid wasn't thinking what he looked as if he were thinking.

"Blackjack," Sid answered Kay's question. "I'll teach you how to play that first. I think you'll like it better than craps."

"Blackjack," Kay repeated. "Yes. I'm sure you're right. Just the name, *craps*, sounds a little..." She gave Sid a ladylike shrug. "And after that," she went on, turning to Holly, "it'll be time to dress for the captain's welcoming cocktail party. You haven't forgotten that's before dinner, have you, dear?"

"No, Mom, I haven't forgotten." But when had her mother decided to join the ship's social whirl with such a vengeance?

"Well, good luck," Mac offered, shifting Jason in his arms and grinning over the boy's ruffled hair at Sid. "Guess I'll see you at dinner—since we're booked for the same time sitting, I mean."

"Oh. Oh, yeah! That's great. See you then." Sid returned Mac's grin.

Holly gazed from one man to the other. What did Mac mean "good luck"? With the races and black-jack? Of course, that's what he was referring to. Then why did those grins seem so conspiratorial?

She looked at her mother again. Kay had risen and crossed to the wardrobe. She stood staring at her clothes, fidgeting with one of the pearl buttons on her cover-up. "I'll just take something into the bathroom and change out of this bathing suit," she murmured, glancing back at Sid. "I'll only be a minute."

"Yeah," Holly muttered, reaching for the door handle. "I'll only be a minute, too. I might even get back before you leave for the races."

JASON HAD FALLEN ASLEEP by the time they reached Mac's cabin. Holly sat waiting while Mac settled the boy into bed. He barely stirred.

"I certainly wasn't necessary as a 'tucker-inner,' was I?" she murmured when Mac sank into the chair on the opposite side of the window from hers. "But I did want a minute to talk with you alone—a chance to apologize for that scene I made in the bar. I don't normally rant and rave at people."

Mac watched her as she spoke, his midnight eyes unreadable. She glanced away, suddenly nervous. Until a few moments ago she'd barely been aware of the way they were dressed—Mac in his tank top and bathing trunks, she with only a T-shirt over her bikini. Suddenly she was very aware.

She looked back at him, determined to make this apology fast. Inviting herself to Mac's cabin hadn't been one of her all-time great ideas.

"I don't know what came over me, Mac.... Well, I do, actually. I had no idea you'd asked Sid to watch out for Jason. I assumed you'd simply left him on his own. And then, when I found you in the bar...saw you'd been sitting drinking while Jason needed you...." She realized she was starting to babble but seemed incapable of stopping. "When I spotted you, you were downing that drink as if you were desperate for it, Mac. I thought you must be as drunk as a skunk. Of course, I realize now you couldn't have had too many of them. And it's certainly none of my business if you like to drink. But I'd been so upset, thinking Jason might have been seriously hurt, and the sight of you just—"

"Just drinking a seasickness remedy?"

Mac's quiet interruption took a moment to register. When it did, Holly felt her face begin to flush. "A seasickness remedy?"

"Uh-huh. Called a stabilizer. Sid suggested I try one. Tasted like hell, but darned if it doesn't seem to have worked."

"But I smelled liquor, Mac."

"That was the remedy—a mixture of brandy and port."

"You're telling me the truth, aren't you?"

"'Fraid so."

"Oh, good grief! I almost wish you weren't. It makes me feel like even more of a fool."

Mac laughed his deep laugh. "I think *fool*'s a little strong. I can't imagine that anyone gets through life without misjudging the occasional thing they see. And, as far as my leaving Jason on his own goes, you were right. I should have waited for him to get back to the pool before I took off. But my stomach was telling me I'd better not."

"Well, thanks for being so gracious, Mac. From now on I'll try counting to ten before I let my temper explode. Or maybe I'd better make it twenty."

"Or maybe a hundred," Mac teased.

"We'll have to stop there, or I'm going to be spending half my life counting. At any rate, I do apologize."

An errant lock of dark hair had fallen over Mac's forehead. Holly had an almost overwhelming urge to reach across and brush it into place. She resisted.

"Holly, I think maybe instead of you apologizing to me I should have been thanking you for looking after Jason. I'm glad someone he liked was close by to take charge. By the time I saw him he wasn't the least bit upset. You really have a way with children."

"That's just as well, since I work with them."

"I should have guessed. A teacher?"

"No. I'm a child psychologist."

Mac stared at her with the strangest look in his eyes. The silence stretched out until it became uncomfortable.

"I said psychologist, Mac, not witch doctor."

"I...I... Sorry, I was just thinking how young you look to have a doctorate."

Holly laughed. "Some people say I look young to have a high school diploma. But I'm glad that's all you were thinking. For a minute I suspected you had a deep-seated hatred of psychologists."

"No. No, of course not." Well, not of this particular one at least, he thought. Holly Russell must be an exception to his conclusions about the profession. She didn't seem at all like his ex-wife or her friends. Maybe child psychologists were vastly different from adult psychologists. Yes. That was probably it.

He'd grant that Holly had come on pretty strongly about how he should have been watching out for Jason. But that wasn't being a know-it-all the way Margaret was. Holly had just been worried.

And that was all right. In fact, he liked it. Not many people would have cared enough to lecture him on Jason's behalf. And, now that he recalled the scene, she'd looked so damn cute...glaring up at him... spitting mad...

"By the way, Mac, I almost forgot to mention that you're supposed to wake Jason after a couple of hours and make sure he's not confused at all. The doctor thought a concussion was unlikely, but he said just to be safe..."

Mac nodded. Holly was looking at him with a concerned expression. He liked that, too. He met so many bimbos whose main purpose in life was getting through each day without breaking a fingernail. But Holly wasn't that way at all. She was clearly a caring person.

Jason had picked up on that immediately. And Jason had great instincts about women. He'd disliked Judy at first meeting. And, if he were really honest, Mac had to admit that Judy was pretty shallow. But Holly Russell was something special.

She was pushing her palms against the arms of her chair. Mac realized she was about to rise. "Wait. Don't go just yet." Without thinking he leaned across the space between them and firmly covered her hands with his own. He definitely didn't want her to leave.

It wasn't merely her good looks that were attracting him...or the way that T-shirt she was wearing seemed innocent yet provocative at the same time...or her incredible perfume. There was something about her that...

Holly looked down, startled by Mac's unexpected touch. His body heat was penetrating her skin, flowing into her bloodstream. Her hands were completely hidden by his. She stared at them.

Architect's hands. According to Jason, the hands of the best architect in Denver. Yet they were large and strong—not what she'd think of as *artistic*.

And they were so warm. And, with Mac's face mere inches from hers, she was keenly aware of the warmth of his breath. It still smelled faintly of brandy. Strange how the smell seemed enticing now, when she'd shrunk from it in the bar.

She sat stock-still, simply staring at Mac's hands, knowing if she looked up she'd meet his eyes...and afraid to. That unsettling, exciting sensation his presence had caused earlier was back.

"Holly...what are you thinking?"

What was she thinking? It would be insane to tell him.

"Holly?"

She had no choice, she had to look up. His gaze captured hers, and he sat watching her exactly the way she'd known he would. How could her mind have pictured, so precisely, the facial expression of a man she'd met mere hours ago?

"It—"

She jumped when he started to speak again.

He smiled. "I didn't intend to say anything frightening. I merely wanted to ask you whether—"

"I have to go, Mac. I promised my mother I'd meet her at those silly horse races." She shrugged ruefully, as if having to meet Kay were the only reason for leaving, as if Mac's nearness wasn't sending an electric current of arousal racing through her body. She desperately didn't want this to be happening.

Too fast! a little voice inside Mac's head was shouting at him. Yes. Right. He was moving too fast for Holly's comfort. He'd only met her this morning. It just seemed so much longer ago.

He was certain she felt the same attraction between them that he was feeling. But rushing her might mean disaster. He didn't want her to think he was a lecher. He wanted her to think he sincerely liked her... because he did.

As casually as he could, he sat back, freeing her hands from beneath his own. "Come on." He stood up, praying she wouldn't notice what her nearness had done to him again. "I'll walk you to the door."

Holly laughed a nervous-sounding laugh and pushed herself out of her chair. "It's not much of a walk, is it? Not very far across to the door, I mean."

"Well, I'd escort you all the way back to your cabin, but I know how you feel about me leaving Jason alone."

"I think I can find my way. Although I'm really awful at directions."

"Well... if you're worried about getting lost..."

"No! No, that wasn't a hint. I'll be fine. I just should watch more closely where I'm going. The Aphrodite Deck's the second one beneath this, isn't it?"

"Yes. And I'll point you in the direction of the stairs." Holly's cabin was on the Aphrodite Deck, he reflected. Aphrodite... the goddess of love.

They stopped at the door. "Well, Mac, maybe we'll see each other around the ship."

He smiled, tempted to tell her about the dinner arrangements, deciding to leave them as a surprise. He reached for the door handle, but Holly beat him to it by a split second. Instead of the handle, he was touching her hand once more. It felt so small beneath his . . . so soft. He forced his own from hers. "Well . . . yeah . . . maybe we'll see each other around the ship."

He stood, gazing down at her, thinking how tiny she was. He'd never kissed a woman this short before. It might take a little practice to get things right. Not that practicing would be any hardship, but it would be nice to do things perfectly the first time. If he just put his hands on her shoulders . . . and bent forward . . .

Oh, Lord! He was doing it. His body had switched onto automatic pilot. His eyes closed; his lips met hers. She had the softest, warmest lips he'd ever kissed.

His arms tightened around her. His hands moved instinctively down her back, drawing her nearer. No problem. No need for conscious thought. Tiny as her body was, it fit perfectly against his. The feel of her curves pressing into him was incredibly arousing.

He struggled to keep his kiss gentle, but then Holly's lips began responding to his and gentleness gave way to desire. Vaguely he sensed she didn't mind. Hazily he realized the desire wasn't one-sided.

But the only thing he was intensely aware of was the delight of her kiss—yielding, then demanding, then yielding again when he responded to her demands. His hands drifted lower and rested on her behind. It was the loveliest, firmest little behind that—

"Mac," she murmured breathlessly, ending their kiss. "Mac, I have to stop. I have to go."

Don't push, that annoying little voice inside his head cautioned.

He managed to wrench his hands off her body and leaned back against the wall. "Right. I know you have to go."

Oh, hell! His ragged breathing was a dead giveaway.

"Holly, I didn't mean to—" Why was he lying? Of course he'd meant to. And she knew he'd meant to.

"It's . . . it's all right. But, Mac, there's something I have to tell you. I'm . . . I'm . . . I have to go, Mac." She pulled the door open and raced out.

Mac stepped into the passageway, checked that Holly was headed in the right direction, then turned back into his cabin, thinking forward to the eight o'clock dinner sitting and smiling.

HOLLY PUSHED her cabin door closed behind herself and leaned against it, telling her heart to stop pounding and her breathing to slow down, trying to force some semblance of regimentation into her thoughts. She gazed unseeingly across the cabin. Then her eyes focused on the roses David had sent. Her feeling of guilt took a quantum leap. She wouldn't have believed it possible.

Why hadn't she told Mac she was engaged? She'd meant to. And she'd tried to. She really had. So what had happened?

She ordered herself not to play dumb. She knew perfectly well what had happened. The words had caught in her throat. Her mouth had gone completely dry when she'd tried to speak. Sigmund Freud would have had a field day with that.

But it didn't take a psychoanalyst to figure out what had been going on in her subconscious. Deep down she hadn't wanted to tell Mac about David. Because...

Because she was a total fool! What on earth had she been thinking? She hadn't been thinking at all. That was the problem in a nutshell. It wasn't her thought process. It was her damn hormones. The fireworks that were lacking between her and David had exploded at Mac's kiss like a Fourth of July display.

She concentrated on breathing deeply, regulating the oxygen flow to her brain so that she could think sensibly. All right. There was an even stronger chemistry between her and Mac than she'd realized. But so what? They were adults. Chemistry could be ignored... well, it could at least be controlled.

So Mac's kiss engendered a pyrotechnic extravaganza and David's kisses didn't. That didn't mean much in the long run. Fireworks were momentary razzle-dazzle—a blazing flash in the dark that quickly vanished forever.

As long as she dealt with this physical magnetism rationally, it wouldn't be a serious problem. Just because two people were attracted to each other, they didn't have to throw reason out the window. And the pull she felt toward Mac was entirely... well, that wasn't quite true.

Setting aside Mac McCloy's sex appeal, she genuinely liked him—liked his sense of humor and his easy manner with Jason and the way he'd so kindly taken her apology and turned it into thanking her and the fact that he treated her as a woman, not a child.

But that got back to the basic problem, didn't it? He definitely saw her as an attractive woman ... And she definitely saw him as an attractive man.... And she should be ashamed of herself for letting that mutual attraction lead to anything at all. And she was. She was going to marry David. David was perfect for her. And Mac was...Mac was clearly as dangerous as hell.

She certainly wasn't going to betray David. At least not any more than she already had. If she found herself within six feet of Mac McCloy during the remainder of the cruise, she'd start talking a blue streak about David. That was what she'd do.

She grimaced, thinking about how embarrassing that would be after the way she'd kissed Mac. Well, she definitely deserved any awkward situation she had to face.

But maybe if she could simply avoid Mac for a day or two, he'd decide she wasn't interested and turn his attention to someone else. And avoiding him might not be incredibly difficult. The *Taurus* would be in a port almost every day after today. Tomorrow they'd call at Margarita Island, a duty-free port. Her mother had said she wanted to try the shopping there. So that took care of the immediate future. They'd be off the ship all day tomorrow.

Of course, there was tonight. But her odds on running into Mac tonight couldn't be very high. Most people with children along likely booked the early dinner sitting. Or Mac might even stay in his cabin all evening. Maybe Jason would feel sleepy right through till morning.

Holly took a deep breath and exhaled slowly. There was no point in worrying...and no real harm had been done. All there had been was one innocent kiss.

Well . . . maybe not exactly innocent, but still merely a single kiss.

She sank onto her bed, deciding to forget about the horse races and casino. She'd be doing well to get herself pulled together in time for that cocktail party. And she'd definitely had enough excitement for this afternoon—if acting like an idiot qualified excitement.

Well, she'd probably have to pay the consequences, probably end up having to confess her idiocy to Mac. But maybe not. All she needed was a little luck.

CHAPTER FIVE

"HOW COME you didn't want to go to the captain's cocktail party, Dad?"

"Because, despite your opinion to the contrary, Jason, I think you're a little young for cocktails." Mac eyed his son closely, looking for any sign of after-effects from his fall. "You're sure you feel fine?"

"Yup. The bump only hurts when I touch it. And I'm as hungry as a bear. But I can't get this tie to work."

Mac knelt down and began fumbling with the tie.

"Ties are dumb, Dad. Why do we have to wear suits, anyway? We didn't last night."

"The rules were different last night because dinner was a buffet."

"But why were the rules different?"

"Well, a buffet's more casual than a formal, sit-down dinner. Tonight we'll be sitting at our assigned table."

"With Holly. Right, Dad?"

Mac nodded.

"And from now on we'll be sitting with Holly every night. Right?"

"Right. With Holly and her mother and Mr. Lambert. And possibly a sixth person. If someone's on their own, they might be seated at our table."

"But every night. Right?"

"Uh-huh."

"How come, Dad?"

"What do you mean, 'how come'?"

"How come you asked for them to sit with us?"

"Well . . . I thought I'd make sure we got to sit with people we like."

"You really do like Holly, then, huh, Dad?"

"Jason, knock off the questions, okay? You sound as if you've decided to become a detective."

"I might. I'm going to ask Mr. Lambert all about it. But you must like Holly if you want us to sit with her."

"All right, Jason. I like her. Are you satisfied?"

Jason grinned broadly. "Did you tell her?"

"Tell her what?"

"That you like her."

"Jason, that isn't the way it works."

"Well, how does it work?"

"I'll fill you in when you're older."

"Well, does she like you?"

Mac couldn't help grinning. "Yeah. I think so. I think she likes me."

"Did she tell you?"

"No. Not exactly."

"Then how do you know?"

"That's something else for when you're older. We'd better get going or we'll be late." Mac gave Jason's tie a final tug and stood up.

Jason played "acrobat" with the hand railing in the passage while Mac locked the cabin. Then the boy raced ahead, leading the way to the dining room.

By the time Mac caught up, Jason was waiting on one side of the wide doorway. "She's over there, Dad! Holly and Mrs. Russell are over there. But they haven't seen me. We'll really surprise them, huh, Dad?''

"Yes, I imagine we will, son. Let's go surprise them.''

Mac winked at Jason as they neared the table. The boy winked back, clearly trying to keep from giggling. "Well, what a coincidence. Imagine Jason and I being assigned to the same dinner table as you two.''

Holly looked up from her menu and stared in disbelief as Mac slipped into the chair on her left and gave her a warm smile. So much for the little luck she'd hoped for.

He was wearing a navy pinstripe...its tailoring emphasizing his broad shoulders. And a white shirt that clung with custom-made perfection. And a dark blue tie that brought out the depth of blue in his eyes. He looked gorgeous. And looking at him was making her more depressed by the second.

"Why, yes, Mac," Kay agreed. "It's a wonderful coincidence. And I'm so glad you're feeling well enough to eat dinner, Jason.''

Holly glanced across the round table, managing to smile at Jason. He was standing beside Mac, watching her with a knowing grin.

This was no *coincidence* at all!

"Why don't you sit here beside me, Jason?" Kay patted the chair next to her.

"That one's reserved," a gruff voice announced from behind Holly.

Her spirits sank another notch. They'd be hitting ground zero any moment now. She eyed Sid unhappily as he stepped into her line of vision and pulled out the chair on the other side of Kay. He looked every bit as rough and tough a character in his suit as he had in that dreadful Hawaiian shirt.

Kay smiled warmly at him. "I thought we might have seen you at the captain's cocktail party."

"'Fraid cocktail parties make me uncomfortable, Kay."

"Well, you didn't miss anything exciting," Kay assured him. "Unless you wanted to have your picture taken with the captain."

Jason plopped himself down beside Mac. But there was still a vacant place at the table. Undoubtedly, Holly thought, the way things were going Count Dracula would be joining them.

"Did we really surprise you, Holly?" Jason asked. "With us sitting together, I mean. It was my dad's idea."

"Yes. I was definitely surprised, Jason. You could have knocked me over with a feather." Holly eyed each of the three males in turn. They were all wearing "cat that swallowed the canary" grins. This promised to be a fun meal.

A waiter materialized, took their dinner orders, then began removing the sixth place setting. Holly was almost disappointed. The count would have lent a perfect finishing touch to their little band of merry men.

She studiously examined the crisp white tablecloth while Mac spoke to the waiter about bringing wine. Then she focused her attention on Sid, who was telling Jason about the silly program that had been printed for the horse races this afternoon. She'd already seen Kay's copy, but listening to Sid was better than having to talk to Mac.

Jason giggled as Sid recalled some of the names and lineages that had been invented for the horses. "No

Commission, by Salesman out of Orders. And there was one called Margarine, by Chef out of Butter.''

Holly smiled, feigning fascination. From the corner of one eye she could see Mac watching her with unconcealed interest. She simply *had* to tell him about David. And fast. But not here. Not with the others listening. She'd catch Mac as soon as dinner was finished and talk with him—explain, as best she could, why she hadn't said anything earlier.

That certainly gave her something to look forward to.

But her imagination was undoubtedly blowing this situation out of proportion. She barely knew Mac, so how bad could the scene possibly be? He'd undoubtedly think she was a silly twit, but at least that would be the end of her problem. Except for these damn dinner arrangements, of course.

After tonight, though, Mac might feel as uncomfortable about sitting with her as she did about sitting with him, in which case he'd be happy to change tables. And, if he'd just take Sid with him . . .

"I keep trying and trying to get the elevator to come!" Jason exclaimed, drawing her attention back to the table conversation. "I push the button every time I go by it and the light lights up but the elevator never comes. It must be broken."

Sid shook his head. "They can't operate it while the ship's moving. The motion could throw the elevator off kilter and someone might get stuck inside. Try the button tomorrow after we dock."

The wine, Holly noticed, had arrived while she'd been lost in thought. Mac was tasting it. He nodded to the waiter, and the man poured a little into each goblet.

"Since it's our first meal together, we should have a toast," Mac suggested. "Would you like the honor, Jason?"

"I've only got milk."

Sid laughed. "Even more reason for you to have the honor."

"Okay." Jason raised his glass in an exaggerated gesture. "To Christmas Eve! Did everyone remember tomorrow's Christmas Eve?"

"To Christmas Eve," the adults murmured in unison, each clinking a goblet against Jason's outstretched milk glass, then sipping the white wine.

"I have a toast to propose, too," Sid announced. "Let's drink to surprises—both Mac's surprise of arranging for this table and the one I've got for us all."

Holly smiled weakly. Mac's surprise had been more than enough. Whatever Sid's was, it was bound to be overkill.

"What is it, Mr. Lambert?" Jason asked. "What's your surprise?"

Sid took a white envelope from his jacket pocket and handed it to Jason. "Here. Have a look."

The boy eagerly opened the envelope and pulled out a little stack of paper slips. He stared at the top one for a moment, then whooped excitedly. "The *Long John Silver* pirate cruise! For all of us?"

"Right. Five people, five tickets. Someone told me it was the most popular of the daytrips for tomorrow. I thought I'd better stop by the excursions desk and get the tickets early—in case they were sold out by the time we dock in the morning."

"Wow. That's neat. Thanks, Mr. Lambert. The kids were talking about the *Long John Silver*. They all want to go on it. It's a real pirate ship with a skull-and-cross-bones flag and everything. And they take you to this deserted island and you have lunch on the beach and you can explore by yourself and everything. And one of the kids said you have to walk the plank if the captain doesn't like you."

"You shouldn't have bought all those tickets, Sid," Kay murmured. "They must have been very expensive. But thank you. It does sound like fun. Isn't this a nice surprise, Holly?"

Holly gazed at her mother. How many times in twenty-nine years had she heard Kay prompting her to thank someone for something? And how many times had it been for something she didn't want or like in the least? She had no idea. But she couldn't recall a single instance when she didn't want or like something as much as this. What were the fates doing to her?

There was an unmistakable order in Kay's eyes.

"Thank you, Sid," Holly managed. "It was nice of you to include us...*awfully* nice. But Mom and I have been planning on shopping all day tomorrow. Margarita Island's a duty-free port. I'm sure you could get a refund for—"

"Oh, but we can change our plans, Holly—now that Sid's bought these tickets. St. Thomas is a duty-free port, too. We can do our shopping when we're there. I'd much rather go on the *Long John Silver* tomorrow."

Kay turned away and began speaking quietly to Sid. Clearly, as far as she was concerned, the matter was settled.

Terrific. Holly sat watching the waiter serve their salads, trying to decide whether she'd rather suffer through a day on a stupid fake pirate ship that Mac would be on, or go shopping by herself and leave her mother alone with Sid . . . on a deserted island. What options to choose between.

But maybe, after they'd had their little talk, Mac wouldn't want to go on the excursion—wouldn't want to be anywhere she was. She glanced across at Jason. He was still grinning from ear to ear at the prospect of a cruise on a pirate ship. Of course Mac would go. He'd have no choice about it.

Holly munched a few forkfuls of salad, then pushed it aside. It tasted like cardboard.

The waiter swiftly replaced it with soup. She sipped a spoonful, trying to remember what kind she'd ordered. It was too bland to be identifiable.

Her entrée, when it arrived, was also tasteless. But the problem had to lie with her rather than the food. Everyone else seemed to be enjoying their meals thoroughly. She picked at another bit of meat, wondering whether it was beef.

Kay flashed Holly a concerned glance. "This lamb is wonderful. Your portion is all right, isn't it, dear?"

"Mmm . . . wonderful."

"David would certainly enjoy it, wouldn't he—the way he loves lamb?"

Holly felt the food in her mouth turn to a solid, impossible-to-swallow lump. She stared straight down, pretending she hadn't heard Kay. If she didn't pick up on the remark, maybe none of the others would, either.

"Who's David?" Jason demanded.

"Holly's fiancé," Kay answered brightly.

No one said another word.

Holly concentrated on chewing the lump, half wishing she'd choke on it before anyone spoke again.

Jason finally broke the silence. "Holly's fiancé?" His voice had jumped an octave. "You mean you're going to marry someone, Holly?"

Holly nodded miserably, not looking up from her plate, feeling Mac's eyes on her.

"When?" Jason demanded.

"Well...we haven't set a date yet, Jason, so I'm not exactly sure."

Mac leaned closer to her. "You aren't exactly," he snarled into her ear, "wearing an engagement ring, either."

Holly pasted what she thought might pass for a smile onto her face, then looked at Mac, hoping the others would think he'd merely passed a humorous remark. "I was going to talk to you about this after dinner," she whispered.

"Wonderful," he whispered back. "I can hardly wait."

"So," Mac said after the bar waiter had delivered two snifters of cognac to their table, "tell me all about this fiancé of yours."

There was no missing his sarcasm and, even in the dim light of the bar, Holly could see that the smile on Mac's face was far from friendly. "Look, I apologize for not mentioning David earlier. I'm not really sure why I didn't. I guess there just didn't seem to be an appropriate time."

"Oh, really? Well, that's certainly strange, Holly, because I can think of one particularly appropriate time. As I recall, it was around three o'clock this afternoon. We were in my cabin. You were just leaving, in fact and—"

"Mac, I said I was sorry. You're perfectly right. I should have told you then. I ... I tried to. The words just wouldn't come out."

Mac took a sip of his cognac and shrugged. "Well, I'm just damn glad you're not *my* fiancée. You and David must play by rather peculiar rules."

"I..." Holly paused. She should probably leave well enough alone—simply let Mac have the last word and get out of here. But she didn't want him to think she was the sort of woman he clearly thought she was. Silly as it seemed, she cared about his opinion of her.

"Mac, my engagement's perfectly traditional. I love my fiancé. And I don't make a habit of kissing other men. In fact, you're the one and only other man I've kissed—like *that*—in years."

"I'm honored." The sarcasm was even more pronounced. "You don't bother leading on every Tom, Dick and Harry. I simply struck you as the perfect 'one and only.'"

"I was not," Holly said, enunciating carefully, "leading you on. What happened was...Mac, I don't know what the hell happened. But it won't happen again."

"You're damn right it won't. Because I resent being played for a fool."

"I wasn't playing you for a fool!"

"Oh? Then what were you playing me for? What did you expect me to start thinking this afternoon? That you weren't every bit as interested in me as I was in you? Was I supposed to say to myself, 'This sexy lady is kissing me like there's no tomorrow, so that undoubtedly means she has a fiancé back home.'? Would you consider that a logical conclusion on my part?"

"No, of course not, but—"

"What were you intending to do—before your mother threw a wrench into your game plan? Did you want to see just how interested I'd get in you? Then you'd fill me in? What kind of game is that?"

"I don't believe this, Mac! Talk about making a mountain out of a molehill. All I did was kiss you. No. I didn't even kiss you. All I did was kiss you back. You were the one who started it. And now you're over-reacting. Your wife's perfectly right. You overreact."

"What the hell does my wife have to do with this? And what do you know about her? And she's not my wife. She's my ex-wife. And I don't overreact! Only a damn psychologist would accuse me of overreacting."

Holly bit her lip and silently started counting. She reached a hundred and kept going.

"All right," Mac finally offered. "I wish Jason would learn to be more circumspect when he talks about his mother or me, but sometimes I do overreact a little. In this instance I guess it was feeling like a fool in front of my son that got me going."

"Mac, Jason wouldn't realize anything—"

"You don't know Jason. He homed right in on the fact that I liked you and figured...well, that's why he was so surprised to hear you were engaged."

"Oh. I'm sorry about that, Mac. About Jason thinking... Oh, not merely about Jason. I'm sorry about the entire stupid misunderstanding. And...and I have to admit to sometimes overreacting myself. In fact, it's one of my specialties. Remember I told you I'd won this cruise on a game show?"

He nodded.

"You should have caught me immediately after that. I was mortified at the prospect of people seeing me playing a stupid game on TV. My mother does a very embarrassing imitation of my performance after the taping. And…and, well, you saw me in action for yourself this afternoon."

The hint of a grin appeared on Mac's face. "I guess it's a good thing you *are* engaged. If we'd gotten something serious going between us, we'd have spent the rest of our lives overreacting to each other. Never would have worked out."

"No. I'd give great odds that you weren't the eldest child in your family."

"What? Well, no. I'm the youngest. But what does that have to do with anything?"

"It has to do with what you just said about us. I did my doctoral thesis on birth order—its ramifications for adult relationships. And, scientifically speaking, you're right—about people like you and me never working out, I mean. I'm an only child. That makes me incompatible with youngest children."

Mac chuckled. "Sounds like the kind of theory that gets a lot of play in pop psychology magazines. I'll buy birth order influencing personalities, but not its ruling people's lives. I'm not knocking your thesis," he added quickly. "Just saying it identifies a probability rather than a carved-in-stone certainty."

"Of course. Nothing's carved in stone. But the probability's pretty strong. I'm living proof. I've been married once, Mac. To a youngest child, in fact. And 'happily ever after' lasted about three months. The remainder of the time was far from great. It seems that only children need to marry eldest children to make a go of it."

"And I suppose your David is an eldest sibling."

"Yes."

"I see." Mac swirled the cognac around in his snifter, then drained it.

Holly watched him quietly, one of the things he'd just said echoing in her mind. *If we'd gotten something serious going between us... If.* Life was full of ifs. What *if* she'd met Mac before she and David...

No. Crazy to even wonder about. The second part of Mac's statement had been the critical one. *We'd have spent the rest of out lives overreacting to each other. Never would have worked out.*

"Mac... I really am sorry I didn't tell you about David earlier. And I honestly did intend to talk to you about him right after dinner. I'm not a scarlet woman. I'm not even pale pink."

Mac smiled. "And I'm not a sex-crazed maniac, so now that I know how things stand, I'll keep my hands to myself. And I assume," he teased, "that I can trust you to keep your hands off me."

Holly returned his smile. "I'm perfectly trustworthy—despite my aberrant behavior this afternoon. So... friends, then?"

"Sure. Why not? But right now I'd better go and collect Jason."

"Yes. I guess it's past his bedtime."

"Not really. He's a night owl. He can generally outlast me. But I think tonight he and the lump on his head should get to bed early. Besides, I don't imagine your mother and Sid want to sit out on deck with him for hours. Sid's probably itching to get into the casino."

Holly put down her half-finished drink. "I'll come with you and see what they're up to. But before we go, what do you want to do about dinner?"

"About what dinner?"

"The table arrangements, I mean."

"Why do anything? Friends are allowed to eat together."

"Oh. Well, as long as you won't feel awkward. I just assumed that with Jason thinking—"

"Holly, I'd feel a darn sight more awkward changing the arrangements than leaving them as they are. After I specifically had the maître d' seat the five of us together, I'd feel like a fool asking him to rearrange things."

"Oh. Of course. I hadn't thought of that."

"And, besides, there's a lesson here for Jason."

"What do you mean?"

"Well, he doesn't seem to believe men and women can be friends. He sees me talking to a woman and, as far as he's concerned, she becomes an instant stepmother candidate. It'll be good for him to see me being friendly to a woman he knows is engaged."

Holly nodded, suddenly wishing she hadn't raised the friends issue, hoping Mac didn't have any ideas about being too friendly too often.

Eating together was one thing, but spending any more time with him would be tempting fate. Men like Mac McCloy should be forced to wear flashing red lights . . . assuming there were any other men like Mac McCloy in the world.

JASON NOISILY PUNCHED his pillow into a ball and stared across the dimly lit cabin again. Mac shifted in his chair, pretending not to notice. He turned a page of his book, hoping Jason would give up the game of twenty questions and go to sleep.

"Dad?"

"It's getting late, Jason."

"But, Dad, I need to ask you something else."

"What?"

"When people are engaged, do they *always* get married?"

"Usually."

"But not always?"

"Almost always."

"But not *always* always."

"No. Not *always* always."

"Why not?"

"Well...sometimes people change their minds. That's partly what an engagement's for, I guess—to give the couple time to be certain they're doing the right thing, that they're each marrying the right person."

"You mean Holly thinks David might not be the right person?"

"No, Jason, that isn't what I said. And it's not what I meant. I was simply trying to explain why engagements don't always lead to marriage."

"But, Dad?"

"Yes?"

"You said Holly liked you."

Mac closed his book. "Son, Holly likes you, too. She probably likes a whole lot of people—men and women and children. But liking people and loving them are two different things."

"And she loves David?"

"Yes. That's why she's engaged to him."

"Then why doesn't she know exactly when she wants to marry him?"

"I couldn't say."

"Maybe she doesn't really want to marry him at all. Maybe it's like you and Judy. You know? The way you always tell me you aren't going to marry her—that she's just gotten to be a habit? Maybe David's just a habit, too."

"Jason, Judy and I aren't engaged. We've never been engaged. And she doesn't want to marry me any more than I want to marry her. That isn't the way things are between Holly and David."

"But then why doesn't she know *when* she wants to marry him, Dad?"

"Jason, I'm not a mind reader. And what Holly and David are planning isn't any of my business—or yours. Holly can be our friend. That's it. Got it?"

"I guess."

"Good. Then I'll turn this light down and you close your eyes and go to sleep." Mac reached over and switched the wall-mounted reading lamp to its lowest intensity, then reopened his book. The light was too faint to read by now. He flicked it off and sat in the darkened cabin, staring out the window.

The moon was an enormous pale globe in the black sky. A full moon—the wide swath of its light sweeping the water, illuminating the waves that rolled toward the *Taurus* until they clashed with its wake and churned into silver bubbling foam.

Romantic was the only word to describe the view. Romance.

It had been a long time since he'd thought about romance. And then suddenly...this afternoon...Of course those thoughts must have been among the most short-lived in history.

But why Holly Russell? Why had he merely looked at her and felt those unmistakable twinges? And when he'd kissed her the twinges had intensified into unde-niable aches of longing. What on earth did she have? Aside from her damn David, of course.

Mac shrugged in resignation. *C'est la vie.* Regard-less of what she had, she was off-limits. He wasn't about to bird-dog another man's fiancée. As he'd told Jason, Holly could be their friend . . . and that was it.

CHAPTER SIX

THE LITTLE MOTOR LAUNCH tendering passengers from the *Long John Silver* drifted to a halt, then sat rocking unsteadily as people clambered out.

"I've got to go find my friend Kevin," Jason announced, hopping into the shallow water. "He was on the first trip ashore. Okay, Dad?"

So Jason had found a friend, had he? Good. Mac nodded his permission, then climbed out of the tender and waded the few remaining feet to the beach.

"Here, sit with us, Mac," Kay called with a friendly wave. "We should have saved you and Jason seats beside us on the *Long John*."

Sid raised a hand in greeting; Holly glanced up and gave Mac a quick, noncommittal nod.

"Uh...sure. Thanks." Mac tossed his sports bag onto the sand and spread his beach towel a few feet away from the others. Once settled, he surreptitiously glanced at Holly. She was sitting on her towel, spreading suntan lotion on her legs...her shapely, satin-smooth legs. They looked far longer than he knew they were. He stared at them, trying to figure out what was causing the illusion of length.

Of course. The black fabric of her bikini, where it should have covered her hips, was cut up to the waistband. Or was it a waistband? No. That bikini bottom didn't make it to anywhere near Holly's waist. It hugged incredibly low on her hips.

He glanced around, decided her bathing suit wasn't any more indecent than what most of the other women were wearing, then looked back at Holly... just to double-check his conclusion. She was straightening a corner of her towel. Then she adjusted her sunglasses and lay down on her stomach.

Her neat little behind was covered.... No. *Covered* was a vast exaggeration. Her neat little behind definitely wasn't covered by that miniscule piece of cloth masquerading as the bottom of her bathing suit.

Mac swallowed hard, unable to pull his gaze away from Holly's sexy derriere. Last night, contemplating their being "friends," he hadn't imagined her in a bikini. That turquoise T-shirt had been bad enough.

But now all he could think about was that moment yesterday when he'd been kissing her, when his hands had drifted lower and rested on her firm behind. Lord! He was feeling precisely the same reactions now that he'd felt then.

He forced himself to look away—out across the bright expanse of sparkling water to where the *Long John Silver* was moored. The tender had motored back out the three hundred or so yards from the island and was bobbing gently beside the two-masted "pirate ship."

His gaze strayed back to Holly. She'd propped herself on her side, facing in his direction, and was rummaging in her beach bag. If he didn't know a lot about architectural design, he'd swear her bikini top—what there was of it—was about to fall down.

He hadn't realized her breasts were so large...or her waist quite so tiny. He could easily span it with his hands. He felt another strong stirring of desire and reminded himself he was a grown man, not a perpetually horny teenager.

That didn't work, so he reminded himself that Holly was engaged. That didn't work, either. It merely annoyed him. What on earth was wrong with this David fellow?

If Mac was engaged to Holly, he wouldn't want her traipsing around the Caribbean without him. And certainly not almost naked!

But he wasn't engaged to Holly. Why had that *if* even crossed his mind? He barely knew her . . . and he was simply her friend.

He looked at the sea again. What he needed was a cold swim. But that water was at least eighty-five degrees.

"Dad! Dad!" Jason rushed up, his feet spraying sand in every direction. "Dad, this is Kevin."

Mac nodded at the freckle-faced boy skittering to a stop beside Jason.

"We're going exploring. Down the beach. Okay, Dad? Kevin's parents said okay."

Mac looked along the coast. It stretched forever. And inland the vegetation was primarily palm trees and the scrub grass. It didn't seem particularly dense.

"You're not to go in the water where I can't see you, son."

"I know, Dad. I know about the under-toad. We're just going exploring."

"All right. But absolutely, positively, stay out of the water."

"We will."

"And be sure you don't go out of sight of the *Long John*."

"We won't."

Mac pulled off his watch and handed it to Jason. "Lunch is at one o'clock. Be back here before that."

"We will."

"And don't get my watch wet—or get any sand in it."

"We won't." Jason and Kevin wheeled in tandem and raced away.

"Mac?"

Mac turned his head at the sound of Sid's gruff voice.

The older man knelt down. "Need a favor," he whispered, his voice sounding like gravel rolling around in a cement mixer.

"Sure."

"It's Holly."

Mac lowered his own voice to a whisper. "What's Holly?"

"Mac, she won't leave Kay and me alone for a minute. Stuck to us like glue last night after you took Jason to your cabin. Sat with us through the late show in the lounge, then followed along when we went to the disco. At three o'clock I finally gave up and escorted *two* ladies to their cabin. And today you probably didn't notice her on the *Long John* but she sat right between us. Sat right between us the whole trip."

Mac nodded. He'd noticed Holly on the *Long John*. And he'd noticed Holly earlier, having breakfast on the *Taurus*. Despite himself he seemed to be noticing Holly whenever she was anywhere within sight.

"I'd like to take a walk along the beach with Kay. I want a chance to be alone with her. So would you mind keeping Holly here?"

"She probably won't need 'keeping,' Sid."

"She will. I guarantee it."

"Look, Sid, I really don't want—"

"Won't be for long, Mac."

"Well...all right. If I can."

Sid grinned. "Thanks. I owe you one." He ambled back over to Kay and spoke quietly to her.

She turned to Holly. "Sid and I are going for a little walk, dear. Do you want to come along?"

"Sure." Holly pushed herself up.

Mac swore silently. Why hadn't she said no and made things easy for him? Possibly, he realized, because she didn't want to be left alone with him any more than he wanted to be left alone with her. But couldn't she see what was going on between Sid and her mother?

He eyed Holly, trying to think of something to say that would keep her where she was, but it was difficult to think about anything except the way that gold chain she was wearing disappeared tantalizingly into her cleavage. And about how, if that bikini top was even a centimeter lower, it would be exposing her—

He forced his eyes down. Even worse! He'd forgotten about the miniscule bottom.

He tried looking at her face. Good. Her sunglasses were hiding her luscious eyes. "Holly..."

"Yes?"

"Holly, I wonder if I could talk with you for a minute. About Jason."

"Ahh...sure. I'm just going for a walk, though. Can it wait till I get back?"

"No. I mean, could we talk now? While Jason's not around?"

"Oh. I guess so." She sounded hesitant, but turned to Kay. "Think I'll pass on the walk, Mom."

Sid waited until Holly looked at Mac once more and then, from behind Kay's back, shot him a grin and a thumbs-up sign.

Holly pulled her towel over closer to Mac's and sat down again. The scent of her perfume was mingled with the smell of suntan lotion...coconut. She smelled good enough to eat....

"So? What's the problem, Mac?"

"Uh..." He watched Sid and Kay starting off, thinking furiously. Problem. He needed a problem. "I'm not sure it's really a problem, Holly. But I figured that since you're a child psychologist, you're the ideal person to ask."

"All right. Shoot." Holly pushed her sunglasses onto the top of her head and gazed at him attentively with her big brown eyes.

"Well, I only get to spend a few weeks a year with Jason. And I don't have much to do with any other kids his age."

"Yes...and...?"

"Well, it's just that he's always on the go—and always at top speed. Did you see the way he took off just now?"

"Uh-huh."

"He's always running, never walks. I've been wondering if that's perfectly normal." Oh, Lord! Couldn't he have come up with something that sounded better than that? Holly was going to think he was a complete moron. He'd like to kill Sid.

She was staring at him curiously. She did think he was a moron.

"You mean you're worried that Jason might be hyperactive, Mac?"

He nodded . . . undoubtedly a moronic nod.

Holly smiled reassuringly. "Based on what I've seen, I don't think there's anything to be concerned about. Clinically hyperactive children generally manifest behavior disorders of one type or another. But Jason's well behaved. In fact, he's a darling. He probably just has a high energy level." Holly glanced along the beach as if she might be considering heading after Sid and Kay.

"So you don't think I should worry?"

She turned back, shaking her head. "No. But I think it's a good sign that you were. When children from divorced homes have problems, it's often because the parent who doesn't have custody—and that's still generally the father—withdraws and loses touch. That's especially common in a situation like yours, with you living in a different part of the country from Jason. But you've obviously worked on maintaining a close relationship with him. It's nice to see. You're a good father."

Mac smiled at the compliment. "That's not what you implied yesterday," he teased.

"Don't remind me, Mac. Yesterday was my day for making a fool of myself. I just want to forget it—pretend it never happened."

Mac nodded. That was a pretty clear message—in case he'd been having any further thoughts about . . . But he hadn't, of course. He could maintain a platonic relationship with Holly the same way he could with any other woman. It might just require a touch more effort. He lay back on his beach towel and closed his eyes, relying on the principle, "out of sight, out of mind."

"Mac?"

He tried to hold on to his dream. In it he was devouring the most delicious chunk of coconut cream pie he'd ever tasted.

"Mac?"

His mind identified the voice; he let the dream slip away and opened his eyes to blue sky and sunlight so bright that he squinted. Bending over him, blocking some of the brilliance, was Holly, still smelling, ever so faintly, of coconut tanning lotion.

Light sparkled like a halo around her tangle of ginger curls. She was wearing that turquoise T-shirt over her bikini again. But even thought her body was covered, he was using all of his willpower to keep from reaching up and pulling her down on top of him.

Just as he felt his willpower fading, Holly sat back on the sand out of reach. The sun struck his eyes with full force, and he shaded them with one hand and looked at her.

"Mac, I thought I should wake you before you burned to a crisp. And lunch is being served."

"Mmm...I never burn. What time is it?"

She shrugged, then turned and relayed his question to Sid.

"Almost one-thirty," he called.

Mac struggled into a sitting position and glanced around. A large barbecue had been set up on the beach and people were milling around it. "Holly, have you seen Jason?"

"No."

Mac swore quietly and stood up.

"Isn't he with a friend, Mac?"

"Yes. A kid named Kevin. But I told them to be back before one. I . . ." He paused while Holly scrambled to her feet.

"We'd better go and look for them, Mac."

He managed a weak smile. "I was about to say that. To say *I* was going looking, I mean. But I hoped you'd tell me I was overreacting."

"Well, probably you are. Just in case, though..." Holly glanced back at Kay. "Mom, we're going to find Jason. If he shows up while we're gone, don't let him escape."

They hurried along the beach in silence. Gradually the sand became smoother, and the number of footprints in it diminished.

"With any luck," Holly murmured, "we'll hit a trail of two sets of little prints."

"I thought Sid was the detective."

"His specialty's homicide, remember? I likely know more about the minds of little boys. If they walk far enough to reach perfectly smooth sand, they'll decide they're the only two people in the history of the universe who have ever explored that part of the island. Now how could they drag themselves back for lunch in the face of such an experience?"

Mac grinned, his concern lessening somewhat. "Given the number of shells on the sand, I'd say the tide washes this beach clean of footprints pretty regularly."

"Well, if that thought occurs to them, they'll simply ignore it. Don't you remember what being a little boy's like, Mac? They aren't going to let reality get in the way of an adventure."

"And reality probably includes keeping track of the time."

"I'm sure that's all that's happened."

Mac looked back along the beach and shook his head. "I told Jason not to go out of sight of the *Long John*. Unless we've missed him, he obviously did."

"'Fraid the ship's part of reality, Mac. If they can't see it, they can pretend they're marooned forever."

Mac and Holly walked on until there wasn't another person in sight. Waves lapped quietly to their left. Raucous blackbirds called messages from the tops of palm trees on their right.

Finally Mac heard a faint but familiar-sounding whoop. His anxiety vanished. Holly shoved her sunglasses onto the top of her head and glanced a question at him.

"Yes, that's the little monster."

They turned away from the water. The sounds of shouts grew gradually louder as they left the beach and started walking inland.

A few yards into the palm grove Holly touched Mac's arm, then pointed ahead to their right. "I think that's where the sound's coming from. See the opening in that rock face over there? Must be a cave."

"Sometimes I wonder about Jason's brain," Mac muttered. "He might have come across a snake in a cave."

"Or maybe a pirate with a hook for a hand . . . or a monster with red eyes that shoot fire . . ."

Mac grinned. "Or maybe they found nothing and were disappointed. Let's see if we can give the little beggars some excitement."

As they walked up to the cave, Mac picked up a couple of loose rocks and motioned Holly to stay to one side of the opening. He could hear the boys inside the cave, giggling loudly. Gently he tossed one of the rocks. It hit the cave's wall, then dropped to the dirt below with a resounding thud. The giggles ended in sharp, audible intakes of breath. The only remaining sound was the chatter of blackbirds in the trees.

Mac waited until he heard whispering begin, then threw the second rock. A split second after it hit the ground, two small figures dashed from the cave and headed, full tilt, in the direction of the beach.

"Jason," Mac called loudly.

The boy wheeled around in midstride. "Dad! Dad, you scared me to death!"

Kevin stopped running and looked back uncertainly.

Mac managed to keep a straight face. "Well, you scared me to death, too, Jason. Half to death at least. It's past two o'clock. I thought the ghost of Long John Silver must have gotten you boys."

"We just thought he was going to, Dad! Or we thought maybe you were a monster."

"And what if I had been? Or," he added, flashing a grin only Holly would catch, "what if I'd been a snake or a pirate with a hook for a hand or a dragon with red eyes that shoot fire?"

"Oh, Dad."

"Never mind the 'Oh Dad', Jason. You walked a good two miles down the beach. And I had no idea precisely where you'd gone. And I'll bet your parents are concerned about where you've gotten to, Kevin. What if you'd run into trouble? What would have happened then?"

Jason stared at the ground, scuffing one bare foot. Kevin carefully examined the trunk of a palm tree.

"I don't know," Jason finally mumbled.

"Well, just stick closer after this. Okay?"

"Okay."

"Good. Now let's get back before we miss lunch."

They started in the direction of the shoreline, walking single file between the palms—Kevin in the lead, followed by Jason and then Holly.

Mac trailed along behind the others, trying not to watch the cute way Holly's hips moved when she walked. It was impossible.

This *friends* idea wasn't going to work at all. Every minute he spent with Holly he liked her more. And not just as a damn friend, either. He was going to have to stay away from her as much as he could. Having dinner together every evening would undoubtedly stretch his honorable intentions about as far as they could stretch.

The little troup reached the sand and spread out, walking four abreast.

"Tomorrow's Christmas Day, Holly," Jason offered.

She grinned at him. "That's the way it generally works all right, Jason. The day after Christmas Eve has been Christmas Day for as long as I can remember."

"And Santa Claus is coming onto the *Taurus*," the boy continued, ignoring Holly's teasing. "In the morning. Right after we dock in Grenada."

"Yes. You mentioned something about that the other day. And are you boys planning to go and see him?"

Kevin shot Jason a knowing glance, then focused on Holly. "Well, we don't really believe in him anymore."

"Of course not. I guess you're way too old for that."

"Yup. Way too old. I'm ten. Same as Jason. But Santa's bringing presents for all the kids on the ship."

"Oh. Well, maybe you should think about going to see him—even though you don't believe anymore. You wouldn't want him to be disappointed because there aren't as many children as he's expecting."

"Yeah," Jason agreed. "We don't want to disappoint him, Kevin."

Jason turned to Holly. "If I go to see him, you'll come, won't you? To watch, I mean. He's going to be in the Euripides Lounge."

"Of course. I love watching kids visit Santa Claus."

"Good. Then Dad'll have someone to sit with. Come on, Kevin. Let's race."

Holly glanced at Mac as the boys ran ahead. "I...I hope you don't mind, Mac. I should have thought before I spoke. It's just that I really do enjoy that sort of thing. I guess maybe I won't belong there, though. If you'd rather I didn't come..."

Mac managed a smile. "Holly, I'd like nothing better."

"MERRY CHRISTMAS, HOLLY."

"Merry Christmas, Mac," she murmured, slipping into a chair beside him.

"Kay's not with you?"

"No. She's gone to breakfast. Said she doesn't intend to do the Santa Claus routine again until she has grandchildren."

Holly glanced around at the dozen or so other adults who comprised the "watchers." Across the sunlit lounge sixteen or eighteen children sat on the floor in front of an empty, thronelike chair.

One little girl, about four years old, was jumping up and down, her red curls bouncing, her brown eyes shining. Some of the older children, including Jason and Kevin, were giggling among themselves.

Beyond the excited-looking little group, the lounge's picture windows afforded a tantalizing view of St. George's, Grenada's capital. Under an incredibly blue sky and impossibly bright sun, the town nestled within the semicircular inner harbor. Along the waterfront a row of shops were mirrored in glass-smooth water. Behind that, colorful little houses climbed up steep emerald hills.

The only visible people were women tending tiny stalls along the pier. Spice sellers. *Taurus Today* had mentioned them and recommended purchasing their handmade baskets of spices as souvenirs of the "Spice Island."

"Looks like a postcard, doesn't it?" Mac observed.

"Mmmm. Definitely not like a Christmas card. Every time I look out here, I have to remind myself what day this is. Winnipeg's probably forty below and shrouded in three feet of fresh snow."

Mac laughed. "Winnipeg sounds a lot like Denver. If you only had mountains..."

Strains of "Here Comes Santa Claus" began drifting in from the hallway, and a young woman—one of the entertainers from last night's show—scurried into the lounge. She was decked out in a forest-green elf costume and flourished a tambourine. "He's coming! Santa's coming, kids! He'll be here any second."

The little red-haired girl shifted her jumping into high gear, then stopped, practically midbounce, as Santa burst through the doorway, a large canvas sack slung over his back. Despite the padding and flowing beard, Holly recognized him as another of the ship's entertainers.

With a series of "ho, ho, hoes," he settled into the large chair, adjusted his "stomach" and eyed the children. Finally he focused on the red-haired girl and motioned to her. She squealed with delight, then shyly stepped forward.

Holly smiled at Mac. "Isn't she darling?"

"Yeah. She looks like . . ."

"Looks like what?"

Mac shrugged. "Looks like she's awfully excited."

The little girl climbed hesitantly onto Santa's knee and started chattering excitedly. Santa ho-ho-hoed at everything she said.

One by one the other children also climbed onto Santa's knee and received their presents. The younger ones were clearly thrilled with Santa's visit. The older ones looked marginally embarrassed.

After Santa had made his way out of the lounge, Jason raced over to Holly and Mac. "Neat, huh?" He held out a handful of candy canes and an inflatable ball for inspection. "We can take this to the beach today, Dad."

Holly saw her mother in the doorway and waved. Kay started over . . . then Sid appeared behind her, sporting another ugly Hawaiian shirt. Holly could feel the smile fading from her face. Didn't that man have any taste? And didn't he need any sleep?

The three of them had been up late the past two nights. She'd hoped Sid might be wearing down—she and Kay certainly were. But here he was, bright-eyed and clearly intending to spend another day with them. And he'd probably taken it on himself to plan their activities again because Kay was carrying a beach bag instead of her purse.

"Merry Christmas, all," Kay trilled as she and Sid drew near. She gestured across the lounge to the cluster of children who'd lingered there. "Did you notice that cute little redhead, Holly? She makes me think of you as a child."

Holly caught the expression that flickered across Mac's face and realized he'd been thinking along the same line. The realization gave her a moment's discomfort. She didn't want Mac McCloy thinking about her.

"What would you like to do today, dear? Sid says there's a famous beach on Grenada called Grande Anse. We thought we might try it. I'm all packed," Kay added, patting her beach bag. "There are change rooms on the beach. Sid checked."

"Mom . . . aren't you beached-out after yesterday?"

"Oh, Holly, I think spending Christmas Day on a beach is a wonderful idea. Maybe I'll write some postcards and make people back home jealous."

"But, Mom, we didn't see anything at all of Margarita Island. My entire recollection of Venezuela consists of the *Long John Silver* and an uninhabited island. And St. George's looks so quaint. Shouldn't we explore it? See something besides sea and sand?"

"There won't be anything open, Holly. Not on Christmas Day. That's why the town looks so deserted."

"Oh . . . I guess you're right."

"So Grande Anse is fine with you, dear? Sid's keen on seeing it."

Holly glanced at Sid. If she'd been reading him correctly, what he was keen on seeing was Kay Russell in her bathing suit again.

This . . . this *thing* between her mother and Sid was really becoming a worry. Holly was going to have to talk with Kay about it—soon.

Kay undoubtedly thought she was in the midst of a harmless flirtation. But her previous flirting experience had been garnered in the 1940s. The ground rules had changed drastically since then.

Her mother was aware of that, of course. But she probably wasn't thinking of those changes in relation to herself and Sid. She probably imagined the two of them were in a forties time warp. And even if she didn't, it was one thing to be aware relationships had changed and another to find herself in the midst of a situation she couldn't handle. Sid undoubtedly played by 1990s rules. And heaven only knew how outrageous those rules had become in the Big Apple.

"Don't feel obliged to come along with us if you really don't want to, Holly," Sid said politely.

"Well . . . I guess there's not a lot of point to sitting on the ship."

"Fine, dear. You just run back to the cabin and grab your bathing suit."

"We're going to the beach, too," Jason piped in. "Are we going to the famous one, Dad? To Grand Aunt's beach?"

Mac nodded.

"Can we all go together then?"

"No."

"No."

The replies popped out in unison.

Holly smiled weakly at Mac, realizing he'd also seen the wisdom of mutual avoidance. That would certainly make the remainder of this cruise less stressful.

Strange that her sense of relief was tinged with another emotion. She wasn't sure what it was, though. It almost felt like... No, it couldn't possibly be disappointment. That would make no sense at all.

"But why can't we all go together, Dad?"

"I... we wouldn't all fit into one taxi."

"Oh. Well, maybe we'll see you there then, Holly."

She nodded at Jason. "Yes. Maybe." But why keep testing the strength of her wisdom? Another day of looking at Mac McCloy's muscular chest would do nothing to heighten her resolve. Maybe Sid could be persuaded to try a not-so-famous beach.

CHAPTER SEVEN

THE ROAD SNAKED among Grenada's lush volcanic hills, climbing sharply to offer breathtaking views of the sea below, then cutting between towering slabs of rock and through dense tropical vegetation.

Holly sat beside her mother in the taxi, glaring at the back of Sid Lambert's head and adding *stubborn* to her mental list of his character flaws. She hadn't noticed before that he had a neck like a bull. A somatologist would have pegged him as stubborn on first sight.

She'd merely made a suggestion. But listening to Sid anyone would think Grande Anse was the only beach in Grenada.

And her mother! When Kay started siding with that man—against her own daughter—things had definitely gone too far.

The driver slowed his car and began talking about the American troops that had liberated the island nation a few years earlier. Their barracks still sat, now deserted, in the open field to the right.

Sid asked a few intelligent-sounding questions about the invasion. But, of course, it was only logical that he'd know more about what had happened than Holly did. The news coverage must have been much more extensive on American networks than on Canadian television.

The taxi turned down a heavily treed side road and, a few hundred yards along, an absolutely gorgeous beach materialized before them. It was surprisingly uncrowded.

Their driver pulled into a little roundabout, obviously designed for discharging and picking up passengers. Holly stared through the windshield. All right. She'd have to admit that Grande Anse was spectacular—a secluded stretch of white sand sheltered at either end by craggy cliffs. But the country was an island for heaven's sake. Practically its entire coast was beach.

She listened as Sid arranged with the driver to return for them, grudgingly admitting to herself she wouldn't have thought about doing that. Common sense, however, she decided as they climbed out of the car, didn't make up for his faults.

"Those must be the change rooms over there." Kay pointed to a log white one-story building.

"I'm wearing my trunks under my pants," Sid announced. "I'll find a good spot for us to sit."

Holly glanced along the broad ribbon of sparkling sand. Sid's idea of a "good spot" was undoubtedly one next to Mac and Jason. She didn't see them. Maybe Mac had decided on a different beach.

"Don't go too far, Sid," Kay said, smiling sweetly. "We don't want to lose you."

"Speak for yourself," Holly muttered under her breath.

"Pardon, dear?"

"I said let's go and change."

They started off, Holly trying to think of a good way to begin the conversation they had to have about Sid. She'd keep it casual, simply suggest they not spend so much time with him. Hopefully her mother would go along with the idea.

If Holly could avoid getting into the rest of her concerns—about Kay's flirting and what Sid was undoubtedly thinking—she would. She and Kay had never been the type of daughter and mother who discussed sex, aside from the physiological basics. And Kay probably didn't want to change that pattern any more than Holly did.

Now, if the appropriate words would just come to mind... But they didn't. This apparently wasn't her day for inspired opening lines.

The change rooms' signs indicated men's facilities were on the building's right and women's on the left. Inside, the structure was divided across the middle into halves. The women's side was empty except for the two of them.

Holly tossed her beach bag and floppy sun hat onto the bench running along the center wall. The words she'd been searching for still hadn't come but the time was right—overdue, in fact.

She couldn't take another day of watching her mother and Sid making cow eyes at each other. Or another day of worrying about where that might lead.

"Mom?"

"Yes, dear?"

"Mom, tomorrow... when we're in Curaçao..."

"Yes, dear?"

"Could you and I spend the day together?"

"Of course, Holly. You don't think Sid and I would go off and leave you on your own, do you?"

"No. That isn't quite what I mean. I mean could we spend the day *just* together—as in you and me. Without Sid."

Kay paused, her blouse half-buttoned, eyeing Holly curiously. "Well...I wouldn't want to hurt Sid's feelings. And he's already been talking about what we'll do in Curaçao. He says the major hotels there all have elegant casinos. 'Serious casinos,' he calls them. He wants to take me to one in particular. And, of course, he wants to take you there, as well," Kay added quickly.

"Of course. I'm sure he'd feel awful if I didn't come along."

Kay glanced at Holly quizzically, then went on, apparently deciding her daughter wasn't being facetious. "I think the casino he was talking about is in the Curaçao Plaza Hotel. Yes, I'm sure that's the name. Sid's heard it's especially nice. And he says I'll enjoy gambling in a 'serious' casino much more than in the one on the ship. And there's a swinging pontoon bridge that Sid says is world-famous. And a floating market we have to see. He says we can buy fresh sugarcane at it. And there's a fort. Fort Amsterdam. Sid says—"

"Mother! Do you have any idea how many times you've just said 'Sid says'?"

"Oh. I'm sorry, dear. Am I being repetitious? I didn't realize—"

"It's not the repetition itself, Mother. It's what you're repeating. Sid says. Sid wants. Sid's heard. Sid this. Sid that. Mom, I've had it up to my eyeballs with what Sid says and what Sid plans for us to do." Oh, damn! What had happened to counting to a hundred when she felt her temper flaring? What had happened to the casual conversation she'd planned.

"I see," Kay murmured.

Holly shrugged, feeling like a spoiled brat, trying vainly to remember what number came after twelve.

"Perhaps... perhaps I shouldn't keep insisting you come with us everywhere then, dear. The next time you'd rather not come along, I promise not to nag you."

"Mother! Are you being intentionally obtuse?" Oh, Lord! Why couldn't she learn to calm down as fast as she heated up? Why couldn't she make herself shut up—bite back the words that were about to escape?

"What I'm saying, Mother, is that I came on this cruise with you. Not with you and Sid Lambert. I have nothing in common with the man. And neither do you. So I don't see the point of spending every waking minute with him."

Kay finished unbuttoning her blouse. "Holly," she finally said sharply, slipping her Bermudas down and digging her bathing suit out of her beach bag. "Holly, I don't like your tone. Let's not forget who's the mother here."

"Who's the mother here? What does that have to do with anything? I'm an adult, too."

"Yes. You are. And it's been a long time since I've tried to run your life. I certainly don't think you should be trying to run mine."

"I am not trying to run your life. I'm simple pointing out that we're on this vacation together—with each other. Not with a Bronx cop."

"Not a Bronx cop," Kay said tersely. "A New York Police Department detective. A retired detective. And what," Kay went on, slipping into her bathing suit and studiously adjusting it, "became of your suggestion—I might even call it your ultimatum—that I not be a clinging vine? That I make an effort to meet other

people? That I not spend all my time on this cruise
with you?"

"I meant other people as in women, Mother.
Women with similar interests to yours. I didn't mean
a man who's as different from you as day is from
night. For goodness sake, Mother. Surely you don't
want to spend the rest of this cruise doing things only
because Sid wants to do them. He doesn't like the
same things we do."

"That isn't entirely true, Holly. You have to admit
this beach looks very nice."

"All right. I admit the beach looks fine. But why on
earth would you want to go to casinos in Curaçao?
Why are you even gambling aboard the *Taurus*? And
what about Sid surprising us with tickets for the *Long
John*? That wasn't your type of activity at all. I remember Daddy used to surprise you with tickets to the
symphony—not tickets for an outing on a dumb 'pirate ship.' "

"Perhaps," Kay said icily, shooting Holly a frosty
glare, "Sid wasn't able to turn up a symphony performance on Margarita Island. Perhaps the Venezuelan
orchestra was playing in Caracas."

"Oh, Mother—"

"That's quite enough, Holly. You've had your say.
Now listen to me. Sid and I do have something in
common. Apparently you haven't picked up on it, but
we like each other."

"Of course I've picked up on it. I'm not blind. But
your liking Sid is just . . . just . . . well, I don't exactly
know what it is. Opposites attracting maybe."

"That may be precisely what it is. Dear, I realize Sid
and I aren't alike..." Kay paused, smiling faintly. "We

probably even look funny together. He's such a big man.''

Holly tried to return her mother's smile...but couldn't manage it.

"On the other hand, perhaps the attraction doesn't stem from us being opposites at all, Holly. Maybe it's that I feel secure when I'm with Sid.''

"Oh, Mother!''

"I know, dear. That sounds terribly old-fashioned. Well, I'm afraid I'm not as liberated as you are. I like the feeling of being taken care of. Here we are, everything around us unfamiliar, and Sid seems to know precisely what's going on and how to cope with it.''

Kay paused once more. When she spoke again, her words were hesitant. "Holly, maybe the attraction is something else entirely. I feel a little self-conscious talking to you about this...and I guess I feel a tad foolish that at my age...but I want you to understand.

"Whatever's happening, Holly—and for whatever reason—the tingle's there. And I haven't felt that for years. Not since your father died. So I think we'd better end our conversation right here and now. Before you say something you may come to regret.''

Holly started undressing, her mind whirling. This situation was even worse than she'd thought. Kay had practically mentioned Holly's father and Sid Lambert in the same sentence!

And "the tingle''? Just precisely how did her mother define "tingle''? Just where did a "tingle'' fit into the turn-on scale? Was it a tiny twinge of interest or a high-voltage electric shock of desire? What if her mother wasn't flirting harmlessly? What if she was thinking that she and Sid . . . Sid with his 1990s New York rules.

Oh, Lord! What if they began playing more serious games? That could turn out to be disastrous for her mother. She'd become emotionally involved while Sid wouldn't. Then, when the cruise was over, Sid would go home to the Bronx—where Holly just knew that men-starved widows abounded—while Kay would go home to Winnipeg and pine for him.

And Sid had serious games in mind. That was only too apparent. He watched Kay with a look that said she might be a reincarnation of Mae West—the real live, hot-blooded Mae West. Not a damn orange life vest.

And every time Holly caught that look, she recalled Mae's asking Cary Grant whether he had a gun in his pocket or was just glad to see her. At Sid's age!

Holly grabbed her bikini bottom and began tugging it on. Kay couldn't know what she'd be getting into. She'd been married at twenty—in an era when nice girls were virgins on their wedding night. And that marriage had lasted until her husband's death.

Her becoming interested in men again was a good thing. But not this way. And certainly not this man. Kay needed to take things more slowly.

If she met someone in Winnipeg, fine. They could date for a few months and see what developed. But a shipboard romance with a totally unsuitable man who'd be gone at the end of the cruise? That definitely wasn't the way to get back into the swing of things.

Kay Russell simply wasn't prepared for dealing with the Sid Lamberts of the world. She'd end up being hurt. She might be the mother here, but there was an awful lot she didn't know.

Holly realized her thoughts were racing at breakneck speed and attempted to rein them in. Maybe things weren't as bad as she was imagining them to be; maybe she was overreacting. She had to try to ignore the fact that it was her mother involved in this situation and consider it clinically, determine the precise lay of the land.

Yes. That was it. She needed to learn exactly what Kay was thinking. Maybe, if Sid made a serious move, her mother would simply slap his face. Or maybe she wouldn't. What if Kay let that damn tingle she'd admitted to feeling...?

Just how powerful was it? Perhaps that was the key question. But Holly couldn't be too obvious about asking it.

She finally managed to fasten the clasp on her bikini top and pulled her pink T-shirt on, taking time for a couple of deep breaths. "Mom?"

"Yes, dear?" Kay's voice had a distinctly wary edge.

"Mom...I'm glad you explained things to me. I just want to ask you...this is a bit awkward... I know we haven't had a lot of mother-daughter heart-to-hearts, and maybe I'm a little old to be starting, but I wonder if I can ask you about something you said?"

"Why of course you can, Holly."

Good. The wariness had diminished. Now, precisely how should she phrase this?

"I DON'T HAVE to change, Dad." Jason snapped the waistband of his bathing suit. "So can I just go with Kevin?"

Mac glanced at the boy's parents.

"No problem," Joe Pritchard said. "We'll wander down the beach and get settled."

"Great. I'll follow you in a minute." Mac headed for the change rooms, glad he and Jason had run into the Pritchards on their way off the ship. The boys would both have a better time at Grande Anse with someone to play with, and Joe and Betty were good company.

They made an unlikely-looking couple—Joe with his tall, dark, Latin looks, and Betty, a short blonde who, when she wasn't pregnant, was probably tiny. Their appearances might be mismatched, but they obviously had fun together. The kind of easy fun that Mac and Holly would have if—

He banished the thought, turned into the entrance marked Men and crossed over to the bench that ran along the center wall of the building. He plopped his sports bag down and reached for his zipper.

"Holly?"

He stopped midzip at the sound of Kay's voice. It had come from directly on the other side of the wall.

"Holly, you look uncomfortable, dear. Whatever it is you want to ask me, go ahead. I'm your mother."

"I . . . Mom . . . I'm just a little confused. It's what you said about a tingle."

Mac stepped closer to the wall. Holly's voice had cracked. What sort of conversation were those two having?

"Yes, dear?"

"Well, Mom, you're going to figure I'm being dumb, but I don't want to misunderstand you. And I think maybe the word *tingle* has changed its meaning a bit over the years. Would you mind explaining a little more precisely what you mean—by *tingle*, that is?''

"Why... Holly, are you teasing me?''

"No. Really.''

"Well, I wouldn't have thought that was an outdated term, dear. Its meaning can't have changed much. You know how it is—you meet a man and there's an instant attraction. A tingle. You feel it every time you see him.

"And then...when he kisses you....well, when I was a girl we used to say we felt weak in the knees. Of course I haven't kissed Sid, but . . .''

Mac swallowed self-consciously. He shouldn't be listening, but it was too late to call out that he was over here. He'd better leave. No. He still had to change, after all. He simply wouldn't listen.

The other two men in the change room began talking—an inane discussion about the heat. Mac glared them into silence. They gave him curious glances in return and headed for the door.

A nervous little laugh drifted from the other side of the wall. Mac wished he could see as well as hear. Operating on only one of his senses, he might be missing something important. He wasn't even certain which woman had laughed.

Kay began speaking once more. "I'm sure you must understand what I'm talking about, dear. So I don't know why you've got me babbling on. You know perfectly well what I mean by a tingle.''

"Not perfectly, Mom. I really don't.''

"Oh, Holly. Now you're the one who's being obtuse. It's the feeling you get when you see David.''

David. That damn David. No doubt Holly would launch into a recitation about how wonderful he was.

Mac rested one foot on the bench and leaned forward. He waited impatiently as the silence lengthened. They hadn't left, had they?

Finally Kay spoke again, her words tentative. "Holly, is anything wrong? You look...you look unsettled."

"No. Nothing's wrong, Mom."

Of course something was wrong. Mac could hear it in Holly's voice. *Come on, Kay. Ask Holly about what's wrong.*

If it had anything to do with David, Mac wanted to know. As ungentlemanly as eavesdropping undoubtedly was, since he was already guilty he might as well take full advantage.

He fumed at the deathly quiet. They wouldn't just let the subject drop, would they? They'd get back to what was wrong, wouldn't they?

"Holly, I don't mean to pry..."

"There's nothing to pry about, Mom. There's absolutely nothing wrong."

More damn dead air!

"But, Holly...you look as if... Holly, I've always just taken this for granted, but you *do* feel that way about David, don't you? Feel tingly when you see him? Feel weak in the knees when he kisses you? You do, don't you, dear?"

Mac held his breath, resisting the urge to punch a hole in the flimsy wall so that he could see Holly's expression. Was she grinning because her mother's questions were absurd? Or was she looking uncertain.

"David's perfect for me, Mother. Whatever would make you suspect I don't love him?"

Mac waited. These silences were frustrating as hell. Holly hadn't sounded entirely convincing to him. But maybe that was merely wishful thinking.

"Holly, I'm beginning to feel as if we're playing a game of definitions. But I wasn't exactly talking about *loving.* I was talking about being *in* love. You are *in love* with David, aren't you? You do feel a chemistry...feel there's something special between you?"

Well? What was going on? Why didn't Holly answer?

"Why are you shrugging, Holly?"

She was shrugging! She wasn't declaring her undying love for that damn David! She was shrugging!

"I'm not shrugging, Mom."

She wasn't shrugging! Hell's bells! Was she or wasn't she? Which one of them was wrong?

"Of course there's something between David and me. There's a lot between us. And it has a far better basis than oogly-boogly tingles. Our relationship is built on having so many things in common and enjoying each other's company and wanting the same things out of life. You know—the home and children bit. And David will be a wonderful father."

"Yes...yes, that's all well and good, dear. And you know how fond I am of David. I just...Holly, you've taken me aback. I've always just assumed. But darling, as wonderful as David is, if that chemistry's not there, I'd hate to see you settle for less than—"

"Less than what, Mother? Less than fireworks exploding when I kiss someone? Neither of us has forgotten about Brad. We know precisely how long fireworks last."

Brad? Who the heck was Brad?

"Between your father and me, Holly, the fireworks lasted for over thirty years."

Holly mumbled something. Damn! Mac couldn't make out her words.

"Brad," Kay said emphatically, "was far too immature for marriage. He couldn't have stayed married to a woman with the patience of a saint."

"And I'm not likely to be canonized," Holly muttered.

Aha! So Brad was the husband Holly had mentioned the other night—the "youngest child" she'd been unhappy with.

"Look, Mom, I don't know how we started off talking about you and ended up talking about me, but let's stop. I'd be crazy to even think about marrying anyone except David."

The sound of footsteps trailed faintly out of the women's side of the change rooms.

Mac slumped down on the bench. Holly would be crazy to even think about marrying anyone except David, would she? She'd be a darn sight crazier to marry him. She'd practically come right out and admitted she wasn't in love with him.

Some man would be doing her a major favor by taking her away from a fiancé she didn't really love. Hell! Marrying the wrong man would ruin her life.

But her life, Mac reminded himself sternly, was her own business. Hadn't he decided he'd be crazy to try involving himself in it? Hadn't she made it plain that she didn't want him to?

Kay had been right, though. Holly shouldn't settle for less, shouldn't settle for companionship and children without those fireworks she'd been talking about. Apparently she didn't feel them with David.

What about with Mac? When he'd kissed her had she felt . . . ? Lord, he certainly had.

But if Holly was so foolish that she actually believed being in love didn't matter, did he really want to . . . No. The conversation had simply taken him by surprise, had started him thinking insane thoughts. And that was precisely what his thoughts were—insane. He'd be far better off leaving well enough alone.

In barely any time at all he and Holly would be flying home. To separate homes in different countries. Of course . . . that wasn't an insurmountable obstacle to a relationship. On the other hand, there were enough other potential impediments to make him think twice. No. There were enough to make him think fourteen or fifteen times.

Holly being engaged would certainly be classed as a serious obstacle, although it was patently clear that her Mr. Right was actually Mr. Wrong. Then there was her ludicrous research on birth order, her ridiculous conviction that only children were incompatible with youngest children.

Of course, the fact that Mac was a youngest sibling, the same as Holly's ex-husband, was merely a coincidence—not at all significant. But then there was . . . Well, there were just too many problems even to consider what his imagination had momentarily toyed with.

He glanced at his watch and realized how long he'd been sitting, fantasizing. It was time to get back to reality and check on what Jason was up to.

CHAPTER EIGHT

"SORRY TO BE SO LONG," Mac apologized to the Pritchards. "I got involved in a conversation in the change room."

"That's all right," Betty told him. "It would have been at least another five minutes before I decided that you'd abandoned Jason to us forever. But I'll admit my imagination was gearing up. And the prospect of trying to cope with *two* ten-year-olds, after the baby arrives, was pretty scary."

Mac laughed, spreading his towel and sitting down. "I'm impressed that you're coping with *one* ten-year-old—*before* the baby arrives. There must be something about being on a ship that zaps boys with extra energy."

"I certainly hope that's all it is, Mac. I haven't been able to decide whether Kevin's actually been getting worse or I've simply been getting more irritable."

"Can I vote for both possibilities?" Joe asked with a rueful grin. "By the time that baby puts in an official appearance—"

The sounds of familiar shrieking interrupted. Jason and Kevin were closing in at top speed.

"Did you see him?" Kevin squealed.

"Yeah, Dad, did you see him?" Jason repeated, stopping beside Mac and pointed across the beach.

"We were playing in the water and he went whizzing right by us."

The three adults shaded their eyes and gazed out to sea. Betty began laughing.

"What am I looking for?" Mac demanded.

"Santa Claus, Dad! He's water-skiing. Right there." Jason adjusted the direction of his pointing finger.

Sure enough. Skimming over the water behind a large white motorboat was Santa—wearing his full regalia, right down to high black boots. The tail of his long red hat trailed out behind him. As they watched, he took one hand from the tow bar and waved merrily toward the beach.

Mac grinned. "You know, for as long as I can remember, people have been telling me how tired Santa is by the time his annual run's finished and that he heads straight back to the North Pole and sleeps for a week. Now I finally know the truth. This is what he does once his presents have been delivered."

"Maybe he's just started this routine since the fitness craze took hold," Joe offered.

"Do you think Holly's noticed him, Dad?"

Betty glanced from Jason to Mac, her curious expression hinting that Jason had been talking about Holly.

Mac shrugged. "She's just a friend."

"Kevin and I ran all along the shore, Dad. She's down the beach—with her mom and Mr. Lambert. We should go and tell them about Santa, Dad. In case they haven't seen him yet. He might leave soon."

"Well..."

"Come on, Dad. She likes Santa. And if we don't go tell her, she might miss him."

Well . . . why not? Mac shoved himself up, glancing at the Pritchards. "Excuse us for a couple of minutes?"

"Maybe," Kevin interrupted excitedly, "we should go and look for the reindeer, Jason. Maybe the sleigh's around somewhere."

Betty grabbed her son by the arm as he started off. "You stay right where you are, Kevin. You can go reindeer hunting in a little while. But playing in the water just washed off every speck of your suntan lotion. If we don't grease you up again, you'll burn."

"I'll come right back, Kevin," Jason promised. "We can go looking then. Kevin's mom's nice," he offered as he and Mac started off.

"Yes. Both his parents seem nice."

"All kids should be like Kevin."

"How's that?"

Jason shrugged. "They should have two parents to go places with."

"Jason, you have two parents. And we both take you places."

"But not together."

Mac wasn't sure what to say next. They walked a little farther while he thought about it. "You know," he finally said, "that your mother and I both love you."

"I know."

Mac glanced down. Jason sounded as if he could use some reassurance. "Son, people get divorced because they don't want to be married to each other any longer—not because they want to stop being parents. What your mother and I felt for each other when we got divorced had nothing to do with what we felt for you. Or what we feel for you now."

"I know, Dad. But it's just not like a real family. A real family has a mother and father and kids. And babies. I'm never going to have a brother or sister, am I?"

"I...I don't know. Maybe. If either your mother or I remarry, you might end up with a whole pack of brothers and sisters."

Jason shook his head.

"What's that mean?"

"Mom's not going to have any more kids."

"She told you so?"

"I heard her talking."

"Oh?"

"Yeah. She's been going out with this guy... Robert." Jason rolled his eyes.

"You don't like Robert?"

"No. He's a jerk."

Margaret hooked up with a jerk. That wasn't difficult to imagine. But Mac had to say something in this unknown Robert's defense, didn't he? Wasn't that the appropriate adult thing to do?

"Robert's probably not such a bad guy, Jason. Maybe you just don't know him well enough."

"Dad, Robert's a jerk. A *real* jerk."

Mac merely shrugged. He'd tried. But he wouldn't be at all surprised if his son was right.

"Anyway," Jason continued, "Robert was over at the apartment one night. He's there lots of nights." Jason looked up at Mac, obviously checking on how that sat with him.

"Your mother's entitled to have friends over, son."

"Well...anyway, they thought I was asleep, but I was listening to them."

"Jason, you shouldn't listen in on other people's conversations." Mac cleared his throat. He'd almost choked on those words.

"But sometimes that's the only way to find out about stuff, Dad. Stuff adults don't tell kids but kids need to know. Like that night Mom and Robert were talking about maybe getting married but not having any kids. Robert said, 'Definitely no kids.' And Mom agreed. Said she didn't want any more—that I was enough. Robert doesn't like kids, Dad."

"Well, not having brothers or sisters isn't the end of the world, Jason. Holly doesn't have any."

"But, Dad...I don't think Robert even likes me. So what if Mom marries him? What'll happen then?"

"Well, son..."

Now what? He could hardly say that coming to live with him was a likely option. When he and Margaret had split, he'd been certain she'd fought for custody of Jason as much out of spite as out of actual desire. And, as far as Mac could gather, she was as spiteful as ever.

Not that she didn't love Jason—in her way. And she'd always made an effort at being motherly. But it *was* an effort for her. She lacked maternal warmth. Or any other warmth that Mac could recall.

He shook his head. He wasn't being fair. Margaret had her good points. He'd loved her for them once— in a long-ago world. But in both the long ago and the present, custody decisions favored mothers.

"Well, what, Dad? What were you going to say? What'll happen?"

Mac glanced down at his son, racking his brain for something reassuring to tell the boy. Then he looked along the beach and spotted Holly. He didn't have the faintest idea what he should say to Jason. But she undoubtedly would.

"Jason, I was just going to say that everything will work out fine."

"Yeah. I guess. Maybe it will." *But maybe it won't* hung in the air between them as clearly as if Jason had spoken the words aloud.

"I'm not ducking your question, son. It's just that this isn't the best time to discuss it. Let's have a long talk later, when we're not in a public place. Okay?"

"Later like in later today, Dad?"

"Sure."

"Promise?"

"Absolutely. We'll talk about it later today."

"Okay." Jason dashed ahead, clearly eager to share the wonder of Santa water-skiing.

By the time Mac reached the others, they were gazing out over the water with obvious amusement. "I should have brought a camera along," he said, sinking onto the sand beside Holly. "When Jason tells his pals back in Maine about this, they're going to have a hard time believing him."

"Yes, I imagine they will." Holly managed a quick smile, then turned her gaze to the sea again, trying to concentrate on the skier.

But Mac's presence was both impossible to ignore and distinctly unsettling. It was also the last thing she needed at the moment. That conversation with her mother had been quite unsettling enough.

Phrases from it kept replaying in Holly's mind. And, with each one, she wished more fervently that they hadn't talked at all. For starters, she hadn't succeeded in her objective, hadn't clarified precisely where her mother was heading as far as Sid was concerned. But, wherever Kay was heading, she was going there with tingles and weak knees. Hardly a reassuring thought.

Far more disconcerting, though, was her mother's suggestion that David... Damn! She didn't want to think about what Kay had said. Her words had forced open a secret door in the recesses of Holly's mind, allowing a myriad of nagging little doubts to escape—doubts she'd been managing to keep securely locked away.

What if she *was* settling for less than she should? What if those darn tingles actually were as important as Kay believed them to be? What if somewhere down the line...?

Double damn! She didn't want to deal with this. Sometimes there was a good deal to be said for repression. If she could simply manage to shuffle those doubts back into the recesses, if she could just tightly lock that secret door again—

"Holly?"

Triple damn! Mac McCloy was the last person in the world who'd be any help with her shuffling and locking. "Yes, Mac?"

He reached across and tilted the floppy brim of her hat up, then leaned closer, so close she thought his lips would brush her ear. They didn't, but she felt... Oh, hell! Her mother might not be the world's champion at definitions, but that had been an unmistakable tingle.

"Holly," Mac said quietly, "Jason has a problem. Could we take a walk? I need your advice."

She tried to ignore the warmth of Mac's breath against her skin. How could warmth cause shivers?

"Mac, I've got a distinct sense of déjà vu. Didn't we have this conversation yesterday?"

"No. Yesterday I was...I mean, this is a completely different problem."

She glanced at her mother and Sid. How was it she kept tagging along with them only to keep leaving them on their own?

"It's serious, Holly. And I really don't know how to handle it."

"Well, if you think I can help."

Mac leaped to his feet, offered her his hand and pulled her up.

"I...let me put something more on. I burn." She freed her hand, tossed the hat down, tugged her T-shirt over her head and mumbled "Be back soon" to Kay.

"Where are you going, Dad?" Jason pushed himself up from the sand.

"Just for a little walk."

"Can I come?"

"No. You promised to go reindeer hunting with Kevin, remember?"

"Oh. Right. Okay." Jason glanced from Mac to Holly, his face sprouting a knowing grin.

Holly grabbed her hat from the sand, forcing herself to grin back, wondering if this new problem Mac was worried about had something to do with Jason having an overactive imagination. The boy began backing down the beach, still grinning.

"Tell the Pritchards I'll be along in a while, son. And tell Mrs. Pritchard I specifically said I wasn't abandoning you to her forever. Got that?"

"Got it, Dad."

"The Pritchards?" Holly asked as they started off in the opposite directions from Jason.

"Kevin's parents—Betty and Joe. Jason and I came to the beach with them."

"SO THAT'S ABOUT IT" Mac concluded, picking up a handful of sand from beside his knee and letting it trickle between his fingers.

Holly nodded slowly. Mac sat quietly as she traced tiny circles in the sand, looking thoughtful. She smelled of that good-enough-to-eat coconut tanning lotion again. But she had on a different bikini today. Pink. Hot pink. And *hot* was definitely the operative word. Good thing she'd put that T-shirt on. It helped...although not much. He was trying to wrench his gaze away from her when she spoke.

"Would you like to have Jason live with you, Mac?"

"Definitely. But there's not much hope of that, is there? Of gaining custody from Margaret, I mean."

"It's probably unlikely."

"That's what I figured. That's why I haven't mentioned it to Jason."

"He's ten, of course," Holly murmured. "That's old enough for a judge to take the child's preferences seriously. But unless Margaret's an unfit mother..."

"She isn't."

They sat silently again for a minute.

"Mac, it's worth raising the issue of custody with Jason—even if the situation's not going to change."

"Oh?"

"Yes. It's awfully common for children to believe they're living with one parent because the other one doesn't love them as much."

"I'm sure Jason knows I love him, Holly."

"I'm sure he does, too. But kids are grand masters at adding two and two together and coming up with five. It's important for Jason's relationship with you that he realizes he's with Margaret not only because she loves him but also because of the way judges look at things."

"Is that playing fair, Holly? Margaret would have a fit if I told him that."

"Mac, from what you've said, I imagine that when you and Margaret separated, Jason barely understood *what* was going on, let alone any of the *whys*. He likely was left with a lot of misconceptions. Maybe Margaret's cleared them up. But if she hasn't, then it's fair enough for you to. And Jason should know that living with you is a possibility. Just don't give him false hopes. Make sure he understands it isn't a likely scenario and why."

"All right. And where do I go once I've dealt with the unlikely scenario?"

"Well, in the first place, tell him that Margaret may not even marry Robert. Perhaps Jason hasn't realized he might be worrying for nothing."

"That's a good point. Unfortunately I can hear his response. 'But what if she *does* marry him, Dad? What happens then?'"

Holly smiled. "You should take up doing impressions, Mac. But that 'what if' is a major part of Jason's problem. He needs to know what's actually going on. Why not suggest he talk with his mother when he gets home? He should ask her what she and Robert are planning. And tell her straight out he doesn't like the man and senses the feeling's mutual."

"Really? You think that's a good idea? Margaret hates hearing her friends criticized."

"Well, that's her problem, isn't it? What we're dealing with is Jason's problem."

Mac gave Holly a half grin, impressed by how sensible her advice seemed.

"Children have difficulty expressing their concerns, Mac. You might never have heard a word about Robert if the timing hadn't been right, if being with Kevin and his parents hadn't gotten Jason thinking about families. He needs to be encouraged to talk with Margaret. And he needs your assurance that, if things aren't working out in the future, the three of you will sit down and discuss the problem, that you'll find the solution that's best for him."

"Holly, Jason's just not going to buy that. He's seen Margaret and me in action. We have a lot of trouble sitting down and discussing anything."

Holly shrugged. "Talk to him about that—about how divorced couples often fall into a habit of lashing out at each other, of being intentionally difficult just to punish each other for past hurts."

"Holly—"

"He's old enough to understand, Mac. But the real point you want to make is that even though you and Margaret don't get along with each other, both of you are concerned about Jason's well-being. So if he becomes unhappy, for whatever reason, the three of you will work together to resolve the problem."

"I see what you're getting at." Mac exhaled slowly, feeling as if Holly had lifted a twenty-pound weight from his shoulders. "Now tell me something else. Why do complicated things sometimes seem so simple when another person explains them?"

"You mean things like calculus?"

The teasing smile she shot him made Mac laugh. "No, Holly, I don't mean 'things like calculus.' Calculus never seemed simple to me, no matter who explained it or how many times. I mean things like how to talk to my son. You must be very good at your work."

She shrugged, looking embarrassed. "I try."

"You succeed."

"Well, then, mission accomplished. I guess we should be getting back. I haven't even been in the water yet and I've got to be able to say I was swimming in the Caribbean on Christmas Day." Holly scrambled to a standing position before Mac could beat her to it and help her up.

"Yeah," he agreed, rising, "I guess we should get back. I've left the Pritchards in charge of Jason for long enough. Would you like to take a little extra walk and meet them? I think Betty's curious about you. Jason must have been doing another of his uncircumspect routines."

"Sure. With all that food aboard ship, I can use the extra exercise."

"I wish," Mac offered as they headed along the sand, "there was something I could do to thank you. I feel as if I've been turning your vacation into a busman's holiday."

"No problem. You've merely been keeping me in practice."

"And you've merely been making my life a whole lot easier. I was serious about you being good at your work."

"It's lucky there's at least one area of my life where I've got my act together, Mac. Now if I can just grow four or five inches taller and work on my overreacting and cool my hot temper and learn how to tell directions and..."

Mac gazed down curiously. Why was Holly itemizing her faults? As a defense mechanism? He silently laughed at himself. Which one of them was the psychologist? But if Holly actually was being defensive, what was her defense against? His attraction to her? Her attraction to him?

"There's nothing wrong with having a few imperfections, Holly. You wouldn't want to be boring, would you?"

"Well, no. Just less imperfect."

Mac shook his head. "Why strive for perfection? It's definitely boring. Who on earth would want to spend time with a perfect person?"

Holly merely shot him a strained-looking smile.

He gazed out across the water, absently watching a dark frigate bird gliding against the blue sky, trying to recall precisely what Holly had said about her David being perfect.

HOLLY SLID out of the taxi after her mother and gazed at the *Taurus*. Returning to the ship was beginning to give her a sense of coming home.

"I want to get some spice baskets, Holly," Kay said, pointing at the little row of stalls along the pier. "And I should stock up on saffron. Someone told me it's a wonderful buy in Grenada. And it's so expensive back home. Are you going to get anything, Sid?"

"Anything? Are you kidding? My daughter gave me strict orders to pick up some of every spice that's for sale. Said they'd be even fresher than what she can get in health food stores. She's a real fanatic about freshness."

"Sid's daughter is a naturopath, Holly."

"A fanatical naturopath," Sid muttered. "I told her I'd probably get arrested at customs if I brought back little containers of powder. I hope she's going to be on hand to bail me out."

"Oh, Sid," Kay murmured reproachfully, turning to Holly. "Christie's only two years younger than you are, dear. And isn't that a pretty name, Christie?"

"Very pretty."

"And isn't it interesting that both Sid and I have only one child each? And that you're both girls?"

"Yes. What a coincidence." Holly glanced at the ship again. It was looking more and more like a refuge. She didn't want to hear about spices or Sid's daughter or anything else. She simply wanted a little time alone. "Mom, I'm going to head straight back to the cabin. Would you mind picking me up in a couple of spice baskets?"

"Of course. And some saffron?"

"Sure. Thanks."

"You aren't feeling ill, are you, dear?"

"No. Only a little tired from all the sun and fresh air and swimming."

Kay nodded absently, turning her attention to Sid as Holly started toward the *Taurus*. She clambered gingerly up the metal stairs of the gangway, clutching the mahogany handrail tightly and thinking her imagination needed an overhaul.

It had always pictured a gangway as being a wide wooden plank, gently sloping up to a ship. But this contraption that stretched down the side of the ship was more like a ladder than anything else. If she wasn't careful, she'd lose a sandal through one of the gaps between the stairs. She looked down into the yard-wide strip of water separating the ship from the pier and curled her toes more tightly.

Once aboard, she located a wall-mounted You Are Here deck plan guide and studied it, trying to get her bearings. There was undoubtedly some rhyme or reason to lowering the gangway from different decks in different ports, but it was darn confusing. Now...if she was here, and the Aphrodite Deck was down there—

"Need any help?"

Holly looked over her shoulder. No. That wasn't quite accurate. The head of the man who'd spoken was leaning directly over her shoulder, so, correctly speaking, she was looking into his face. He was in his thirties—not unattractive but a little jowly and, she suspected, a little drunk.

"No thanks. No help necessary. I've just figured out where I'm going."

"Looks like you've been to the beach."

She smelled his breath. Suspicion confirmed. He was definitely a little drunk. Maybe more than a little. "Yes. I've been to Grande Anse."

She managed to contain a sarcastic question about what his first "beach" clue had been. Even though she'd pulled shorts on over her bathing suit for the ride back, she was carrying her beach bag, her hair was still a wet salty tangle from swimming and her T-shirt was clinging to the not-quite-dry top of her bikini. She certainly wasn't going to award the man an A for perception.

"Where are you going now?"

"To my cabin."

"Oh. Would you like a drink before you go? Must have been hot at the beach."

"Yes."

"Great." The man grinned, grabbing her bare arm. "Bar's this way."

"No. Wait." Holly pulled free from his grasp. "Sorry, but I meant, yes, it was hot at the beach, not, yes, I'd like a drink."

"Oh. Well, how about just a quick one? A little Christmas cheer?"

"Thanks, but I have to go."

"Okay. I'll walk you."

"No, really. I'm fine on my own."

The man shook his head. "Nope. You're not. I've already heard a lot of stories about this crew. Some of them have been away from Greece for almost a year, you know. There's a single woman sitting at my dinner table, and you wouldn't believe what happened to her—the first night out, too. One of the waiters followed her onto the deck and suggested that—"

"Look, I'm sure—"

"No. No problem about my walking you. Absolutely no problem. In fact, now that I've met you, I feel positively obliged to escort you safely to your cabin. To tell you the truth I'm the most perfect gentleman I know."

Holly took a step backward. The phrase, *To tell you the truth*, always set off an alarm in her brain.

"Name's Randy," the *gentleman* persisted. "Randy Niebuhr."

"Look, Randy—"

"Nope. No arguments. You sure of the way?"

Holly swore silently. What was she going to do? Randy clearly wasn't about to be politely dissuaded.

So she could be rude or let him tag along or go and sit outside until Kay and Sid boarded.

The tagalong definitely wasn't a wise option. And, if she sat outside, Randy would probably follow her and keep her company while she waited. The last thing she wanted was company—particularly his.

Oh, hell! Why should she let herself be annoyed by this nerd? "I really don't need an escort, Randy." She pushed by him and hurried down the stairs, not looking back. He was likely the type who'd read a fleeting glance as a come-on.

Holly reached the Aphrodite Deck, paused momentarily to check the arrows indicating cabin numbers, then headed along the corridor. One right turn...then one left...and here she was.

She stopped outside her cabin door, finally looking back before digging her key from her bag. No one on her tail. Of course not. Randy was probably back in the bar again, well into another glass of Christmas cheer.

Once inside the cabin, she pushed the door closed behind her, clicked the lock and threw herself onto her bed. She lay motionless for a moment, eyeing the ceiling, trying to decide whether she had the energy for a shower.

A noise riveted her attention to the door. She stared...the handle turned...the door opened...and Randy stood in the doorway. Holly's breath caught in her throat; her heart stopped in midbeat.

"Well, well," Randy said, a sloppy grin spreading across his face. "Straight to bed? Without even telling me your name? And here I figured you were playing hard to get, sexy lady."

She tried to speak, but no sound came out. Randy stepped into the cabin, shoved the door shut with his foot and reached for the lock.

Click . . . click.

The tiny sounds reverberated in Holly's head like gunshots in an echo chamber. Two little clicks. Two clicks to lock the door. She hadn't actually locked it. But he had.

CHAPTER NINE

AT THE LOCK'S CLICK a mixture of fear and disbelief knotted Holly's stomach. Her mouth went dry, her lips felt parched. She licked them nervously, staring at Randy Niebuhr, an animal instinct within her silently screaming, *danger!*

"Nice," he murmured.

The word sent a chill through her.

"I like that, sexy lady. I like ladies who lick." He slid his tongue suggestively over his own lips. "I like ladies who lick all over...lick and suck." Randy took a step toward the bed. "Oh, yeah...licking and sucking, sexy lady. Just you and me."

Holly's final shred of disbelief was drowned in a fresh wave of fear. But with it came a rush of adrenaline that jolted her to her feet. Heart pounding, mind whirling, she raced through her options.

She could scream. But who would hear? What about escape? He was blocking her path to the door. And he weighed twice what she did.

Her glance flickered to the bedside phone. Did ships use O for operator? Nine-one-one for emergencies? Hardly likely.

There was a sheet of numbers beside the phone. But what would Randy be doing while she searched for a promising one? Silly question!

Take control. Yes! That was it. She couldn't act like a victim. Her only hope lay in gaining control of the situation.

Randy took another step forward, tugging his shirt loose from his pants. Holly thrust her hand out in front of her. "You're in the wrong cabin, Randy." Oh, Lord, she hoped she sounded far more in control to him than she did to herself.

He glanced around with exaggerated innocence. "Looks fine to me. I don't see anything wrong with it at all."

"Well I don't want you in here. That's what's wrong. I want you to go—immediately." She tried to manage a glare, but Randy merely leered at her. "I said I want you to leave. You've come into the wrong cabin. *By mistake.*" She emphasized the final words, praying he'd grasp that she was offering him an excuse for his behavior thus far, praying he'd decide to go along with it.

"Oh, no, sexy lady. It was no mistake. Now let's knock off the game. I think you and me—" He paused and glanced at the door.

Oh, thank heavens! Holly's knees almost gave way at the relief that flooded her. The pounding she heard was no longer just her heart's furious hammering. Someone was knocking on her cabin door. Her mother. Oh, please let Sid be there with her! But why was her mother knocking?

"Holly? You in there?"

Not her mother. Mac!

"Mac! Mac, don't leave!" Holly darted past Randy and twisted the lock . . . then the handle.

"Mac!" Oh, no! She could feel tears forming. "Mac! Don't go! I can't get the door open!"

"Holly? Holly, what's the matter? You sound hysterical. Calm down. All you have to do is turn the lock to the left until you hear it click twice."

Turn the lock.

Click . . . click.

"Good. You've got it. Now twist the handle."

It moved! She yanked the door open and threw herself into the passageway, flinging her arms around Mac's neck.

"Holly? Holly, what's wrong?" Mac hugged her to him.

She was safe! She was safe and secure, her face buried against Mac's chest, his arms firmly around her.

"Holly?"

She felt his body tense as he spoke her name. She glanced up, her vision blurred. Tears had been making good their escape without her noticing. But through them she could see that Mac was staring into the cabin.

"What the hell is this?"

"On my way," Randy muttered, bolting through the doorway and past them.

"Hold it a minute, fella!" Mac released Holly and started after Randy.

"No! Mac, wait! Don't leave me alone!"

He looked around, glancing at Holly uncertainly.

"Just . . . just let him go. Nothing happened."

"Right," Randy agreed, backing rapidly down the passageway. "Nothing happened. I wandered into the wrong cabin. That's all." He wheeled and began running. An instant later he rounded the corner and disappeared.

Mac stared after Randy for a moment, then turned back. "Holly, are you sure nothing happened? You're crying."

"I know. And I hate crybabies. I'll be all right in a second. Really."

Mac wrapped one arm securely around her shoulders and propelled her into the cabin. He shoved the door shut, then guided her across to her bed. "Just try to relax," he murmured, drawing her down beside him, his arm still protectively encircling her.

Holly leaned against Mac's shoulder. He felt so solid and strong. How could one man make her feel so horribly threatened and another so incredibly protected?

She wasn't in any danger now. Randy was gone and Mac was with her. She willed her body to stop trembling and tried to breath normally.

"Holly? I was sitting on deck a few minutes ago and saw you boarding the ship—alone. What the hell happened after that?"

"He . . . he just followed me. And I didn't lock the door properly...and he came in and..." A fresh trickle of tears slid down her cheek.

Mac brushed them gently away. When he spoke, his voice was anything but gentle. "I'm going to kill that guy, Holly. I'm going after him."

"No. Please don't, Mac. I need you right here. I need hugging more than vengeance. He doesn't matter. But if you weren't here...if you hadn't come..."

Mac shifted his position and folded his other arm around Holly, ensconcing her snugly within his embrace. "You're sure you're okay? You're still shaking. He didn't—?"

Holly shook her head. "He didn't touch me. But, oh, Mac, he would have. And he said... the way he looked at me and I knew... I've heard about how frightening it is, but... Oh, Mac, I was scared spitless."

Mac drew her even closer so that the top of her head rested in the hollow of his neck so that she could feel the reassuring rhythm of his heart.

"We'll just sit here, Holly. We'll just sit here." Mac lapsed into silence and began tracing tiny circles on her back.

She could feel his concern... his warmth... the masculinity of his body against her... the responses within her that were saying... saying things she shouldn't be listening to.

But at least, she mused ruefully, they were telling her that Randy Niebuhr hadn't frightened her off men in general. And when it came to one man in particular...

Mac stroked her hair, his fingers catching in its wet tangles. She realized how irritating the salty dampness must be against his neck and glanced up at him, determined to sound collected.

"Sorry, Mac. My hair's all yucky from swimming. It must feel terrible. And look. I got tears all over your shirt."

"Do you think I care?" He smiled down at her—the warmest, sexiest smile she'd ever seen.

She realized he was about to kiss her... and she was about to kiss him. And then she heard the cabin door open. Her heart jumped crazily. She twisted in Mac's arms, her gaze darting fearfully across the cabin.

"Holly!" Kay stood in the doorway, a picture of surprise.

"Mom!" Holly giggled with relief.

Behind Kay, Sid stood grinning.

"This isn't at all what it looks like," Mac said, his tone deadly serious.

Sid's grin vanished.

Mac took his arms from around Holly; she felt bereft. He rose, walked across the room and closed the door behind Sid and Kay. "Holly just had a bad experience. Some jerk followed her into the cabin. Luckily I—"

"Holly!" Kay rushed to the bed and sat down where Mac had been, putting one arm around Holly's waist. "Are you all right, dear?"

"Yes. I'm fine. He frightened me, but I'm okay."

"A passenger or crew member?" Sid demanded.

"Passenger."

"Do you know his name?"

"He said it was Randy Niebuhr. But I don't know if—"

Sid crossed to the phone and began running his finger down the list of numbers beside it. "The captain's in charge of law and order aboard ship. Let me—"

"No, Sid," Holly objected anxiously. "I just want to forget about it."

"You can't do that, Holly. Did he force his way in?"

"I . . . I didn't have the door locked properly."

"Damn locks," Sid muttered. "They're a stupid design. Look, Holly, I'll call and get things started here, but you'll have to talk—"

"No, Sid! Really. I don't want to."

"Holly, I realize that's a common reaction after an attempted . . ."

Holly swallowed hard. Would Sid's saying the word make her feel even worse?

He glanced from Holly to Kay, then back, without completing his sentence. "Holly, what if this creep does the same thing to someone else? What if they aren't as lucky as you were?"

"But, I...but he'd been drinking. Maybe..." Holly felt tears welling in her eyes again and looked pleadingly at Mac.

"Sid," Mac said, crossing from the door, "leave it for the moment. Holly's too upset to deal with anything more right now. Let's give her a chance to calm down. Then she can decide what she wants to do."

She tried to smile at Mac. Instead, her mouth merely twitched and she sniffed loudly.

"Mac, you just can't—"

"Come on," Mac ordered, gazing at Holly and ignoring Sid's objection. "Let's go sit on the deck, get you out of this cabin. You could use the fresh air."

He reached for her hand and, as if he hadn't heard Kay's clucking protests, whisked Holly out of her mother's embrace and into the passageway.

"HOW ABOUT SITTING there, Holly?" Mac pointed to a couple of lounge chairs on the almost deserted promenade. "I don't know how much more gorgeous blue sky and water I can stand in one day."

"If that's a concern, this looks like the perfect spot."

They settled themselves onto the loungers. Above, a row of lifeboats hung suspended from the Zeno Deck, affording shade from the late-afternoon sun.

Directly below, on the Grenada pier, stood a long, low shed, its green tin roof boldly proclaiming Geest Industries (WI) Ltd., Banana Reception Depot.

"Do you suppose," Holly murmured, "that sign is a snide comment about the tourists who arrive at this dock?"

Mac smiled. "I take it you're feeling a little better."

"Much more than a little, Mac. I don't know how to even begin thanking you."

"No thanks necessary. It was nothing that any other wonderful, red-blooded American hero wouldn't have done. I'm just glad," he added seriously, "I was in the right place at the right time."

"Not nearly as glad as I am. But what exactly were you doing in the right place?"

"Coming to see you. I wanted to tell you that Jason and I had our talk when we got back from the beach. And it went well."

"That's good, Mac. I'm pleased. Where's Jason now?"

"Gone to watch a movie. But he really did seem relieved, Holly. So thanks for the advice."

"No thanks necessary. It was nothing that any other wonderful, red-blooded Canadian heroine wouldn't have done. I was just in the right place at the right time."

Mac laughed, his gaze lingering on her.

She looked down at her pink T-shirt and rumpled shorts. "I'm surprised you're willing to be seen in public with me." She fluffed her damp curls self-consciously. "I'm a mess."

"No, you're not. I've always been partial to the natural look."

The silence between them grew, as if they both realized they'd stepped onto dangerous ground but were uncertain whether to continue or retreat.

"Besides," Mac finally offered, "I figured I'd better hustle you away from Sid before he got you crying again."

Holly nodded. Much as she didn't want to, she was going to have to think through what had happened, and what she should do about it. "Sid isn't going to want to let this drop, is he, Mac?"

"No, but whether you report it is your decision, not Sid's."

"Mac, I simply don't know. What do you think I should do?"

"Your decision, Holly. Not Sid's or mine. But I'll be a sounding board if you want to talk about it."

"There's not really much to talk about, is there? I realize Sid's right. Randy might pull his stunt on someone else. And I don't want to be responsible for that. But you can imagine what would happen if I made a big deal of this, Mac. I'd say Randy came bursting in on me and he'd say I invited him. It would simply be his word against mine. And what did he actually do, except scare the hell out of me? I mean, I know what he intended, but he had no weapon and he didn't actually touch me. I didn't even scream. I'd be naive to think pursuing this would do anything but embarrass me. Maybe it's cowardly, but I just want to forget about it."

"That's understandable, Holly. But I'd hate to see that jerk walk away scot-free. I've been thinking maybe Sid and I could set him straight, without even involving you."

"What do you mean?"

"Well, suppose I tracked Randy down. Even if that's not his real name, I'll recognize him when I see him. Then Sid and I could have a private talk with the creep. I suspect Sid would know the right things to say."

"Would you do that, Mac? Do you think Sid would agree to it?"

"Would I do that? I'm the one who was going to kill Randy, remember? And I think Sid would go along with me." Mac paused, chuckling. "I guess Sid wouldn't go along with murdering Randy. But if Sid and I talked to the guy, all of us would probably feel better—except Randy, of course."

"Oh, Mac! I know I'd feel better. A whole lot better. I guess it's taking an easy way out, but we're on a vacation. I don't want to turn it into an episode of *Miami Vice*."

"Well, wait a minute, here. Let's not discard that idea too fast, Holly. Would I get to play Don Johnson?"

"I doubt it. I'm sure Sid would insist on playing the cop role."

"Well...okay, if I'm not going to be in line for hero worship, let's forget Miami Vice. I'll discuss the talking-to-Randy plan with Sid before dinner."

"Thanks, Mac. I really do appreciate that."

"But first I'm going to get you a little treat. I want to be certain you've calmed down completely before I take you back to your mother."

"I'm calm, Mac. I don't need anything."

"Trust me. It's a magic elixir that banishes all fears and woes and makes you feel a hundred percent again. My special remedy. It always works for Jason and me."

"Oh, well, if it's magic, how can I dare resist?"

Mac pushed himself up. "Don't run off anywhere."

Holly watched him walk away. In a tiny corner of her mind a barely audible voice was repeating the word *run.... Run for the hills,* it whispered. But she couldn't quite make sense of why it was saying that.

Holly noticed a few passengers scurrying down the pier and absently wondered if anyone ever missed a sailing. The *Taurus* would be weighing anchor for Curaçao in half an hour.

She glanced along the promenade, her pulse quickening. Mac was headed back, carrying a mug, grinning his disarming grin. She tried to picture David, but his image wouldn't form in her mind. There was no point in pretending she didn't know why. The "why" was walking toward her.

The strength of her physical reactions to Mac still amazed her. But it was her emotional response—the way her feelings for him were growing stronger by leaps and bounds—that was truly dangerous.

Dangerous and guilt-provoking. She couldn't possibly let herself fall for a man she'd barely met. No. More than that. She couldn't possibly let herself fall for a man who wasn't David.

"Voilá!" Mac held out the mug.

Holly gazed at him, wondering what there was about his smile that tempted her to throw common sense to the wind. She swung her legs over one side of the lounge chair and sat sideways on it, reaching for the drink.

"This is what you call a treat?" she teased, peering into the mug and smelling the tartness. "Hot lemonade? Mac, it's at least eighty, even here in the shade.

Isn't hot lemonade only legal on cold winter days in the far north?''

Mac assumed a phony-looking hurt expression. "It's not plain, ordinary, garden-variety lemonade, Holly. I told you, it's a magic elixir. Try it."

Holly obediently took a large sip and almost choked. "You give this to Jason? Take my advice, Mac. Don't let the child welfare people find out about that or they'll have you thrown into jail."

"Well, actually, I leave the white rum out of Jason's. But I figured you could do with it." Mac lowered himself onto the lounge next to Holly's again, facing her, his knees almost but not quite touching hers.

She eyed the two sets of bare legs . . . well, she eyed Mac's, intensely aware of how close he was to her.

Sometime over the past few days, simply being near Mac McCloy had become a turn-on. And his all-American hero act had just added a whole new wrinkle to her attraction to him. Now being close to him made her feel safe, as if she was still cuddled reassuringly in his arms.

But that safe feeling was undoubtedly a symptom of developing insanity. Because *safe* was the last thing Mac was—at least for her. He was exciting, tempting and dangerous, but definitely not safe.

She took another sip of the potent lemonade, then put it on the deck. She should go back to her cabin and make sure Kay wasn't fretting about what had happened.

Just as Holly was about to tell Mac that, he reached across and took her hands in his. She stared down at them, her mind ordering her hands to pull away, her hands disobeying. She looked up at Mac's face.

"Holly... I want to talk about us."

"No, Mac. That's not a good subject." Her mind began sending a sterner message to her hands, and she made a halfhearted attempt to free them.

Mac merely tightened his grip. "Okay. Not about us, then. Let's have a philosophical discussion."

"About what?"

"Don't sound so suspicious. How about fate? Do you believe in it?"

Holly shook her head firmly, aware of where he was leading. "I'm a scientist, Mac. Not a fatalist."

"Well, we don't have to call it fate if you'd rather not. We can call it kismet or serendipity if you'd prefer. But whatever we call it, don't you think it explains how we met? Don't you think it's amazing we met at all?"

"It's amazing a lot of people meet each other, Mac.'

"Yes, but the odds against our ever meeting were astronomical. You're only here because you won this cruise on a game show you didn't even want to be on. And I booked on a last-minute impulse, only because Margaret had an unprecedented spurt of generosity about letting me have Jason. Now how can you say some form of fate, by whatever name you want to call it, didn't decide we should meet?"

"Mac... you're being silly. You know you are."

"No. That's not true. Not everything has a rational, scientific explanation. But that doesn't mean it's silly. Holly, I know I shouldn't push, especially today when you've been so upset, but we don't have much time. And things have changed."

"Mac, nothing's changed. I'm still as engaged as I ever was." She looked away, focusing on the improbable Banana Reception Depot sign.

Mac released one of her hands, then gently turned her chin back toward him and captured her gaze. She felt in danger of melting under the midnight intensity of his eyes.

"Holly, you may be engaged, but you're sitting here holding my hand."

"That's only—"

"Look," he rushed on. "Look, I know this isn't the right time or place for what I'm going to tell you. But I don't think there ever will be a right time or place."

"Then you probably shouldn't tell me, Mac."

He smiled slowly and her danger of melting multiplied by a million. "I have to, Holly. Otherwise I'd go through life with an extremely guilty conscience."

Guilty conscience? Even if there was more than one guilty conscience lurking, the most extreme one couldn't possibly belong to Mac.

"Holly, I was in the change house at Grande Anse this morning. I heard you and your mother talking."

"Talking?"

"About you . . . and David . . . and tingles . . ."

"You eavesdropped!"

"I didn't. I just happened to overhear. Another example," he added with an infuriatingly smug smile, "of fate intervening in life."

"Oh, Mac!" Holly wrenched her hand from his, more embarrassed than she could remember ever being. She tried to rise, but he quickly leaned forward and placed his arms on either side of her, trapping her where she sat.

"Holly, listen to me for a minute. I apologize. I didn't mean to overhear, but I did. And I got the distinct impression that you and David aren't—"

"Don't, Mac! Don't say it. I love David."

"But he doesn't make you tingle, does he?"

He asked the question so quietly that Holly barely caught his words. "That's none of your concern, Mac."

"What about when I kissed you, Holly? That's my concern, isn't it? Did you feel tingles then? Or excitement? Or fireworks? Or whatever you want to call it?"

"Fireworks are for kids."

"That doesn't answer my question. And I'd really like an answer. Because I sure felt something. And holding you, Holly—when I was holding you in your cabin I felt... Hell, I feel something every time I look at you. I'm feeling something right now."

Holly took a deep breath and looked down at Mac's hands. They were resting a millimeter on either side of her bare thighs.

Tingles? He wanted to know if he made her tingle? Why only ask about that? This very moment his nearness was sending tingles and quivers and a little aching throb and a hundred other wonderful sensations through her body. And she had no right to be feeling any of them.

"Holly?"

She shook her head, staring at his hands. "No, Mac. I didn't feel anything at all special when you kissed me."

He didn't speak.

She waited.

He outwaited her.

She looked up, knowing it wasn't wise. His face was so close to hers that she could feel the warmth of his breath.

"Is that the truth, Holly?"

The truth? The last thing she wanted to deal with was the truth. But she owed Mac so much after this afternoon. The least she could give him was an honest answer.

"All right, Mac. You didn't even really have to ask, did you? There's obviously a chemistry between us—tingles and fireworks and a fire alarm bell to boot. I enjoyed kissing you, far more than I should have. And, yes, it excited me. But that isn't the point."

"Oh, Holly, that's very much the point."

"No, it isn't. The point is..." Remembering what the point was suddenly became difficult. Mac had begun gently caressing her bare thighs.

He had to stop. She had to stop him. But he was making her feel so... Maybe he'd stop on his own in a minute or two.

"Mac, the point is that I'm going to marry someone else. And I don't intend to cheat on him—before or after we're married."

"That's admirable of you."

"Are you being sarcastic?"

"No. I'm not. I think scruples are admirable."

"Then I think you should stop stroking my legs."

"All right. There." He took her hands in his again. "And I think what you should do is give us a chance."

She eyed him uncertainly. "What do you mean?"

"You and me—*us*. Holly, the first time we met I realized there could definitely be an *us*. I don't know for sure how terrific an *us* it would be, but I suspect somewhere between fantastic and unbelievable. And what I mean is that I don't think we should turn our backs on that possibility."

"Mac, I—"

"Let me finish. I don't think we should spend the next week and a half running away from each other when that just might be the stupidest thing in the world we could do. Holly, I think we should be spending every moment we can together."

Holly stared at Mac, thinking of her impetuous first marriage, trying to recall whether the feelings she'd had for Brad had been anything like the ones that had been swirling so crazily inside her for the past few days.

Yes. They were definitely similar. But this time those feelings were a thousand times more intense—and a thousand times more hazardous. The stupidest thing in the world she could do was to go along with Mac's suggestion.

"Mac, we keep losing sight of the central issue here. I'm engaged to be married. And spending time with you would be tempting fate. I'm willing to admit that. And my tempting fate wouldn't be fair to David. It just isn't right."

"Holly, you know what I don't think is right? After that conversation I overheard, I don't think David's right. Not for you. And I don't think your mother thinks David's right for you. And maybe, way deep down, you don't even really think so."

"Mac, do you want to know what I really don't think? I really don't think this is any of your damn business! Or my mother's business, for that matter. David's perfect for me."

"Except for the lack of fireworks," Mac said softly.

"To hell with the fireworks! I'll live without them! Mac, I don't want you and any damn fireworks complicating things for me. Hormones screwed up my life once. Now it's firmly on track and I'm not about to jeopardize that for... for a tawdry affair on a ship."

Mac took a deep breath and leaned back. "Holly, I'm sorry. I didn't mean to get you upset again. And I certainly wasn't thinking in terms of a tawdry affair. Holly... I honestly wasn't going to get into this. Even after I heard you and your mother talking, I decided to just leave you alone, not say a word. But then... Holly, I'm not even certain what all the *thens* were, but I think they included Jason talking about brothers and sisters and Betty Pritchard being pregnant and that little red-haired girl in the lounge this morning. And suddenly I was thinking about having more children. I've never thought about that before, but there I was, thinking away. And then I started imagining you having babies with David whatever-his-name-is—"

"Lawrence. David Lawrence."

"Well, anyway, when I saw you boarding the ship earlier, I was thinking about all those things. That was when I decided to go down and talk with you for a bit—but just to tell you about my conversation with Jason. Then, after I got there, well, sometime between Randy leaving and your mother and Sid arriving, I realized how much I already care about you. I realized that I couldn't just let you wander back out of my life without saying a word about..." Mac gazed at her for a long moment, then shrugged. "Guess it turned into a pretty long word. I only meant to tell you I wasn't thinking in terms of a tawdry affair. I was thinking in terms of seeing if you and I really had something."

"Mac, it just wouldn't be right for me to—"

Mac released her hands and silenced her with his fingertips, brushing them softly across her bottom lip. "Holly, what wouldn't be right is if you passed up something that might possibly fall between 'fantastic and unbelievable' and settled for just 'companionship and things in common.'"

Holly tried to ignore the little voice that was telling her that what was right or wrong in this situation might not be as clear-cut as she'd thought. The voice refused to be ignored, so she concentrated on resisting the urge to kiss Mac's fingertips. If their gentle touch against her lips could cause the sensations of desire she was feeling at the moment, something between "fantastic and unbelievable" was more a likelihood for her and Mac than a mere possibility. But it wasn't—

Mac took her hands in his once more. "Look, we have a week and a half. We could do a lot of getting to know each other, see how we feel by the end of the cruise. If things aren't as great between us as I think they'll be, if you're still convinced David's right for you, well, there's nothing to lose and a lot to win, Holly. Just spend a little time with me."

Holly tried to think logically. Mac's proposal had a rational ring to it. What if in her determination not to make another mistake, another emotional error, she was being *too* sensible? What if she was passing up...? But how logically was she capable of thinking when she was with Mac?

"Holly, I won't push you into doing anything you don't feel right about doing. I promise. I just don't want to let you walk away without... I just don't want to spend the rest of my life wondering, 'what if?'"

Holly looked down, avoiding Mac's gaze. His hands, holding hers, were distracting enough on their own. Had she already become so emotionally involved that she, too, might spend the rest of her life wondering, 'what if'?

"Come on." Mac rose, drawing her up with him. "I meant what I said about not pushing you, Holly. I'll walk you back to your cabin so that you can get ready for dinner."

CHAPTER TEN

THE LIGHTS WENT OUT, plunging the dining room into blackness. Table conversations broke off midword. Amber glows from cigarette tips floated eerily in the darkened smoking section.

"What's happening?" In the stillness Jason's whisper sounded like a roar.

"I don't know," Holly murmured. "We'll have to wait and see."

A moment later, at the far end of the room, the galley door swung open, creating a beam of light. Suddenly march music blasted forth and, in single file, the tuxedoed waiters strutted through the spotlight into the dark room and down its center aisle. Each man held a platter aloft, its contents flaming. Collective oohs and aahs greeted the presentation.

"What is it, Dad?"

"Must be dessert. The menu promised baked Alaska flambé. But it didn't mention a floor show."

"It looks just like the opening of the Olympic games, huh, Dad? Remember on TV? Remember the torches? This looks exactly like that."

Mac laughed. "Well, maybe not exactly."

The flames died and the lights flashed back on. Applause rewarded the waiters and the trio of musicians who'd sneaked into the darkened room. The waiters bowed slightly, platters still aloft, then headed to their assigned tables and began carving the desserts into gooey slices.

Jason stared, wide-eyed, at the huge portion he was served. "I've never had baked Alaska before," he confided to Holly. "It looks way better than Christmas pudding."

"Is this the most unusual Christmas Day you've ever spent, Jason?" Kay asked as the boy dug into the meringue.

"It sure is. And it's not even over. There's a Junior Cruisers' party in the disco with bingo and games, and I think Santa might be coming again. It's started already. The kids who eat early were going there right after dinner." He paused to devour a spoonful of ice cream from the Alaska's center. "The party doesn't end until twelve o'clock," he continued. "And then Kevin's mom and dad are going to take us to the midnight buffet. And *then* I'm going to sleep over in Kevin's cabin. His mom said we can even play cards if we aren't too tired."

"I still think Mrs. Pritchard must have been suffering from sunstroke when she invited you to spend the night, son."

Jason shrugged, stuffing another spoonful of desert into his mouth. "She says it doesn't matter. She says the baby keeps her awake half the night, anyway, that it almost kicks her out of bed."

"You're going to have to make a tough decision, Jason," Sid offered. "You'll either have to miss a few more minutes of the party or do without a second helping of baked Alaska."

"Yeah. If only it wasn't so melty, I could take it with me."

Holly laughed. "If it wasn't so melty, it wouldn't be so good."

Jason made his tough decision, demolished a second helping of desert, then raced off. Gradually the dining room began emptying.

"Come outside with me for a minute, Holly," Mac suggested quietly.

She hesitated. The more she'd thought about his spending-time-together idea, the more certain she'd become that agreeing to it would be foolhardy.

"For Pete's sake!" he whispered. "You don't have to look at me as if I'm the big bad wolf. I've just got something to tell you."

She glanced quickly at her mother. Before coming to dinner, they'd talked about the incident with Randy, including, of course, Mac's fortuitous arrival on the scene. And, throughout the conversation, Holly had waited for a question about what was going on with Mac.

But Kay hadn't asked a single question about him, not even the obvious one of why he'd been coming to their cabin. That struck Holly as most peculiar. Something was percolating in her mother's mind.

Holly eyed Kay thoughtfully. She was gazing absently about the dining room. Either she'd grown strangely unobservant over the past few days or she was simply pretending not to see what had been happening under her nose.

Holly took the hand Mac was offering, then released it once she was standing. "We're just going to get a little air, Mom."

Kay glanced at them. "That's nice, dear. Do you want us to save you chairs in the lounge? For the entertainment?"

"Yes. At least I'd like one."

"Mac?" Kay asked.

"Sure. Thanks."

Holly followed Mac outside. At the end of the promenade, near the ship's stern, the deck was bright, its mast strung with lights. But the promenade itself was dimly lit. And the shroud of night was heavier than usual. Neither the moon nor stars were visible. The only illumination on the water beneath them came from the *Taurus*.

Glittering bubbles of the ship's wake trailed alongside her and, nearby, tiny wave caps shimmered. But fifty feet out blackness reigned. Blackness and silence—disturbed only by the throbbing hum of the engines and the lapping of the calm sea below.

Mac walked a few yards along, then stopped, resting his arms on the railing. Holly leaned against it too, carefully keeping her distance from Mac but unable to keep her gaze from tracing his profile. Even in the semidarkness she could make out the straight line of his nose and the strong definition of his jaw.

"Well?" she finally prompted. "What were you going to tell me?"

Mac smiled at her. "Sorry. Didn't mean to keep you in suspense. Watching the water's hypnotic."

Holly nodded. Watching the water was hypnotic and the setting was pure romance. This wasn't the place to be alone with Mac McCloy. She shifted a fraction of an inch farther away from him, wishing he didn't have the world's sexiest smile.

"Sid and I talked to Randy."

A tiny chill raced through her. Even thinking of the man upset her. "You did? Already?"

"Yes. He was no challenge to find. He'd gone back to the bar."

"And?"

"You want the details or simply a synopsis?"

"I . . . maybe I'll make do with a synopsis."

"That's probably just as well. Sid did most of the talking and a lot of what he said I wouldn't want to repeat. Turns out that cops' vocabularies on television are pale versions of the real thing. At any rate, Sid introduced himself as a detective. Of course, he didn't bother mentioning that he was retired, or that he had nothing to do with security aboard ship. Then he introduced me—clearly implying I was a cross between Rambo and Mr. T. Then he proceeded to frighten the devil out of Randy, told him about sex offenders getting thrown into jail cells with other prisoners and being raped themselves. Apparently it's a great example of criminal justice by the criminals. He finished off with a very explicit description of what would happen to Randy if we heard about him even looking at another woman on this ship."

"What? Explicitly what would happen?"

"That's a detail," Mac teased her gently.

"I think maybe I'd like to hear just that one."

"Well, Sid said we'd, uh, castrate him. Of course, he used more colorful language and he went into great detail about exactly how we'd do it."

"Oh."

"And that was just with reference to Randy bothering *any* of the female passengers. If he sees you again, Holly, I expect he'll set a new world's speed record trying to get away from you. Course I wouldn't be at all surprised if Mr. Niebuhr stayed in his cabin for the remainder of the cruise."

Holly exhaled slowly, realizing how anxious she'd been feeling and how much Mac's news had relieved that anxiety. "Thanks, Mac. I only wish *thanks* didn't sound totally inadequate after you've made me feel so much better."

"Well, as I said, Sid did most of the talking. You should be thanking him."

"I will."

They stood silently for a few moments.

"I guess we should be heading back inside, Mac. The show will be starting soon."

"It'll be a while yet. Jason and I are going to explore Curaçao tomorrow," he added casually. "If you'd like to join us, we'd be delighted."

Holly gazed along the railing, wishing decision time hadn't come, wishing she didn't want to take a chance she'd be crazy to take. "Thanks, but I...I don't think I can. Sid has plans for Mom and me."

Mac looked away, staring into the darkness, then abruptly wheeled around and started away back toward the door. After several strides he stopped and turned. "Would you mind coming inside with me, Holly? I really don't want to leave you alone out here in the dark."

And she didn't really want him to leave her alone at all. But she didn't want to go inside into the light. If she did, Mac would see she'd begun crying.

"I'm not afraid of the dark, Mac," she managed. "I'm not a child."

"Damn it, Holly! Don't be too sure about that. I'd say you still have an awful lot of growing up to do."

She couldn't answer. She merely gazed into the black night, not wiping away her tears until after the sound of Mac's footsteps faded to silence.

HOLLY SLIPPED into the chair beside her mother just as the lounge lights fully dimmed and the master of ceremonies stepped onto the raised dance floor that doubled as a stage.

"Where's Mac?" Kay whispered.

Holly shrugged, staring studiously at the MC.

The first act he introduced was a comedian. At least the man claimed to be a comedian. There was nothing humorous about his patter. In fact, it was making Holly feel like crying again.

"There's Mac now," Kay whispered, waving across the lounge.

He was standing in the doorway, glancing around the almost full room. He started in their direction but stopped about twelve feet away, spoke to a young woman sitting alone, then sat down in the chair beside her.

"Who's she?" Kay demanded.

Holly glared at the back of Mac's head.

"Do you know her, Holly? The blonde Mac just sat with?"

"No."

"Isn't she the girl we noticed by the pool yesterday? You know the one I mean. The one who had on the incredibly indecent string bikini? Remember? Sid said she could be arrested for wearing it in New York State. I didn't realize Mac knew her, dear. Did you?"

"No." Holly continued glaring.

Mac leaned closer to the blonde and spoke to her.

She laughed, touching his arm as she replied to whatever stupid thing he'd said.

And then Mac smiled at her.

Only seeing his profile, Holly couldn't be certain if he'd produced one of his incredibly sexy smiles. But she'd bet he had! And he was leaning toward Miss String Bikini again whispering another undoubtedly asinine remark into her ear.

And now they were standing up...and walking out. Mac's hand was on the small of Blondie's back. Holly watched, unable not to.

Once they'd disappeared, her gaze drifted back to the entertainment. The comedian was bowing his way offstage. The audience was applauding. And Holly felt as if she were dying.

"Are you all right, dear?" Kay rested her hand solicitously on Holly's arm. "You don't look well."

"No. I don't feel quite right. Mom, I'm going back to the cabin."

"We'll come with you. I don't want you going alone."

Kay turned, spoke briefly to Sid, then they all rose and headed for the doorway. Holly followed the others blindly, grateful for their company. Without them she wouldn't have found her way in a million years.

But how could she be so upset? Mac was obviously complete and total slime. He'd wanted to spend his time with Holly Russell, had he? He'd wanted to see how fantastic they were together? Ha!

Despite his Mr. Wonderful routine, clearly all he'd really wanted was to spend time with a warm female body. Any warm female body—although a young one with bleached hair, big breasts and a string bikini was apparently right near the top of his list.

How could Holly even have been tempted? It was just lucky she was a sensible woman. Lucky she thought things through logically. Yes. She was incredibly lucky.

Then why did she feel so incredibly awful?

Sid and Kay stopped. Holly glanced around. They'd reached the cabin. "I...I didn't mean to spoil the show for you two. If you'd like to go back, I'm fine now. Thanks for walking me, though."

Sid glanced questioningly at Kay.

"I think I'll stay with Holly, Sid." She unlocked the door.

"Yeah. Well, an early night's not a bad idea. We arrive in Curaçao before seven tomorrow, and I'd like to be on deck. The Willemstad harbor's supposed to be the prettiest one in the Caribbean."

"Sid?"

"Yes, Holly?"

"Mac told me about your conversation with Randy. Thanks. I really appreciate what you did."

Sid shrugged. "It wasn't much."

"Well...it means a lot to me. So thanks."

"You're welcome. Night now."

Kay hesitated in the passageway, wishing Sid goodnight, while Holly went inside and plopped herself down on her bed, trying to force the image of Mac with his hand on Blondie's back from her mind. What did she care where he put his hands? As long as they weren't on her. She swallowed hard, wishing that were the truth, then glanced across the cabin, trying to manage a smile as Kay locked the door behind herself.

Her mother walked over and perched on the edge of her own bed. "Sid told me about his conversation with Randy, dear, while we were waiting for the show to begin. Don't you think he and Mac handled things perfectly?"

"Yes. Perfectly."

"Holly? You aren't crying, are you?"

"No." She sniffed, betraying herself.

"Holly? It's still Christmas Day, dear. I'm sure there's a rule that says people can't cry on Christmas Day."

"I have before. Do you remember, Mom?"

"I don't think so."

"I was nine years old. I was certain you and Daddy were going to give me a puppy for Christmas. But instead you gave me clothes and a pair of goldfish."

"Myrtle and Minnie," Kay murmured. "Well... Christmas isn't a good time to give puppies. You know that."

"Oh, Mom, when you're nine years old any time's a good time for a puppy." Holly sniffed loudly again.

"Well, we did buy Major for you the following spring, for Easter. But that isn't what you're crying about now. What's wrong? Did Mac's telling you about the conversation with Randy bother you?"

Holly shook her head.

"Then what is it, dear? When you left the dining room you seemed fine. What upset you? Did Mac do something?"

"He...Mom, he invited me to explore Curaçao with him and Jason tomorrow."

"Well that's nice, dear. I'm sure you'll have a lovely day. But you still haven't told me why you're crying."

"Mother! I'm not going off with Mac McCloy tomorrow! And I told him that. I'm going with you and Sid."

Kay looked genuinely puzzled. "But why would you do that? I don't want you to come with us and be bored, Holly. Not when you have a good alternative."

"I won't be bored."

"But you were objecting to Sid's plans for Curaçao, dear—the casino and all. You'd have more fun with Mac and Jason."

"Fun? Fun? Mother, don't you see what's going on here? Why in heaven's name are you shoving me at Mac? Don't you see that he and I..." Holly stopped speaking and stared at the floor. She'd already said far more than she'd intended.

"Holly? You and Mac are what, dear?"

"I...I just meant he's an attractive man and...well, it's probably a bad idea for me to be...you know, Mom."

"I'll admit to having wondered, dear. But I decided it wasn't my place to—"

"Wasn't your place? Mother, I distinctly recall you promising David you'd be the perfect chaperone on this trip."

"Ah."

Holly waited for Kay to say something more. She didn't.

"What do you mean, 'ah'?"

"I mean...I mean I'm very fond of David. While he was training under your father he became almost like a son to me. But he's not my son, Holly. And you *are* my daughter. And I love you. And I want you to be happy. And I think you're perfectly capable of chaperoning yourself...if you want to."

"If I want to? And what on earth does that mean?"

Kay shrugged. "Well, given the way I've seen Mac looking at you, I thought possibly..."

"What way have you seen him looking at me?"

"You know, dear."

"No, I don't know! At least I'm not sure I know! Mother, this sounds like a replay of our conversation this morning. Why do you keep implying I know what you mean about things when I'm not at all clear. How do you think Mac's been looking at me?"

Kay glanced away. Holly followed her mother's gaze across the cabin and focused on David's roses. They were fading. A guilty lump formed in her throat.

"Mac has been looking at you," Kay said quietly, "the way your father looked at me."

Holly stared at the roses. "And David?" She had to force the words out past the guilty lump. "Does David look at me like that?" She watched her mother closely, uncertain what answer she wanted to hear.

"I'm not sure, dear."

"What do you mean you're not sure? I've known David for years! I've known Mac for days! How can you have noticed the way Mac looks at me and not the way David does?"

"I guess... Holly, I guess since your father died I just haven't been noticing that sort of look. But in the past few days since Sid..."

Holly eyed Kay in dismay. "Since Sid what?"

"I told you, dear. I told you this morning. It has to do with the tingles. The looks go with the tingles."

"Oh, Lord!" Holly threw herself facedown on the bed. "Mom, I wish we'd never come on this cruise! I wish we'd never gone on *Your Knowledge Is Your Ticket*. I wish we'd never gone to California. Oh, Mom! I wish I were dead." Holly heard Kay crossing between the beds, then felt a tentative pat on her shoulder.

"Dear, I think you're overreacting a little. Now tell me exactly what you see as such a serious problem here."

Holly rolled onto her side. ''Which one do you want me to start with, Mother? The one where you're falling for a man who's totally unsuitable for you and who's going to go back to the Bronx at the end of this cruise? Or should I start with the one where I'm in love with my fiancé, but Mac McCloy is causing those tingles you're telling me about and looking at me with those damn looks you've suddenly started to recognize again?''

''Let's not worry about me at the moment, Holly, because I'm not the one who's upset. And I don't consider Sid a problem at all—and he's certainly not your problem.''

''Fine. Then let's get back to Mac. Oh, let's not even bother! What difference does it make? He's already moved on down the line to that bleached bimbo. And Jason's sleeping in his friend's cabin tonight. Which means Mac's probably taken that...that...'' A trickle of tears escaped.

Kay brushed them from Holly's cheek. ''Do you really believe he's that kind of man, dear?''

Holly shrugged miserably.

''Well, I don't think he is, dear. I like him. And so does Sid. I suspect that little act in the lounge was simply to make you react exactly as you've reacted, to make you realize that perhaps you shouldn't be so quick to reject suggestions.''

''What suggestions?''

''Well...you just told me, dear. Mac suggested you explore Curaçao with him and Jason.''

''Oh, no, that's not it! That's not it at all! He wants me to spend my time with him... Mom, he thinks maybe the two of us...that maybe David's wrong for me and...''

"I see." Kay paused. "But what do you think, Holly?"

"I told you. I think I wish I were dead." Holly rolled back onto her stomach and pressed her face into the pillow, hoping she'd smother. "Mac couldn't possibly be right for me," she finally burbled into the pillowcase. "He lives in Denver. And his ex-wife is a psychologist. And I get the impression that's left him with a lot of latent hostilities that he might ultimately direct at me."

"Holly, you know better than to try fooling yourself with pretentious psychobabble."

"Well, aside from anything else, Mac's a youngest child."

"Oh, dear. I'd hoped I'd heard the last about that silly research of yours."

Holly shoved her pillow aside. It was too fluffy to smother against. She glared at Kay. "My research wasn't silly! It was scientific."

"Well...you take its implications far too seriously. You're a psychologist, not a chemist. There are more exceptions when it comes to dealing with people than there are in the pure sciences. You know that, dear."

"What about Brad and me?"

"Holly, you aren't the only woman in the world to have made a bad marriage. So Brad was a youngest child. So what? How many times have I reminded you that your father was an only child and I'm a youngest?"

"That's just one example!"

"And so are you and Brad." Kay stroked Holly's back. "Would you like to know that I think, dear?"

"Why ask me that?" Holly muttered. "You're going to tell me, anyway."

"I think that if seeing Mac merely walk out of a room with another woman has got you this upset, you'd better give some long, hard consideration to the idea of spending time with him."

"Mom! How can you be suggesting what you're suggesting? It just would be unfair to David."

Kay brushed Holly's hair aside and kissed her cheek. "What really wouldn't be fair to David, Holly, is if, deep down, you don't love him enough but you marry him, anyway. I'm going to get ready for bed now, dear. I want to be up early in the morning and watch our arrival in Willemstad with Sid."

Holly buried her face in the pillows again and silently screamed.

SLOWLY THE *Taurus* glided along the narrow stretch of water that was St. Anna Bay. On the far side of the bay stood Willemstad's waterfront. The row of Dutch Colonial buildings looked like delectable iced pastries—tinted softly with food colorings, trimmed with sugary white gables and roofed with candy-red tiles. They stood shoulder to shoulder in the sunlight, their pink, green, blue and yellow reflections sparkling in the harbor. Ahead, on the left, lay the pier. The *Taurus* was inching her way closer to it.

Their arrival had been spectacular and Holly wished she'd been able to give it her full attention. She shoved her fists deeper into the pockets of her white cotton jumpsuit and ordered herself to stop scanning the deck for Mac. He might still be in bed. And wherever he was he might not still be interested in her company.

He could even be with Blondie this morning...
could even have been with Blondie all night. What if
he was with her for the remainder of the cruise?

Holly forced herself to concentrate on the scenery.
Sid had been right. There couldn't possibly be a pret-
tier harbor in the Caribbean. In fact, there might not
be a more picturesque one in the world.

Taurus Today had referred to the Curaçao capital as
Little Amsterdam. But the buildings that lined
Amsterdam's canals were mostly dark brick or painted
in drab browns and grays, whereas Willemstad looked
like a bright, cheery watercolor from a child's story-
book.

Just as the ship came to rest and the crew set about
to secure it, Jason appeared. "*Bon bini*, Holly!"

Holly's glance flickered along the promenade until
she located Mac, standing several feet away. Alone.
She exhaled slowly, shot him a smile that she hoped
looked warm rather than nervous, then focused her
gaze on Jason. "Bon what, Jason?"

"*Bon bini*. It's...what is it again, Dad?" He turned
expectantly to his father.

Mac moved a single, hesitant step nearer. "Papiamento."

"It's Papiamento," Jason repeated. "It's a mixture of a whole bunch of languages. It's what people
speak on Curaçao. Well, they mostly speak English,
too. But Papiamento's neat."

"I didn't realize you were a polyglot, Jason."

"A what?"

"A language expert."

Jason grinned. "I'm not an expert anything yet,
Holly. It's Mrs. Pritchard who knows about lan-

guages. She's got a little book called *Island Phrases*. But she taught me and Kevin some words. *Bon bini* is kind of like *have a nice day*. And she was calling Mr. Pritchard *dushi* this morning. That means *dear*."

Holly smiled. "Well, Jason, my little *dushi*, I'm impressed. You certainly know more Papiamento than I do." She glanced at Mac. "I gather the Pritchards survived spending the night with Jason and Kevin."

Mac merely nodded.

Holly bit her lip. If a question about who Mac had spent the night with escaped, she'd die.

"We just saw Mr. Lambert and your mother, Holly. He was telling us about the bridge that opened to let us pass. It's called the Queen Emma Bridge. And it's a...a..."

"A pontoon bridge," Mac supplied.

"Right. And it opens about thirty times a day. And whenever it's open a ferry goes across from near where we dock to the town. But only when the bridge is open, so Dad said we could wait at the ferry landing until the bridge opens again."

"And take the ferry to town," Holly concluded.

"Yeah. And then we can walk across the bridge coming back."

"I guess," Mac offered, "you and Kay and Sid are going over to Willemstad as soon as the boat's cleared."

"Well...well, actually...actually I don't think they want me along."

Mac said nothing.

"I think they'd like some time alone."

Oh, no! He still wasn't saying anything. He didn't want her along, either. Mac had had a change of heart.

He'd had a change of heart, and she was making an absolute fool of herself.

Why was she doing this, anyway? What had possessed her? She didn't want her mother and Sid having time alone. And did she really even want—

"You can come with us, Holly. Can't she, Dad? If she doesn't mind waiting for the bridge to open again?"

Mac stared at her evenly, his midnight eyes unreadable. "Of course, Jason. She's welcome to come. But she probably has other plans."

Now how the hell was she supposed to read that remark? Was Mac simply being a gentleman, offering her an easy out if she was still determined to avoid him? Or was he telling her he didn't want her with them?

"Do you, Holly? Do you have other plans?" Jason asked.

"No. No, I have no other plans, Jason." Oh, Lord. Had that really slipped out? Before she'd decided whether Mac still wanted her along or not? She had no plans and she apparently had no pride or self-respect, either. And her loyalty to David left a lot to be desired. And she—

"Well, that's fine then." Mac beamed at her.

He did still want her company! That was wonderful! Wasn't it?

"Good morning, ladies and gentlemen," a female voice said over the public address system. "It is 7:00 a.m., the temperature is seventy-seven degrees and Curaçao customs has cleared us for disembarkation. I hope you enjoy your day on the island."

Holly glanced at Mac, uncertain whether she really wanted to enjoy her day or not. The more she enjoyed, the deeper she was digging herself.

Mac smiled one of his devastatingly sexy smiles at her. "Let's hit the dock ... *dushie*."

CHAPTER ELEVEN

ON THE PIER BELOW dark silent figures were casting off. The throaty departure whistle blasted at the stroke of midnight, and moments later Mac felt the engine's initial throb as the *Taurus* shuddered to life.

The ship inched from the dock and began its slow sail past Willemstad's waterfront toward the sea. He glanced down at Holly and smiled. She was staring over the observation deck's railing with an expression of childlike fascination.

"Enjoy our day, Holly?"

She flashed him her thousand-watt smile. Every time he saw it he wanted to hug her.

"The day was absolutely wonderful, Mac."

Wonderful. That was a good word. Wonderful and fantastic and incredibly unbelievable.

Of course, he'd be hard-pressed to recount a single detail about what they'd done or seen on Curaçao. But every new moment he shared with Holly seemed like the best moment of his life. What would forever with her be like?

"I wish we had more time here, Mac."

More time. Yes, that was definitely what they needed. More time here or anywhere else—as long as they were together. Enough time for Holly to accept the reality that was staring her in the face.

She could deny believing in fate all she liked, but surely she couldn't deny cosmic truth. Holly Russell and Mac McCloy were destined for each other. That was the clearest example of a cosmic truth he'd ever come across.

How many women had he met whom he'd thought about every moment he was awake? Whom he'd dreamed about every night? How many women made his pulse race each time he looked at them?

One. Only one. And she was standing mere inches from him. Yet it might as well be a million miles unless she changed her mind about marrying that faceless David . . . unless Mac could make her change her mind.

And how could he accomplish that in the short time left on this cruise? She might admit their day had been wonderful, but every so often he'd sensed her feelings of guilt about being with him. If he pushed, she'd likely back right off.

He had to take things slow and easy. But that was difficult when they had so little time. And when it was all he could do to keep his eyes, and his hands, off her.

He gazed out over the railing at the fantasyland they were passing. Their arrival at Willemstad had been merely enchanting; the departure was breathtaking. The pastel waterfront buildings, softly bathed by floodlights, shone like jewels set in the black velvet of the Caribbean night. Occasionally one of the people walking along the street or sitting at an outdoor café waved farewell to the *Taurus*. And each time Holly waved back.

"Jason should be out here with us," she murmured.

Mac glanced at her once more. A wisp of breeze was playing with a strand of her hair...her long, sexy hair. He had difficulty thinking of a coherent response to her remark.

"I guess Kevin's more fun to be with than old folks like us, Holly. And scenery apparently rates second to the midnight buffet if you're ten years old. Or if you're pregnant. I'm lucky Betty wants to eat twice every night, or I'd be stuck with the late-night parenting detail."

Holly smiled at his comment. How could her smile be so sensual? How could it be so arousing?

"Oh, look!" She pointed ahead at the Queen Emma. The little bridge, swinging open as the *Taurus* neared, was fancifully decorated with sparkling red and green lights. "Willemstad's like a fairyland, isn't it, Mac? It's almost as if we're in an unreal world."

Mac draped his arm lightly across Holly's shoulders, unable to resist the lure of her closeness any longer. He felt her tense at his touch. "Relax," he whispered. "I just wanted to reassure myself that you're real, that you're not a figment of my imagination."

She smiled a nervous-looking smile but didn't pull away. He remained motionless, afraid to move a muscle, simply relishing the warmth of Holly's body next to his.

"We're in Aruba tomorrow," he finally offered.

"Yes. Cruising gives you a peculiar sense of time and space, doesn't it? It's strange to wake up in a different country each morning."

"Would you ... Holly, would you like to spend the day with Jason and me again?" His heart stopped beating while he waited for her answer.

"I ... I'm not sure, Mac. I'll have to see what my mother wants to do. And I don't have any idea where she and Sid are right now. Can I let you know in the morning? I'll call your cabin before breakfast."

"Sure. No problem." No problem unless she turned him down, that is—in which case hara-kiri would undoubtedly be appealing.

Mac stood silently, unable to ignore the urgent messages of desire his body was sending to his brain, using all his willpower to keep from folding Holly into his arms and kissing her. He had to resist doing that. Playing this game by her don't-touch rules might be driving him insane. But trying to play by any other rules might drive her away.

WHILE SHE WAITED for Kay to finish dressing, Holly absently flipped through the growing stack of *Taurus Today* issues. On top was the current one, featuring information on Martinique. Beneath was yesterday's—Bonaire. Then the previous day's copy about Aruba.

It was just as well she'd decided to keep the newsletters as souvenirs because her memories of the past few days focused far more on simply being with Mac than on what they'd seen together. She really shouldn't be spending so much time with him. But he kept asking. And she kept finding it impossible to say no.

Just as Kay walked out of the bathroom, a sheet of paper was slipped under the cabin door.

"See what that says, will you, dear? I haven't been able to find my glasses for two days now."

Holly picked up the paper. Information Update was splashed in huge red print across the top of the page. "It's datelined today, December 29, Martinique. It says, 'Tendering. Due to heavy traffic in the port to-day, the TSS *Taurus* will be required to drop anchor in the harbor. There will be a berth available in Fort-de-France at noon. Until that time the ship's tenders will run between shore and ship on a regular basis. Those passengers taking part in the tours will have priority on the first tenders. Please be prepared to show your tour tickets at the gangway. Please listen carefully to all announcements. Thank you.'"

"Oh. Well, I'm sure Sid will have everything figured out," Kay said.

"I take it you and Sid have made plans again."

Kay gave Holly a sheepish-looking smile. "He was talking about hiring a taxi for the morning and going across the island to St. Pierre. You know, dear, the city that was destroyed by a volcano."

"Mmm. I noticed something about it in *Taurus Today*."

"Would you like to come with us, Holly? Although Fort-de-France is supposed to be a charming city."

"I . . . I'm not quite sure what I want to do." Well, actually she was sure. What she wanted to do was spend another day with Mac. But she felt guilty about wanting that. He was like a growing addiction. The more time she spent with him, the more time she wanted to spend, even though she knew she was playing with fire.

She should probably be sticking like glue to Kay and Sid. That would be in her best interest, not to mention her mother's. Kay hadn't come in last night until after Holly had fallen asleep. Lord knows what she'd been doing. Thus far Holly hadn't gotten up the courage to ask.

"Do you have any other options for today, Holly? I certainly don't intend to abandon you."

"Well, I could always do something with Jason and Mac. In fact, I promised to phone them before breakfast again this morning and tell them what my plans are."

She glanced anxiously across the cabin, knowing her mother would mentally translate "them" to "him," wanting to know what Kay thought about her daughter spending so much time with Mac. But Kay's expression was impossible to read.

"Dear," she finally said hesitantly, "you look unhappy. I hate to see that, especially when I'm enjoying this vacation so very much."

This *vacation*. Yes. They all had to keep in mind that this was merely a break from their normal lives. And cruising created a totally artificial, temporary environment.

"I'm not really unhappy, Mom. And I don't mean to be a drag. It's just that I'm having trouble keeping things in perspective. And I'm worried that you are, too."

"What do you mean, dear?"

"I mean, that this isn't reality. And in no time at all we'll be going home, back to the real world. And...Mom, I just don't want anyone to be hurt. Not you or me or David." Her glanced flickered involuntarily to the roses. They'd almost completely withered. Before she left for breakfast she'd throw them out.

"I see," Kay murmured. "But people do get hurt at times, Holly. It can't always be prevented. There's certainly no reason to be concerned about me, though. I know what you've been thinking, dear. But New

York City isn't Timbuktu. And Sid's already invited me to visit him—to meet his daughter and see the city. He suggested," she added with a tiny sigh, "that I spend Valentine's Day there. Isn't that romantic?" Kay beamed happily at Holly.

She tried to smile in return. But the news flash didn't diminish her worries in the least. Far from it. Kay was going to New York. As Sid's Valentine date. To meet Sid's daughter. And then what?

Back in the real world Sid and Kay led totally different lives. Sooner or later those differences were going to smack one or the other of them in the face. If there were ever two ships that should pass in the night, they were her mother and Sid.

"So, Holly, are you going to come with us to St. Pierre?"

"I . . ."

"Darling, why don't I run ahead and get us a table for breakfast while you make that call to Mac. Then you can let me know what you've decided.

"So," HOLLY elaborated, sipping a final few drops of coffee, "the Pritchards are taking Jason and Kevin to a special beach—one that's a ferry ride from the port."

"That'll be the beach at Anse Mitan," Sid said. "It's supposed to be like the French Riviera. I thought about us going there," he added, turning his attention to Kay, "but I decided we'd be pushing ourselves just to see St. Pierre this morning and Fort-de-France this afternoon."

"Well, anyway," Holly continued uncomfortably, "that leaves Mac on his own, so I thought I should . . ."

She gave up on her explanation in the face of Sid's grin. She wasn't fooling either him or her mother. It was extremely embarrassing.

"That was thoughtful of you, dear," Kay murmured. "And what are the two of you going to do?"

"Well, I threw my beach things into my bag, but we've pretty well decided just to look around Fort-de-France. I noticed Mac and Jason leaving the dining room a few minutes ago," she added, rising. "Guess I'd better head up to the Zeus Deck."

"The gangway's lowered off the Euclid Deck today, Holly."

"Oh, thanks, Sid. Then I guess that's where I'd better head. Enjoy your trip to St. Pierre."

She fled, half wishing she'd had the willpower to turn Mac down on the phone earlier, half dying to spend another day with him. When she reached the Euclid Deck, he was standing just inside the exit to the gangway. Even in Bermudas and a casual checkered shirt, he was undoubtedly the most handsome man in the world.

She dragged her gaze from him and smiled at the Pritchards and Jason. "Hi, everyone."

"Hi, yourself," Mac said softly. "How would you feel about a last-minute change of plans—about hitting the beach this morning and saving Fort-de-France for this afternoon?"

"The real question," Betty offered, patting her stomach, "is how you'd feel about playing surrogate mother for a few hours. Joe and I promised the boys we'd go to Anse Mitan. But it turns out that I'm stuck aboard ship until we dock. Take a look down the gangway and you'll understand why."

Holly stepped out and peered down. Usually the metal stairs led directly to a pier. This morning they led to nothing but sea—a rather rough sea.

A crew member stood on a tiny platform attached to the bottom of the steps. One of the lifeboats sat bobbing a few feet from the *Taurus*'s hull.

Betty followed Holly out. "I watched a couple of people getting into the tender. That fellow at the bottom hoisted them across the water. If he tried to hoist me, he'd probably get a hernia. And my balance is so off-kilter that I'd likely end up in the drink. I don't dare risk it."

"You sure don't. Why not just sit on deck and relax for the morning? Mac and I would absolutely love to have the boys."

Betty laughed. "Spoken like a true nonparent. But that would be terrific. I'd hate to disappoint them. And if you bring them back to the ship for lunch, Joe and I will take them both for the afternoon—give you and Mac some time alone together."

Holly smiled uneasily. Was everyone pushing her at Mac or was she simply imagining it? She glanced inside at the others. "Are we off?"

"Yeah!"

"You bet!"

The boys raced down the gangway.

"Want me to go ahead?" Mac asked. "Break your fall?" he added with a grin.

"There'd better be no fall to break. I hate to sound like a scaredy-cat, Mac, but my legs aren't very long. And it's a giant step across to that boat."

"Don't worry, short stuff. We'll get you aboard safely."

Holly started apprehensively down the metal stairs after Mac.

"Have fun," Betty called out.

Jason and Kevin easily scrambled into the tender, but Holly didn't like the way the addition of their little bit of weight set it rocking.

"See," Mac said, glancing back up at her. "Those two don't have long legs, either."

"Yes, the boys are half monkey. I'm not."

Mac swung himself into the lifeboat, then reached back, placed his hands firmly about Holly's waist and lifted her over the water.

"You're a show-off," she whispered as he put her down. "You did that as if I weigh nothing at all."

Mac merely stood grinning at her... until she realized he was still hugging her securely, even though her feet were firmly planted on the floor. She glanced about. She and Mac were clearly providing amusement for the twenty or so passengers already seated.

"I think we're supposed to sit down, Mac."

"Oh. Right."

Once they were settled on the bench seat behind Jason and Kevin, Holly looked around again. Three crew members sat by the open engine in back. It was putting noisily, pumping a fog of gas fumes into the air.

Beneath the seats narrow wooden planks—separated by half-inch gaps—formed the tender's floor. Between the planks and the hull several inches of water lapped audibly with each rocking movement.

Holly pointed down, nudging Mac. "That doesn't augur well for a dry run."

"Where's your sense of adventure?"

"It must have jumped ship during the night."

Mac laughed. "Well, at least the ferry to the beach is likely to seem safe in comparison. Here," he added, "I'll just put my arm around your waist, then you won't have to worry about falling overboard."

No. All she'd have to worry about then was how much she liked having his arm about her. She tucked her bag securely against the side of the lifeboat, trying to decide if her outside seat was the best place to be.

"Check how gorgeous Fort-de-France looks from here," Mac suggested.

Holly gazed obediently across the mile or so of water between the *Taurus* and shore. The town did look lovely, like a village in France with picture-pretty houses rising up the sides of hills that finally disappeared into billowy white clouds. A high church spire dominated the left-hand side of the town while a large fort sat to the right. Moored in the inner harbor were fifty or sixty sailboats, all flying the French tricolor. Between the *Taurus* and shore sat another cruise ship—apparently also without a place at the pier.

Holly glanced back at the gangway as three more passengers braved the leap into the tender. Then one of the crew members revved the engine and they were off.

When they hit the first wave, Holly realized an outside seat hadn't been the smartest choice. Little droplets of spray splashed up over the side. They quickly increased in number and turned into more substantial drops as the boat gained speed.

Another tender passed them on its return trip to the *Taurus*. The crew of the all-but-empty craft waved. And then the two wakes clashed and a serious wave washed into the lifeboat and over Holly.

She let out a shriek of surprise and glanced down. She could easily be a refugee from a wet T-shirt contest. Her blue jersey was clinging to her breasts, clearly defining her nipples, and her wet white shorts were almost transparent.

She looked at Mac. He was obviously trying not to laugh—and obviously not making any effort to pull his gaze from her body. She finally caught his glance.

He grinned. ''Too bad the *Taurus* is in line for a berth, huh, Holly? We won't have the enjoyment of a return trip by tender.''

''Very funny.''

''Dad! Dad!'' Jason shrieked from the bench in front of them. ''Look at that ship! Look at its name!''

Mac and Holly gazed at the moored cruise ship they were passing.

''It's the *Pacific Princess*, Dad! It's the Love Boat! Boy, is it ever bigger than the *Taurus*. Do you think Gavin MacLeod's aboard?''

''Anything's possible, son.''

Jason and Kevin continued to stare back in apparent awe of the *Pacific Princess* for the rest of their trip to shore.

''I'd hate to think,'' Mac muttered, ''that seeing the Love Boat is going to be Jason's major recollection of Martinique.''

''Boy, that was neat, Dad,'' Jason said as they climbed from the tender onto the pier. ''The real Love Boat. Just like on TV.''

Mac shook his head. ''Jason, what you should have been watching just now was our approach to the Island. What's special about cruising is the different places and unusual things to see. Here we are, starting our second week already, and all you seem to be seeing is the ship's pool and dining room, and beaches.''

"But those are all different, Dad."

"Well, how about starting to pay some attention to the scenery? I'm beginning to think you'd have been happier at a resort with a poolside snack bar than on this cruise."

"Nope. I like this cruise, Dad. If we hadn't come, I wouldn't have met Kevin . . . or Holly."

"See," Mac whispered to Holly as they started along the dock after the two boys. "Even Jason recognizes the significance of fate."

"That's only because he's your son," Holly whispered back. "You've likely brainwashed him."

Mac laughed, wrapping his arm around her waist and drawing her closer. She knew she should pull away, but the twinge of guilt she felt over Mac's growing familiarity wasn't nearly as strong as the rush of pleasure his touch sent racing through her. In fact, his arm encircling her felt so right that she found herself musing about fate all the way to the ferry . . . then all the way across the bay to Anse Mitan.

When the ferry docked, the boys raced off it. "Which way?" Jason demanded, looking back. "Which way's the beach?"

Mac gestured at a sign reading La Plage. It pointed to a trail leading through a heavy stand of tropical growth.

"What language is that, Dad?"

"It's French for beach."

"Boy, *la plage*. Wait till Kevin and I tell his mom we've learned another foreign language. We'll see you at the beach, Dad."

"Just a minute, Jason."

The boys paused with clear reluctance.

"Don't go into the water until we catch up with you."

"Okay, but hurry."

Mac grinned down at Holly. "Ah, *ma chérie*. Alone at last." He casually took her hand.

That gesture seemed every bit as right as him putting his arm around her.

You are, a little voice whispered into her ear, *really asking for trouble.*

Shut up, a second little voice ordered. *She's not doing anything wrong. What harm is there in holding hands?*

Terrific. Now she was having audible arguments inside her head. Hearing one voice was bad enough. But two? A full-blown schizophrenic episode was probably imminent.

"I'll have to change when we get to the beach, Mac. I'm not wearing my bikini under my clothes."

"I noticed that when you had your shower in the tender."

Before she could think of a reply, the foliage thinned and the beach appeared before them. Just as it came into view, so did Jason and Kevin, racing back. They stopped amid imitation brake screeches and loud giggles.

Holly tried to pull her hand from Mac's. He merely tightened his grip. The boys didn't seem to notice; they were bubbling over with excitement.

"What's up, son?"

Mac's question sent them into a fresh fit of giggles.

"We were just looking at the scenery, Dad, like you told me I should. You were right. It's real neat."

Holly glanced at Mac. He clearly had no more idea of what was going on than she did. She looked back at Jason. He was eyeing her with one of the phoniest expressions of innocence she'd ever seen.

"Are you going to put your bathing suit on when you get to the beach, Holly?"

"Yes. Of course. I was just saying to your father that I hope there are change rooms."

Kevin practically doubled over with laughter.

"Come on, Dad," Jason urged with another giggle. "Hurry up. You'll like the scenery, too."

Mimicking the noise of roaring engines, the boys took off toward the beach again, this time running backward, watching the adults.

"What do you suppose the little monsters have discovered?" Mac muttered as they passed the last of the growth.

Holly gazed along the beautiful stretch of sand and realized what the little monsters had discovered. She mentally chalked up another point for Sid. The beach at Anse Mitan was definitely reminiscent of the French Riviera.

Mac suddenly stopped walking and swore quietly.

Holly managed not to laugh. "I see a change room over there, Mac. I'm going to hit it—right now. To put on *both* halves of my bikini."

"You aren't leaving me alone to deal with this, Holly!"

"You bet I am, Mac. I'm not the one who offered to bring two ten-year-old boys to a topless beach. You can have the pleasure of discussing French culture with them."

CHAPTER TWELVE

MAC TOYED with the last of his cognac, not wanting the evening to end. "What did you enjoy seeing most today, Holly?"

"Well...it certainly wasn't the beach. If Kevin had asked me one more time why I wasn't taking off my bikini top, I'd have strangled him."

"You? You were considering infanticide?"

"He's too old for it to have been infanticide."

"Adolescentcide, then?"

"Whatever."

"I'm shocked, Holly. Here I've been thinking how good you are with children."

"We all have our limits. But, to answer your question, I liked everything about Fort-de-France. It really reminded me of a little town in France, with all that old-world-style architecture and those narrow streets parked solid with Peugots and Renaults. And some of the signs, Mac. I was sorry I didn't have a camera when we came across that one reading, Salon de the Fast Food."

He smiled, aware how easily Holly made him smile. "That was hardly a challenge to translate, was it? You know, we've been managing pretty well for a couple of gringos. I wonder how we'll do in Santo Domingo tomorrow? I've heard English isn't all that commonly spoken there. How's your Spanish?"

Mac held his breath. For the past few evenings they'd been playing this game—he would pretend to take for granted that Holly would be spending the following day with him and she would go along with his assumption. But each time they played he worried that she might have a change of heart.

"My Spanish, Mac? Let me think."

He breathed again.

"I know *sí, gracias* and *por favor*."

"That's it? Yes, thank you and please?"

"'Fraid so."

"We could be in trouble then. I'm about as fluent as you are. But at least we'll be polite, even if no one understands what we're being polite about."

He lapsed into silence, gazing across the cocktail table at Holly. Something about the filmy white dress she had on was making it difficult to keep his eyes off her.

Its fascination, he decided, lay in the way it exposed her shoulders, with only wisps of straps holding the top up. She had the most gorgeous shoulders he'd ever seen. And the way the thin gold chain she always wore disappeared between her breasts drew his eyes down to... He looked up again, sensing she was watching him.

"I think," she suggested with a trace of a smile, "we should call it a night."

"You'd leave me alone already? It's barely eleven and I have to wait around until the midnight buffet's over to pick up Jason."

"And I have to get some sleep. This fresh sea air is taking its toll."

"All right. Just let me finish my drink." He swirled the remaining drops around in the snifter, wondering how much longer he could make them last.

"Do you want to see the historic sites tomorrow, Mac? The old walled city? Sid told me there's a terrific fort that Jason would love."

"Sounds good." Of course, with any luck, Jason would want to go off with the Pritchards, leaving Mac alone with Holly.

"Well, I was talking with Betty earlier and she told me that she and Joe are planning to explore the colonial section. Maybe the six of us could spend the day together—the six of us and Betty's trusty island phrase book."

"Ah . . . yeah. Spending the day with the Pritchards is a possibility."

"Will you ask them about it when you pick up Jason later?"

"Ah . . . sure. I could do that." Mac swore silently. How had a potential day alone with Holly just turned into a group outing?

"Good." she gave him a devastating smile, then pushed back her chair. "I really to have to go."

"Right. I'll walk you."

They started out of the bar and Mac put his arm lightly around Holly's shoulders. She leaned comfortably against him, absently wondering precisely when she'd stopped jumping each time he touched her. At some point her body had begun ignoring her brain. Or perhaps her brain had reviewed the ground rules and decided that relaxing when she was with Mac wouldn't bring her world crashing down around her, that she could loosen her control without losing it entirely.

After all, no one was being hurt. She and Mac were simply enjoying each other's company during this vacation. Yes, that was all they were doing, she reassured herself. But inside her head she heard a sardonic laugh that reminded her she was a psychologist. She knew all the tricks for fooling herself when she was into self-deception.

She was enjoying Mac's company, all right. But she was also rationalizing her behavior like crazy. And she was trying with all her might to make herself believe they were involved in an innocent friendship.

Because, as long as she didn't admit that she might be falling in love with Mac, it couldn't be happening. And, if it couldn't be happening, no one could get hurt. That was perfectly logical.

Besides, she did have this situation between the two of them under control. She was even avoiding potential problems by thinking of ideas like spending tomorrow with the Pritchards.

That was definitely a good plan because a nagging little fear was lurking in the back of her mind—a nagging fear that too much time alone with Mac might reveal a fallacy in her perfect logic.

They headed down several flights of stairs to the Aphrodite Deck, then along the passageway. "Well," she murmured, digging out her key as they neared her cabin, "I'll see you in the morning. You won't forget to mention my suggestion to the Pritchards?"

"No. I won't forget."

"Night, then, Mac." She unlocked the door, pushed it open . . . and froze where she stood.

"Holly!" Kay exclaimed with a startled gasp, quickly clutching at her unbuttoned blouse.

Holly stared at her mother. The cabin was lit only by the dim glow of a reading light near the window. But her mother wasn't reading. And she wasn't sitting by the window. She was sitting on her bed—with Sid.

Only they weren't exactly sitting. And Holly didn't even want to imagine how unexactly they'd been sitting before they'd realized someone was bursting in on them.

"I . . . I'm just going for a walk, Mom. I'll be back in a while."

Mac watched quizzically as Holly jerked the door closed, snapped the lock and threw her key into her purse.

She shrugged uncomfortably at him. "My mother and Sid are . . . were . . ."

"That's not exactly a surprise, is it?"

"I . . . well, I guess I'd never have believed . . . and those beds are so narrow! Want to go for a walk on deck with me, Mac?"

A CHIFFON DRESS with spaghetti straps quickly proved no match for the late-night breeze. Holly shivered slightly. A second later Mac's suit jacket was around her shoulders.

"Mac, how could you see me shiver in the darkness?"

"X-ray vision."

"Of course. Superman. I should have guessed."

"Let's sit down for a bit, Holly." He took her hand in his and led her along the deserted promenade, finally stopping to sink onto a lounge chair, stretching his legs out in front of himself. "No," he objected when she moved to sit down on the chair next to his. "Over here." He drew her onto his lap.

"Mac, I—"

"It's all right. I just don't want you to be cold. There." He carefully adjusted his jacket over her shoulders, then slipped his arm beneath it and cuddled her against his chest.

"Mac . . . you're making me very nervous."

"Don't be. Platonic you want? Platonic you've got."

She rested her head tentatively on his shoulder, repeating to herself that he just didn't want her to be cold. That sardonic little laugh echoed inside her head once more but, sitting so close to Mac, it was strangely easy to ignore.

"You okay?" he asked quietly.

She shrugged. "I guess my subconscious has been denying that my mother's still interested in sex. I mean, consciously I realized . . . but coming face-to-face with it was a bit of a shocker."

"Everyone has trouble thinking about their parents that way, Holly."

"I know. Remember when you were a kid, Mac? Were you certain that your mother and father had only made love as many times as they had children?"

Mac chuckled. "Definitely. With my parents it was four kids, four times. And of course, after I was born they stopped entirely."

"Silly, isn't it? I mean not being more realistic when I'm an adult? But seeing Sid there made me think about my father and that . . ."

"Sid's a good guy, Holly. I don't think you have anything to be concerned about."

"Oh, Mac, I guess he's all right. But not for my mother. She's only going to get hurt."

"How do you figure that?"

"Because she's falling for him—if she hasn't completely fallen already. And she thinks there may be a future for them. She's excited because he's asked her to visit him in New York. And you know that's not likely to come about. At the end of the cruise they'll go back to their separate lives and she'll probably never hear from him again."

"No? I wouldn't bet on that. I think Sid's fallen every bit as hard as your mother has."

"Mac, even if that's true, they're an impossible match. My mother enjoys bridge and the symphony and the theater. And Sid likes blackjack and craps. And can you imagine him at a symphony performance? And I wouldn't be surprised if he's never been to the theater—despite living in New York. He's all rough around the edges."

"Sure you're not exaggerating their differences, Holly?"

"I don't think so. Even cocktail parties make Sid nervous. I remember him saying that. And, the other day, you told me you wouldn't want to repeat most of what he said to Randy. My mother could never adjust to a man like Sid."

"Holly, he'd never talk in front of Kay the way he talked to Randy. Not in a million years. He treats her as if she were a china doll."

"Right. He thinks she's a delicate china doll when, in reality, she can be stubborn as hell about things. And she thinks he's a take-charge genius who knows everything about everything. But in reality he's simply a man who noses around about what's going on."

"That's merely the cop in him, Holly."

"I realize that. But what I'm saying is that they're looking at each other through the proverbial rose-colored glasses and not seeing how unsuited they are for each other. Just think about it, Mac. Sid spent his life as a cop, seeing the seamy side of life in the Big Apple, while my mother was being a pampered doctor's wife in a quiet Canadian city of half a million. Think about how different their worlds have been, what different people that's made them. And, even setting that aside, I can't imagine either my mother being happy in New York or Sid being happy in Winnipeg."

Mac shifted Holly's weight a little and cradled her head in the hollow of his shoulder. "Holly... sometimes the people you'd think most unlikely to be right together end up fooling you."

"I guess. Sometimes."

"And hasn't your mother managed her life pretty well up till now?"

"Well ... yes."

"And only she can decide what she wants as her future, right?"

"Of course."

"Then it seems pretty futile for you to be worrying about what she might do or what might happen to her. Besides, the only two people who know what goes on in a relationship are the two in it."

"Oh, Mac. I just don't know. Maybe you have a good point. And no matter how much I worry, she'll do what she wants. She's made that pretty clear."

"Exactly. So stop worrying."

Mac lapsed into silence and Holly sat quietly in his arms, relaxing against the warmth of his chest, grateful for his sensible advice. Gradually she became aware of his hand resting on her hip...of the way its warmth was seeping into her bloodstream...slowly spreading through her body, spreading unmistakable tingles of desire. And then, beneath the cover of his jacket, Mac moved his hand upward and began gently stroking her bare arm.

His fingers brushing against her skin were startlingly arousing. How could such an innocent motion cause the ache that began throbbing deep within her?

It was all she could manage to keep from caressing him in return. But he couldn't possibly intend his touch to feel as sensual as it did. He was simply stroking her reassuringly, as one would stroke a child. And yet he was making her want to feel his hands moving over the rest of her body, making her want his lips kissing her, making her want—

Mac slid his hand up the full length of her arm and began to tease at her spaghetti strap, slipping his fingers beneath it, then tracing its flimsy cord of fabric down to the bodice of her dress...then slowly back up to her shoulder.

With each stroke her skin felt more alive; the heat from Mac's fingers seemed to penetrate her body more fully. Her sense of wanting to feel his hands on the rest of her body became an urgent need for him to caress her breasts. His fingers lingered at their swell, and she held her breath, aware of the rapid hammering of her heart.

Then Mac's hand retreated to her shoulder once more, leaving her nipples fully aroused and aching for his touch. She cuddled closer against his chest, unable to resist brushing her breasts against it, sending him an unspoken yet unmistakable message. But his fingers continued upward, softly grazing her neck, then brushing slowly to her ear.

Lord! She'd never realized how sensitive the skin beneath her ear was.

His hand trailed slowly from her neck back to her shoulder, telegraphing tiny electric sparks to every nerve ending in her body.

She overcame the urge to take his hand in hers and move it to her breast but resisting took every ounce of her willpower.

Gradually she grew aware how hard Mac was beneath her—hard with wanting her. She could feel her own body growing liquid with desire, realized she was beginning to move her hips suggestively against him.

This couldn't be happening! Her body couldn't be betraying her. She tried to force her thoughts to David. It was impossible to do. It was Mac's touch she wanted . . . Mac's body she was craving.

"Holly?" he whispered softly against her ear.

The warmth of his breath sent electric currents of longing sizzling through her.

"Holly . . . let's test your imagination."

Test her what? Right now? While her resolve was already in the midst of miserably failing a test? While she was imagining how wonderful making love to Mac would be?

"Holly?"

"What?" she managed anxiously. Mac couldn't possibly have any doubt about what she wanted. And, wherever his game was leading, she was liable to say yes whether she really meant it or not.

"I just want to ask you a test question, Holly."

"A test question?"

"Yes. You said you couldn't imagine either your mother being happy in New York or Sid being happy in Winnipeg. Well, could you imagine me happy in Winnipeg...or you happy in Denver?"

Her body tensed involuntarily. She struggled to sit up but Mac tightened his hold.

"Relax, Holly. It's simply a test of your imagination."

"I...Mac, where you or I might be happy isn't something I've thought about."

"Why not? You've thought about your mother and Sid in different cities. Why not about us?"

"Mac!" She pushed firmly against him. Her momentary insanity had passed. What the hell was she doing sitting on Mac's lap, wishing what she'd been wishing, acting like Holly Hormone?

But he didn't release her. He just stroked her arm until she gave in and leaned hesitantly against his chest once more.

"Holly, doesn't it seem strange to you that you've been thinking about your mother's future and not your own?"

"Mac, my future's set. I've told you that before. I don't know why I ever agreed to this harebrained spend-time-together idea of yours in the first place. And I certainly don't know what I'm doing here at the moment."

"Don't you, Holly?"

"No, I—"

Mac's fingers pressed against her mouth, preventing further words. Silently he traced her lips, his thumb softly caressing their flesh and gently separating them. One of his fingers slid along the bottom of her front teeth, then slipped past them, brushing against the tip of her tongue.

Holly tentatively licked his fingertip. It tasted of salt...incredibly delicious salt. She sucked on the end of his finger, then on another, taking them into her mouth one by one, drawing tiny circles on them with her tongue, gradually pulling them farther in, then releasing them, then sucking them in again until Mac slid them across the outside of her mouth once more, leaving her lips moist to the cool air.

And then his mouth covered hers, warming her lips against the night, moving on them in a kiss that made her heart race with excitement. His tongue explored her mouth as his fingers had just done. And her tongue darted to continue the lovers' game it had instigated with his fingers.

Mac caressed her hip, stroking her thigh. There was nothing between his hand and her body but thin chiffon and delicate lingerie. She could feel the slight tremble in his touch, was certain he could feel that she was quivering beneath it.

With each caress the silky fabric of her dress slipped a little farther upward until she felt the cool air whispering against her bare thigh, until Mac's hand was stroking her skin without even a scrap of fabric between his palm and her nakedness.

She had to stop this. But there was no way on earth she could. And then Mac's kiss subsided. He moved his hand from her leg and cradled her tightly in his arms.

She buried her face in his chest, uncertain whether she felt relieved or disappointed or ashamed. Mac's breathing was ragged, and his chest heaved against her. She didn't move. If she moved, Mac would expect her to speak. And she had no idea what to say.

Gradually Mac began breathing more easily; gradually the throbbing within Holly stilled. Finally he tilted her face up, brushed her cheek lightly with a kiss, then allowed her to burrow her head against his chest once more.

"I'm a total idiot, you know," he whispered.

"Why?" One word and her voice caught. She silently prayed Mac wasn't hoping for conversation.

"I distinctly recall promising you 'platonic.' I must have been out of my mind."

"Mac . . . Mac, thank you for that."

"For being out of my mind?"

"No, silly. You know what I mean."

"Yeah. Right. But isn't there a saying about nice guys finishing last?"

"Oh, Mac." Holly shifted a little so that she could look at him. He was so incredibly appealing it was all she could do not to kiss him again. "Mac, maybe if things were different . . . but they aren't. I told you that up front. I told you David's—"

"Don't say it, Holly. I don't want to hear how David's perfect for you. Especially not at this moment. No. Wait. Maybe I do. Or, better yet, I want to hear what makes you so certain he's perfect for you and I'm not."

Holly peered at Mac in the dim moonlight. "Is that a serious question?"

"Very."

"All right. I'll give you a serious answer. In fact, I'll give you several serious answers. First off, David's a wonderful man."

"And I'm not?"

"Well . . . well, yes you are. At least you seem to be. But I've known David for years. I've known you for a week."

Mac shook his head. "Time's immaterial when it comes to being wonderful. So we're both wonderful men. Continue."

"Well . . . I'm used to the type of life David leads. He's a doctor, like my father was. In fact, David did his cardiology training under my father."

Mac shrugged. "So what? So doctors make a lot of money? Architects don't starve."

"No, Mac. It's not the money. What I mean is I'm used to a doctor's family life. I don't get upset when the phone rings in the middle of the night or when plans have to be canceled at the last minute."

"Architects' phones rarely ring in the middle of the night. And we seldom have to cancel plans. So there's nothing to get upset about."

"Well, at any rate, I'm used to doctors. And then there's the fact that David's an eldest child. Only children tend to be demanding, Mac. And eldest children take that in stride—they coped with demanding younger siblings while they were growing up. I've told you before that only children have to marry eldest siblings."

"As I recall, we agreed that wasn't a carved-in-stone certainty."

"But for me it is. I know some people can adjust their behavior relatively easily, Mac, but I can't. I didn't before. And what with my first husband being a youngest child and youngest children being spoiled and only children not coping well with that and the mess my marriage turned into—"

"Holly, how long ago did you marry Brad?"

"Five years."

"And are you a more mature woman now? Do you cope better with different people?"

"Of course, but—"

"And didn't I hear your mother say how immature Brad was?"

"Yes, but—"

"Well, Holly, I'm not the least bit immature. And I may be a youngest sibling, but I was far from spoiled. And you're going on about the evils of youngest children because you were once married to one is as irrelevant to us as if I insisted I could never be happy with you because Margaret was a psychologist and I wasn't happy with her."

Holly sat quietly for a moment, trying to decide if Mac's logic could actually be as reasonable as it sounded. More likely she was simply growing confused.

"Well, I've already given you at least three valid points about David. And four..." Four. Where the hell was four? "I...David and I have a lot in common," she added lamely. "And David lives in Winnipeg. And everything's all planned."

"Oh, Holly," Mac murmured. "Holly, don't you see what you're doing by trotting out that list?"

"You asked me to, Mac."

"I know I did. But, Holly, nobody's absolutely perfect for anybody else. Not in the one-two-three way you're laying things out. And you know what?"

"What?"

"You got to reason four—or maybe it was five or six you were mumbling about at the end—and you didn't once say David was perfect for you because you loved him."

"I didn't?"

Mac shook his head.

"But I meant to! I mean, that's a given. After all, we're engaged."

Mac began gently caressing her arm again. She wished he'd stop.... Well, she sort of wished he'd stop.

"Holly, I'll admit our not having known each other for very long isn't something we should sweep under the carpet. And I'll admit the *Taurus* isn't exactly the harsh, cold world at large. It's possible things would be different between us once we were back home and got to know each other better. But, if you weren't engaged, after the cruise is over I could visit you in Winnipeg. And you could come to Denver."

"Oh, Mac, it would never work. Winnipeg? Denver? What if... what if we ever did decide on something permanent? Where would we end up?"

"Together," Mac said softly. "Wherever we were it would be together. Architecture and psychology are both pretty mobile professions, Holly. I think you're grasping at straws if you try to make a major issue of geography."

Holly gazed into the darkness. Her mother was caught up in a romantic fantasy that could never end happily back in the real world. And weren't her own feelings for Mac a similarly strange by-product of this vacation? A manifestation of some bizarre *Love Boat* phenomenon?

Odds had to be that they were.

But what if they weren't? What if her feelings were real and what if they were as intensely strong as they seemed to be?

"Holly...all I'm asking is that you think about this. That you don't go on blindly telling yourself how perfect David is for you without actually thinking about the two of you . . . and the two of us.''

"Oh, Mac, here I am, cuddled in your arms in beautiful moonlight in the middle of the Caribbean Sea. And there's no point in denying that fireworks explode between us. You're hardly playing fair.''

"Oh, come on, Holly. All's fair in love and war.''

"Nice guys finish last? All's fair in love and war? This must be your night for clichés. But not all clichés are true, Mac. And, just at the moment, I'm not sure what's true. I'm barely sure if it's night or day.''

"This beautiful moonlight's your best clue, Holly. It's night.''

She couldn't help smiling at him. "You're certain of that?''

"I'm certain of that. I'm also certain I love you, Holly. Remember that when you're thinking about David.''

Mac pulled her against him and kissed her again, preventing her from thinking about any man except him, about anything else except that he'd just said he loved her.

CHAPTER THIRTEEN

HOLLY DIDN'T WANT to die in the Dominican Republic. In fact, she didn't want to die anywhere just yet. But the odds on here and now were frighteningly high.

She wrestled down her urge to start issuing driving instructions from her seat in the back. The driver apparently didn't understand a word of English, anyway. Finally she closed her eyes as the taxi roared through the cobblestoned streets of Santo Domingo's colonial sector.

A mental search through her tiny collection of foreign words produced *muerto*. She was still trying to decide whether that meant *dead* in Spanish or in Italian when the car screeched to a jolting halt.

She peeked. They'd stopped beside a tiny park that was bounded on the far side by a weathered stone wall overlooking a river. To their left sat a row of ancient buildings housing modern-looking shops. Ahead an aged, unpretentious cathedral presided over a small cemetery.

Jason grinned across the back seat at her. "Neat ride, huh?"

"Absolutely the neatest. Like being an Indy 500 passenger in a car without shocks or seat belts."

The driver was rattling on to Mac in Spanish, pointing at some of the nearby buildings. *"Veinte pesos, señor,"* he finally demanded, holding out his hand.

Mac glanced a question into the back. Holly shrugged. "For what it's worth, in French *vingt* is twenty."

Mac handed the man several peso notes.

"Gracias, señor. Hasta luego." He gunned the engine while his passengers piled out of the little car.

"Why," Holly murmured as he sped off in a cloud of exhaust, "do I feel a compelling need to kiss the ground?"

"Don't do it," Mac ordered. "If you shouldn't drink the water, I'm certain you shouldn't kiss the ground, either. And don't go turning nervous on me," he teased. "We're doing just fine. We got where we wanted to come, arrived in the same number of pieces we left the *Taurus* in, and I obviously paid the driver what he asked for."

"I wouldn't be surprised if you paid him *more* than he asked for. He looked pretty happy. I certainly hope the Pritchards and Betty's phrase book haven't gotten lost."

"You don't really think they're lost, do you, Holly?"

"No, Jason. I'm sure their taxi will be along in a minute. I guess they just weren't lucky enough to have a Mario Andretti clone behind the wheel."

"Look at those old cannons mounted on the wall over there, son. Why don't you go and check them out until Kevin gets here?"

"Yeah. Okay."

Mac turned back to Holly as Jason raced off. "I haven't had a chance to ask you what happened when you got back to your cabin last night."

Holly closed her eyes, wishing Mac hadn't raised the subject, not wanting to recall the scene.

"I assume Sid was gone by then?"

"Oh, Mac, the only way things could have been worse was if he'd still been there. My mother obviously felt like a teenager who'd been caught making out in a parked car and she insisted on explaining how they hadn't really been doing anything serious. But her explaining only embarrassed me into babbling like an idiot—about how wonderful Sid is and how I understood her attraction to him."

"Mmm . . . when did you change your mind?"

"Don't joke, Mac. It really was awful. I can't believe some of the things I said just to make her feel better. But, worst of all, she informed me that ships' captains can't legally perform marriages anymore."

"That's the *worst*? I'd have thought you'd be relieved."

"No, Mac. Don't you see? The fact she knew that must mean Sid's asked about it. And there's only one logical reason he'd have asked. Right?"

Mac's expression told her he couldn't think of another. He glanced away, without replying, at the sound of an approaching car. "There's the Pritchards' taxi now, Holly. Try not to worry about your mother. It's pointless. We talked about that last night. Remember?"

Holly forced a smile. Did Mac actually think she'd forgotten their talk last night? A single word of it? Hardly. She'd been awake until dawn thinking about that conversation. But not the part about Sid and her mother. It was the part about David and her and Mac that had kept repeating itself inside her head.

If only she'd been able to figure out what on earth she should do. If only she wasn't still so totally confused.

Kevin leaped from the taxi, waved fleetingly at Holly and Mac and sped across the park to join Jason. Joe climbed from the front seat, then helped Betty out of the back.

"I've got a recommended route for touring the old town in here somewhere," she told them, digging around inside her purse. "Aha!" She pulled out her map, glanced at it, then surveyed the area. "That," she said, gesturing toward the cathedral, "is St. Mary the Minor where Christopher Columbus is buried—or not buried, depending on which source you believe. And it's just a short walk from here to the Alcazar where his son, Diego, lived in the early 1500s."

"I thought your specialty was languages," Holly said, grinning. "Sounds more as if it's history."

"Betty knows a little bit about everything," Joe assured them. "Unfortunately it's usually just enough to get us into trouble."

Betty made a face at him. "Before we get into trouble today, dear, there's the jeweler we heard about." She pointed to one of the tiny shops across the street. "And look, they're just opening up."

"And I'll bet my bottom peso those bars protecting the display window mean the jewelry's expensive. According to Betty," Joe went on, glancing at Mac, "the Dominican Republic is famous for its amber. And, also according to Betty, I'll be a dead man if she doesn't get some."

MAC AND JOE SORTED through their peso notes and left a stack of them on top of the lunch bill.

"Things would be easier," Joe muttered as they all left the restaurant, "if we didn't have to deal with a different currency every time we got off the ship."

"That's part of the adventure of cruising, dear," Betty told him. "Besides, if you were clever about figuring out exchange rates, you'd probably have gone into cardiac arrest this morning when you were paying for my necklace."

"A bazzillion pesos," Joe teased, "and you're carrying it around in your purse. At least Holly's wearing her—"

"Dad?" Kevin interrupted. "Dad, do we have to look at any more old buildings? Me and Jason went to go back to the *Taurus* and play in the pool."

"Jason and I," Joe corrected. "What do you think?" he asked the other adults. "We've seen the major sights."

Mac checked his watch. "We're sailing at five. That doesn't leave us a lot of time, anyway. Okay with you if we head back, Holly?"

She nodded, absently fingering the present Mac had insisted on buying for her. It was a delicate butterfly—unmistakably a monarch—created of gold filigree and tiny amber stones that ranged in color from yellow to dark orange.

It was absolutely gorgeous and had cost far, far more than she should have let Mac spend. But there had been no "letting" involved. He'd been adamant about buying it to hang on her gold chain.

"Are you up to walking back to the cathedral, Betty?" Joe asked. "We'd probably have better luck getting taxis there."

"Sure. Just don't walk too fast."

They started off, the boys dashing ahead as usual.

Mac took Holly's hand. "The butterfly looks nice against that blue dress."

"The butterfly will look nice against anything, Mac. It's beautiful."

They walked silently, hand in hand, along the almost deserted street.

"It must be siesta time," Holly murmured.

"Right. Only mad dogs and Englishmen—and crazy gringos—go out in the midday sun."

Holly laughed. "I wouldn't have imagined you were a Noël Coward fan. What else—"

One second there was no one in front of them. Then, in the blink of an eye, a blur sped past. Holly instantaneously saw the person and felt her chain gouging into her neck. She wheeled around, pulled by the tug that snapped a link. By the time she'd focused on the racing figure, it was already three buildings away.

Mac saw someone dart forward but, for a moment, didn't realize what was happening. Then his mind processed what his eyes had seen and he started running.

He raced after the thief, uncertain whether it was a boy or a slight man. Whichever he was, he ran like the wind, pulling farther ahead with every step.

Mac stumbled on the rough stone road, hopped a few steps to steady himself, then wheeled around a corner and into a side street, still in pursuit. Terrific! The side street was a damn hill. And the incline was sloping up.

They continued running, Mac with a growing certainty he couldn't win the race. He wiped at the perspiration that was pouring down his forehead, blurring his vision.

Ahead, at the top of the hill, he could see a thoroughfare—busy with traffic and pedestrians. "Thief! Stop, thief!" he shouted, instantly realizing he was crazy to use precious effort yelling. Likely no one on the street would understand him. But the figure ahead slowed and glanced back.

Mac wiped at his perspiration again, unable to see the man's face clearly. "Thief! Stop, thief!" If yelling slowed him down, it was worth the energy.

The man glanced quickly from one side of the narrow street to the other, clearly looking for a quick escape route, but apparently not seeing one, since he darted forward again.

"Thief!" A stabbing pain pierced Mac's lungs. That had to be his final shout.

But then, miracle of miracles, two burly men appeared at the top of the hill and stood staring down it. The thief slowed almost to a walk. And then, as he neared the pair, he darted sharply to his left, attempting to spurt by them. But he failed. The men snared him and dragged him onto the main street.

By the time Mac rounded the corner after the trio, the two captors had multiplied into a small circle of men. They were roughly knocking the thief around.

Mac stared at the scene. He'd been chasing a boy— only a couple of years older than Jason. His face already bore red slap marks. His shirtsleeve was torn. And he looked terrified.

"Wait!" Mac grabbed an arm of one of the captors. "Wait, he's just a child . . . a *muchaco*."

"Señor, el muchacho esta un ladrón. No esta solo un muchacho."

Mac nodded. Whatever that had meant, the men had at least stopped shoving the boy around. One of them was now holding him securely, looking expectantly at Mac.

"I . . ."

"Mac?"

He glanced back at the breathless sound of Holly's voice. He hadn't realized she'd chased after them. She was trying to see into the circle of men. She was far too short to be seeing much.

"Your thief's just a boy, Holly. Only about twelve years old."

"Oh, Mac! Just ask him for my butterfly—and my chain. And tell those men to let him go."

"Holly. . ."

The men began mumbling among themselves. "¡Policía!" an authoritative voice ordered.

"No," Mac tried. "No police."

The men ignored him and one of them hurried into the store they were standing in front of—undoubtedly to call for the *policía*.

Another man stepped up to Mac and Holly. "I speak the little English," he offered hesitantly.

Mac breathed a sigh of relief. "The boy snatched my friend's necklace." He enunciated each word clearly and pointed at Holly's neck, wincing when he saw the red line of broken skin. A bruise was already forming.

The man nodded, stepped into the midst of the circle, grabbed the child by the shirtfront and slammed him against the brick wall. The boy let out a wail of pain, then began crying.

"Mac!" Holly grabbed his arm. "Mac, stop this!"

A younger boy, standing on the periphery of the group, called something to the man. He turned back to Mac. "This thief, he throw it away. That one saw."

He shot an order in rapid Spanish to the second boy, who promptly scurried halfway under a parked car, felt around for a moment, then emerged with both the butterfly and chain.

He held them out.

"Oh, *gracias*!" Holly exclaimed, gratefully taking them. "*Gracias* to you all," she added, smiling at the group of men, then glancing at Mac. "Should we be giving them a reward?"

"Good idea." He reached into his pocket and pulled out his remaining pesos.

"No, *señor*," the English-speaking man said firmly. "We do not for the money."

"Well . . . *gracias*, then. *Muchas gracias*."

"Dad! Dad!" Jason and Kevin wheeled around the corner with Joe on their heels.

"I told them to stay with Betty," he muttered, breathing hard. "Instead, they chased after me."

Mac glared at Jason. "The next time you don't do as you're told you're in big trouble!"

"But, Dad, we thought you might need our help."

Jason looked so earnest that Mac almost laughed. He gave up on his lecture and turned to Joe. "Holly's got her butterfly. I just want to see about this boy, then we can head back."

"No, *señor*," the English-speaking man interrupted. "The police will come."

"No," Holly said, shaking her head firmly. "No police. I—"

Her words were cut off by the squeal of brakes. Mac glanced into the street. The police had indeed come— in a Volkswagen Beetle painted official blue and white.

Two uniformed men scurried from the front seat and every man in the circle immediately began shouting at them.

"Let's get out of here, Mac," Holly whispered.

One of the officers pointed at her. *"¡Quedárse!"*

"I suspect," Mac whispered back, "we've just been told we aren't going anywhere yet."

The officer held out his hand, nodding at the jewelry Holly was holding. She turned it over to him with obvious reluctance, then she and Mac stood—listening but not understanding—as the policemen questioned a few of the locals.

Finally one of the officers snapped an unintelligible order at Mac. The English-speaking man stepped forward. "You must go with them. To sign the complaint."

Mac shook his head. "We don't have time. We're just on shore from a cruise ship. We have to get back to it."

The man relayed Mac's protest to the officer. He muttered something and patted his gun holster.

"You must go with them," the man repeated, shrugging. "Not for long. At the station someone will speak the English."

The policeman patted his holster again, then gestured Mac and Holly to the Beetle. The other officer was already herding the child thief into the back seat.

"Mac," Joe said quietly. "That guy doesn't look as if he's going to brook any arguments. You're liable to find yourselves in jail if you don't cooperate."

"You may have a point," Mac muttered unhappily.

"Why don't Betty and I take Jason back to the ship while you sort this out?"

"No, Dad! I want to go to the police station with you. This is neat."

"Jason, do you expect the policemen to strap you to the car roof? You go with Mr. Pritchard. And until I get back, you do exactly as he tells you to. Understood?"

"Yes," Jason mumbled.

"Joe's right," Mac said, taking Holly's arm and turning her toward the police car. "We don't have much choice, so let's get this over with before we miss the damn sailing."

He glanced into the Beetle. The boy was huddled in one corner of its tiny back seat. He'd stopped crying but looked as if he might start again any moment.

Mac maneuvered himself into the car first so that Holly wouldn't have to sit beside the child. But, as they pulled away, she was reaching across Mac's bunched up knees and handing the boy Kleenex.

"Again I must apologize," Captain Villanueva repeated, holding the back door of the police car open for Holly but resting his hand on her arm.

"It's all right, Captain. We understand." She snuck a furtive glance into the back seat at Mac.

He was glowering.

She inched closer to the car, praying the officer would let them escape before Mac's temper blew. For the past hour it had clearly been all he could manage to keep from exploding.

"But, as I explained, my men have their job to do, their rules to follow. The . . . how do you call them . . . ah, yes, the hooligans. The hooligans who frighten tourists must be removed from our streets. To do this we must have complaints signed."

"But Pablo is only a child," Holly murmured for the thousandth time.

"And you will still not change your mind, Dr. Russell?"

"No. I'm sorry, but no."

Villanueva shrugged. "And I am sorry I was not at the station when you arrived, that there was no one to speak the English with you. I am sorry, too, about your ship departing. But I have done what I can."

"Yes. And we do appreciate that. Thank you again for having your radio room contact the *Taurus*. And for booking us a flight to St. Kitts."

The officer nodded. "You will catch up with your ship. But I fear some other will be most unhappy tomorrow. Two some others. They will go to the airport. They will expect to fly to the carnival. But you will have their seats. The plane to St. Kitts was full. I have...how do you say it? I have pulled the string for you. That is it."

"Yes. That was very kind."

"And now my driver will take you to the Hotel Lina. It is one of the finest hotels in Santo Domingo. And I have pulled the string for you there also. Our hotels are full during the festive season. From all over the island people come to Santo Domingo to celebrate Old Year's Night on the Malecon. There are no rooms, no rooms at all...but I have pulled the string."

"Yes. Thank you." She glanced at Mac. I think, she mouthed, he wants a tip.

"Fat chance," Mac growled, leaning forward so that only she could hear. "Just get in the car and let's get to the damn hotel before I punch someone in his damn nose."

Holly turned back to Villanueva, pasting a smile onto her face. "Well, we've taken too much of your time already, Captain. Thank you again for all your help."

He nodded officiously, handed Holly into the car, then closed the door behind her. "Hotel Lina. *¡Rápido!*" he ordered the driver.

"*Rápido*," Mac muttered as they pulled into the twilight traffic. "If anybody had cared about *rápido* when they should have, we wouldn't have missed the damn boat."

"Well…at least Villanueva managed to get us plane reservations. And I suppose with tomorrow being New Year's Eve—or Old Year's Night as it seems to be here—he really did have to 'pull the string' to—" She stopped speaking midsentence and cringed against the back of the seat as their driver swerved sharply to avoid hitting a pedestrian.

"He got us reservations on some interisland airline we've never even heard of, Holly. Its pilots probably fly the same way these drivers drive. We might be better off swimming to St. Kitts."

"I'm not a strong swimmer, Mac. You wouldn't desert me and make me brave that airline on my own, would you?"

He grinned at her, then put his arm around her shoulder and drew her closer. "Of course I wouldn't desert you. Not in a million years. I'm just in a foul mood. Once I've started overreacting it takes me a little time to cool down."

"It's okay, Mac. I understand. I sometimes have the same problem." Holly gazed into the gathering darkness at the lights of downtown Santo Domingo. "I hope Jason isn't terribly upset that you missed the sailing."

"He's probably not the least bit upset. It means he'll get to sleep overnight in the Pritchards' cabin again. I doubt there's any reason to worry about Jason."

"Then I guess I'll worry about Pablo. What do you think the police will do with him, Mac?"

"I imagine they'll give him one hell of a lecture, then turn him loose. There's not a lot else they can do when you refused to sign their complaint."

"I just couldn't, Mac. He's only a child. But you . . . you think I should have signed, don't you?"

"Someone's going to. Sooner or later. Holly Russell can't take care of the whole world's children."

"I know. I just couldn't have it be me who sent him to whatever awful place they'd have sent him to. So thanks for taking my side."

"That's what friends are for. Although I was having visions of us spending the remainder of our lives in that police station. At least you have nothing left to worry about now, though."

"Well, I suppose there's my mother and what she'll be up to tonight without me there to come crashing in on her and Sid."

"Holly, what is this? A new game called Twenty Worries?"

She managed a smile. "Sorry. I guess I'm just upset because the day's been so rotten. And when I'm upset I worry. But I need something specific to worry about."

"Well," Mac said, laughing, "at least you don't suffer from free-floating anxiety. But look." He pointed ahead. "There's the Hotel Lina. Why don't you concentrate on not worrying and I'll concentrate on cooling the last remnants of my anger?''

"Sounds like an eminently sensible plan, Mac.''

"Right. It is. We'll check in and have a good dinner with a relaxing bottle of wine. Things can only improve from here. You'll see.''

"Ah, yes, Senor McCloy! I am Señor Gomez, manager of the Hotel Lina.'' Señor Gomez beamed a greeting at Mac and Holly, dismissing the desk clerk with a flick of his wrist. "Captain Villanueva has called me personally. I am at your service. Anything I can do for you. Anything at all. And your room is waiting.''

"Rooms,'' Mac corrected.

Holly glanced at the manager in time to see his beam lose a ray of its brightness.

"Rooms?'' Gomez looked questioningly at her as he repeated Mac's word.

She smiled hopefully, and he looked back at Mac.

"Rooms. One for Dr. Russell and one for me.''

Another ray dissipated. "I am terribly sorry, Señor McCloy. But the captain did not say two rooms.''

"Well, the captain should have said two rooms. As you can see, there are two people. Dr. Russell and me.''

"But there is only one room, *señor*. And, to arrange for even one room was very difficult. We could do so only for the captain. You must understand. The Hotel Lina is fully booked. All the hotels in the city are fully booked. But it is a very nice room, Señor McCloy. This one room the captain has asked for.''

Mac glared at the manager. The manager glared back.

How, Holly wondered, was he managing to glare when there was still a polite smile on his face? She didn't know. But clearly he and Mac were in the middle of a Mexican standoff. Or was that the wrong term to use in the Dominican Republic? Was there a Dominican standoff? Or a Republican standoff?

She didn't know that, either. All she knew was that she'd spent the day racing around in cars with kamikaze drivers, being robbed, sitting in a stuffy police station while the *Taurus* sailed for St. Kitts without her and Mac, and if she didn't end up somewhere peaceful soon she was going to scream.

"Mac, let's just take the room."

"What?"

"*Muy bien*, Dr. Russell." Gomez's beam reappeared. "You will see that it is a very nice room."

"Holly..."

"Mac! Let's just take the damn room! If we don't, the way our day's been going, we'll probably find ourselves sleeping in a park."

"We'll take the room," Mac snapped.

"*Muy bien,* Señor McCloy. And your luggage is...?"

"No luggage."

Holly swore silently. She'd forgotten about that minor detail. And she felt as if she'd been wearing the dress she had on for the past forty days straight.

She glanced around the lobby, seeing nothing that looked promising. "Is there a shop in the hotel, Señor Gomez? Some place we could get toothbrushes? And clothes? A shop that takes credit cards?"

"*Sí*, Dr. Russell." He pointed to the far end of the lobby. "There are several shops along that concourse. Some are still open. Here, I will give you the room key, Señor McCloy.''

Mac took the key but merely stood staring at Holly.

''Well, Mac?''

''You want to go shopping? Right now?''

''You don't mind, do you?''

''Mind? Of course not. Shopping's one of my all-time favorite pastimes. In fact, it almost beats out sitting in police stations for the top spot on my list. I'm just starting to wonder, though, how much more fun we can pack into a single day.''

CHAPTER FOURTEEN

HOLLY SIPPED the last drops of burgundy from her glass and looked across the table at Mac, deciding the wine had been a major mistake.

No. Not precisely accurate. Not all of the wine. The bottle Mac had ordered with dinner hadn't been a problem. But the one Señor Gomez had sent to their table, compliments of the management...this one they'd just finished drinking...

Yes. It was the second bottle that had been the major...that had been the major whatever it had been.

She was so relaxed that her willpower had nodded off. And now she couldn't keep her eyes away from Mac—or keep her thoughts from drifting up eight floors to their one, shared room.

Of course, Mac would sleep on the floor. Of course he would, she silently repeated for the thousandth time. He'd told her that the moment they'd seen there was only one double bed. But she didn't want to think about what her night would be like in that bed.

Simply showering, earlier, knowing he was in the next room, had almost done her in. She'd begun imagining Mac's hands, rather than her own, washing her body.

And the longer she'd stood under the pulsating water, the stronger had grown her alarming urge to invite him to join her.

She hadn't.

But then she'd listened while he'd showered, picturing him naked. And a second alarming urge had carried her to the bathroom door, hand raised to knock, before she'd regained control.

And those showers had only lasted a few minutes each. Whereas, later tonight, she'd be lying alone in bed for hours, intensely aware of Mac in the room with her, her hormones pumping to beat the band.

By morning she'd be ready to jump out of her skin. Because she'd be awake all night, wanting Mac. Much as she hated to admit it, she knew she would.

Last night, when he'd kissed her, she'd have made love to him on the damn promenade if he hadn't played the perfect gentleman. She'd wanted him so desperately that getting through tonight without giving in to her desire would likely prove the challenge of the century.

She wasn't at all certain she was up to it. But she had to be. No matter what her body was telling her, she simply wasn't going to make love to Mac until—*Until?* what was she thinking? She wasn't *ever* going to make love to Mac because . . . because . . .

She mentally ordered up an image of David. Nothing appeared.

She closed her eyes, but still all she could see was Mac, sitting across from her, his new off-the-rack blazer emphasizing the breadth of his shoulders as if it had been tailor-made for him, its navy blue fabric making his eyes seem even bluer than they actually were.

All she could visualize was Mac. And she knew that when she opened her eyes again she wouldn't see anyone else in the room but him. And she'd probably see him with the X-ray vision she'd developed.

While they'd been drinking the second bottle of wine, she'd realized she was looking right through his blazer and white shirt and seeing his naked torso— every bit as clearly as if he were sitting at the table nude.

He'd been a vision of golden tan, gorgeous muscles and dark chest hair.

She reopened her eyes. Yup. X-ray vision. Every bit as clear as before.

She was fantasizing about reaching over and running her fingers through the crinkly little curls of his chest hair when he caught her watching him and smiled. "Feeling better, Holly?"

What? He'd asked her a question. Was she feeling better than who? She concentrated on processing the meaning of his words.

"Better. Yes, better. Much. It's amazing what a shower and fresh clothes can do. It's a little hot in here, though, don't you think?" She absently undid the top few buttons on the black silk dress she'd bought.

Mac coughed a funny, choking little cough, then loosened his tie. "Yes. The room's a little hot. But this dinner was great, wasn't it? I never though I'd appreciate French cuisine so much—and good burgundy. One more Greek meal, washed down with one more bottle of Apelia, and I'd have turned into Zorba."

Zorba? Who was Zorba? Oh, yeah. That old Greek guy. But there wasn't a chance Mac would ever turn into someone as rough-looking as Anthony Quinn. Not a chance in the world.

If Mac turned into anyone Greek, it would be a Greek god. Of course, that wouldn't take much turning. If there were a Greek god contest right here and now, Mac would be a shoo-in for first prize.

She glanced around at the diners, then at the couples on the small dance floor. There wasn't another man in the room who was even in the demigod category.

She realized Mac was speaking and focused on him. "Pardon?"

"I was asking if you'd like to dance."

Dance? As in would she like to be held in Mac's arms with her body pressing against his... with his hand caressing her back... with her breasts crushed against his chest... with their hips moving to the slow music that trio in the corner was playing? That would be the absolutely worst thing she could do!

"I'd love to dance, Mac."

What? That had been *her* voice! What the hell was happening? Was she fragmenting? Had her voice assumed control over her brain?

Oh, wonderful. Never mind her voice. Now her body was getting in on the act, as well.

Her eyes had seen Mac standing up. They must have told her legs to mimic his. And her hand was reaching out to take his.

And now he was putting his arms around her.

They were undoubtedly the strongest arms in the world, because she began positively floating across the dance floor, secure that nothing could ever harm her as long as Mac's arms stayed exactly where they were. Maybe she could convince him to keep them around her forever.

Why not? He'd told her he loved her.

She smiled. Every time she recalled him saying that she smiled. He loved her and she loved him.

And she loved him.

So there it was. The admission she'd been refusing to make—even to herself. She'd been willing to admit she liked him an awful lot, that she found him the sexiest man she'd ever met, that he made her blood boil. But she'd been holding back on the final truth.

What was the saying? *In vino veritas.* "In wine is truth?"

"Pardon, Holly? I didn't catch that."

Oh, Lord! Had she spoken out loud?

"I...I..."

She looked up at Mac's face. She loved that face. And she loved the way his hand was holding hers and the way the other one was resting on her back.

She slid her own free hand up under his jacket, caressing the muscles of his back. She loved them, too. She'd love them more if there wasn't a shirt over them, but...

Mac smiled down and pulled her closer.

Oh! And she loved the way being near her so clearly turned him on, the way he was so hard against her that he made her ache with wanting him. But if they both wanted the same thing...

"Mac? I'm tired. Let's go up to the room." She snuggled her lower body suggestively against his.

He coughed that funny little choking cough again, making her hope he wasn't coming down with something.

"How about coffee first, Holly?"

Coffee? She didn't want coffee. She wanted Mac. But before she could protest, he dragged her back to the table and signaled for coffee.

"Drink up," he ordered once the waiter had left. "And here," he added, pulling a tiny flat aspirin tin from his pocket. "Take a couple of these. I've been carrying them around in case Jason got too much sun. But they'll help for too much wine, as well."

"I haven't had too much wine, Mac.

"No?"

"Absorootely not."

"You know the Peter Piper tongue twister, Holly?"

"Of course I do."

"Repeat it for me."

"What?"

"Repeat it. Say the tongue twister."

Holly sighed. Sometimes Mac got the strangest notions. "Peter, Peter, pumpkin eater," she said carefully.

"No, not that one. The Peter Piper picked a peck of pickled peppers one."

"Oh. All right. Peter Pecker piped a puck of prickly poppers." She smiled hopefully across the table.

Mac shook his head. "That's about what I thought. Take some aspirin and finish your coffee. Then we'll go outside and sit by the pool for a while. We could use a little fresh air."

Holly drained her coffee, then unhappily followed Mac from the dining room and outside. Beyond the hotel grounds the sounds of Santo Domingo told her that evening was in full swing. But on this side of the Lina's high brick wall all was still. The pool lights had been dimmed for the night, and she and Mac were the only people in sight.

"Mac," she protested as he settled her into a lounge chair. "Mac, I have to talk to you...about what you've been telling me about us and fate and things."

"What about them?" Mac stretched out on the chair beside hers and reached for her hand in the darkness.

She took a deep breath, feeling as if she was about to plunge into frigid water. But plunging was the best way. It got the painful part over with all at once.

"Mac, you've been right about us. I've been trying to deny what I feel for you but you've been right about us having something special. Mac...Mac, I love you."

She whispered the final words, then held her breath, waiting for him to tell her again that he loved her.

He didn't say a word. She swallowed hard and peeked across at him. He was staring at her.

"And what about David?"

"David? Well...Mac, I just don't know anymore. All during this cruise I've been thinking I have to be fair to David. But tonight I seem to be thinking about being fair to me. To you and me. I think maybe you've been right and I've been wrong. Mac...oh, Mac, I'm all confused. But I want to go upstairs with you now. I'm not confused about that."

"Holly, you're a little drunk."

"I'm not! Possibly a smidge squiffed, but definitely not a little drunk."

"Well, I think being a smidge squiffed is affecting your feelings. And that what you're feeling for me right now is plain old ordinary lust."

"Oh, no! It's not plain or ordinary at all, Mac. It's the most extraordinary lust I've ever felt. And it's not only lust. Not even only extraordinary lust. I do love you. I really do. So much. And I thought...well, last night you said you loved me. And I thought you wanted to make love to me. And here we are in this hotel and..."

Mac sat up and took both her hands in his. "Holly, I do love you. And, in my case, I'm certain that's not merely the wine talking. And I do want to make love to you—very, very much. But what I don't want is to make love and then for you to wake up in the morning wishing we hadn't."

"I won't, Mac. I know I won't."

"Tell you what, Holly. Let's just relax here for a while—say until you can manage to get through 'Peter Piper picked' without any major mistakes. Then we'll go up to the room."

Holly closed her eyes, mentally repeating the tongue twister, trying to get it right. With each try she hated Peter Pecker more. Finally she decided a brief nap might help.

She woke from it to the sound of crickets chirping. Overhead, a black sky jeweled with stars stretched forever. Gradually she remembered where she was and half turned onto her side.

Yes, there was Mac. Fast asleep on the chair beside hers. She couldn't make out the time on her watch but they must have been asleep for hours. Beyond the walls of the hotel property Santo Domingo was silent.

She lay quietly, listening to the crickets and thinking back to their evening...ahead to the remainder of the night. Finally she sat up, straightened her hair as best she could, then shook Mac's shoulder gently.

"Mac?"

"Mmrrrphh?"

"Mac? Are you listening to me?"

"Mmmm."

"Peter Piper picked a peck of pickled peppers, Mac. Is that enough or do you want me to say the rest?"

Mac opened one eye. "Are you trying to tell me you'd like to go up to the room now?"

Holly leaned across the space between them and lightly kissed his cheek. "You may not understand Spanish, but when it comes to English you do just fine."

HOLLY TRIED to smile at Mac; his expression told her she wasn't succeeding.

Down by the pool she'd been absolutely certain she wanted to make love to him. But on their way up in the elevator a horde of butterflies had invaded her stomach and now, standing beside the bed...

She watched him remove his jacket and tie. He tossed them onto the chair, then turned and stared at her for a long moment before finally speaking.

"You okay?" he asked gently.

"I...nervous, Mac. I'm nervous."

He stepped across the space between them and took her hand in both of his. "Holly, as much as this kills me to say it, my offer to sleep on the floor still goes. But you only have one more minute to accept it because I can't stand here any longer seeing and not touching."

One more minute. The moment of truth. She looked up at Mac, not knowing what was right or wrong, only knowing she loved him...and that she couldn't live the rest of her life wondering, 'what if'?

She gazed into the midnight depth of his eyes, wanting him so incredibly much that her body was aching. "I think the minute's up, Mac," she whispered, bending to switch off the bedside lamp, leaving only stray moonlight to soften the room's darkness. When she turned back, Mac was a shadowy figure. She could barely see that he was smiling one of his incredible sexy smiles.

She kicked off her shoes, and Mac sat on the bed, drawing her down into the circle of his arms. "That was the longest minute of my life, Holly," he murmured against her ear. The warmth of his breath made her shiver with anticipation. He drew back a little. "Sensitive ears?"

"Mmmm...not that I've ever noticed before... but mmmm," she repeated as he nuzzled her earlobe.

"Holly...would it ease your nervousness if I tell you how much I love you?" he whispered, rushing on before she even replied. "It's so much more than I've ever loved anyone. I've never felt anything even close to the way I feel about you."

His words sent a rush of ecstasy through her. It settled as a dull throbbing, deep within. Then his mouth trailed down her neck to kiss the hollow of her shoulder, and her bones started to melt.

He turned her slowly in his arms and began kissing her mouth, parting her lips with his delicious tongue, making her hot with longing for him, with wanting him to make love to her in this strange room, in this unknown hotel, in this foreign country. The world they were sharing couldn't be unreal—not when she felt as if her world were just beginning.

His hand stroked the outside curve of her breast. She shifted slightly, silently asking for more, and Mac brushed his hands across her breasts to the buttons of her dress.

One by one he undid them, pausing after each one to caress her breasts through the thin fabric—every touch arousing her more than the one before it had done.

Then, once the final button was free, he slipped his hand inside the silk bodice, teased his fingers beneath the neckline of her slip and began grazing her nipples through the thin, lacy veil of her bra.

The friction of lace against her skin, the touch of Mac's hand on her near-naked breast, sent erotic messages racing through her. She reached to unbutton his shirt...then tugged its tails out of his waistband. She felt him suck in his breath and, fingers trembling, she unzipped his pants.

"Oh, gawd, Holly," he whispered, leaving her for a moment to shrug out of his clothes.

She gazed at him in the dimness. He was even more beautiful naked than her X-ray vision had promised he would be.

He drew her to her feet, eased the dress from her shoulders so that it fell to the floor, then knelt before her and began caressing her legs, sliding his hands under the hem of her slip and up the outside of her thighs to her hips.

She quivered as he began easing her panties down. His touch reached right through her, igniting flames of passion, making her want him more than she'd imagined it was possible to want a man.

Standing, he smoothed the straps of her slip from her shoulders. It slid to her waist, stopping at the flare of her hips as Mac discarded her bra.

"Oh, Holly," he murmured, cupping her breasts, bending to kiss her mouth.

His tongue explored the inside line of her lips. They parted invitingly, of their own accord, and he accepted the invitation to probe more intimately. His mouth was warm and wet against hers...she felt his kiss everywhere.

Mac's hands drifted to her hips as they kissed and her slip fluttered slowly down to join her dress, leaving her nude, allowing Mac's naked body to press fully against hers.

Skin against skin, hardness against softness...and a shock wave of desire drowning her, making her feel both incredibly excited and terrifyingly vulnerable.

Mac gently stroked her hips until her need for him overwhelmed her last shred of fear and she relaxed against his body. "Nervousness gone?" he whispered.

She couldn't speak...could only answer him with her body, pressing its desire against his. He drew her down onto the bed to lie facing him and kissed her again, opening her mouth with his tongue once more, heightening her need as he covered her breasts with his hands and began a circular caress. His palms tantalized her nipples into impossibly firm arousal.

Holly moaned, wanting more, and nudged his head to her breasts. He continued stroking one, taking the other into his mouth, suckling it lovingly. His tongue, roughly tender, made tiny circles about her nipple, making it ache every more longingly.

Drenched with love for him, she smoothed her hands across his stomach to encircle his hardness. He groaned at her touch, his own hands sliding down to her hips, to her inner thighs, one finally moving between her legs.

She arched against it, and he began stroking her—gently but intimately—until the pleasure she felt was so excruciating she could scarcely bear it.

Her body moved rhythmically beneath Mac's touch, giving him a message of readiness, but he continued to stroke and caress her moist warmth until her heart was pounding and her blood grew so hot that it turned to liquid fire.

She frantically moved her hands to his hips, verging on orgasm, wanting to share hers with his. "More, Mac. I need more of you. Make love to me now."

He brushed her lips with a kiss and covered her with his body, sliding his hands to cup her behind.

She felt as if she'd been born to lie under him. She was vaguely aware of his ragged breathing, of the racing of his heart next to hers, of his weight pressing her.

And then he whispered her name and she was aware only of him entering her, moving inside her the way she'd craved him to, of her body arching against his, of the wild cresting of her desire...of his desire... and then the flood of relief that surged through her in incredible waves of love.

Love. As the waves diminished, she realized Mac was whispering the word. She opened her eyes.

His face was inches from hers. "I love you, Holly. I love you so much I can't believe it."

"Mac...Mac, I love you, too.... I don't believe you can possibly love me more than I love you."

He smiled. "And that's not the wine talking?"

"No. The wine's effect is long gone. This is me talking."

Mac eased from above her and onto his side, drawing her into his arms. "Let's just rest for a few minutes before we try that again."

"Again? Mac, I'm not sure I could handle *again* without dying. That was...that was...oh, Mac, I don't think there's a word wonderful enough to describe what that was.''

His nuzzled her throat. ''Just wait until we've had a little practice. Practice makes perfect.''

Holly closed her eyes, knowing there could be nothing more perfect that what they'd just shared, nothing more perfect than lying in the shelter of Mac's arms.

THE TAXI CRESTED a hill and St. Kitts's harbor appeared in the distance. Mac squeezed Holly's hand. ''There's the *Taurus*. I wasn't sure we'd ever see it again.''

Holly gazed down at the ship, uncertain that she really wanted to see it again. Last night with Mac had been heaven. So had this morning when they'd made love until they barely had enough time to catch their flight from Santo Domingo.

But the *Taurus* was reality—at least as close to reality as she was going to get before she flew back to Winnipeg. Winnipeg and David.

She glanced at Mac. He smiled at her and squeezed her hand again.

Oh, Lord! What was she going to do—aside from feeling incredibly guilty and fabulously euphoric all at once? Her life had turned upside down last night. Everything rational and logical and sensible had flown out the window of the Hotel Lina.

She loved Mac so much. Being with him was a natural high. But David . . .

David was good and kind and right for her in so many ways. Only he didn't make her feel the way Mac did—as if she were about to die of happiness every instant she was with him.

But David... why did being with Mac prevent her from recalling David's good points? When she was with Mac, she couldn't think of a single thing except how absolutely insane she was about him. But what if it was only temporary insanity?

She had to sort out the emotional tangle she'd gotten herself into... had to figure out whether what she felt for David... whether what she felt for Mac...

The taxi pulled to a stop at the pier. "You don't want to be missing carnival now, man," the driver told Mac. "Old Year's Night starts in the afternoon on St. Kitts. And it be like nothin' you ever seen. You want I should come back to your ship in an hour or two? Drive you into Basseterre?"

Mac glanced a question at Holly.

"We'd better see what's happening before we make any plans, Mac."

The driver shrugged. "Just don't you be missing carnival."

Mac paid for the trip from the airport. Then he and Holly headed into the *Taurus* and along to her cabin.

Kay wasn't inside but there was a note sitting on Holly's bed. She picked it up and read it.

Dear Holly.
Welcome home. The message from the radio room didn't say what time you'd arrive, so Sid and I have gone exploring St. Kitts. We'll be certain to get back long before sailing—not like some people.

Love,
Mom

"Not like some people," Holly repeated, grinning ruefully. "Sounds as if she thinks we intended to get left behind yesterday."

"Sounds to me," Mac murmured, encircling Holly's waist from behind and drawing her back against him, "as if she and Sid are gone for the day…that you and I have this cabin all to ourselves."

Holly tried to ignore the surge of arousal she felt at Mac's embrace. He bent down, brushed her hair aside and nuzzled the back of her neck, making ignoring him impossible. She turned in his arms and gave him a deep, lingering kiss.

"You have," he murmured when it finally ended, "the fullest, sexiest lips I've ever kissed."

"What I have, Mr. McCloy, are lips that are swollen and aching from kissing you."

"Is that bad?" he teased.

"No. Not bad. Just a constant reminder of last night…and this morning." She refrained from mentioning that other parts of her body were aching as well—partly from their lovemaking and partly from the longing she was feeling right now.

One more kiss and she'd find herself in bed with Mac again. She took his hands in hers and backed away to arm's length. She needed time to think. And she couldn't think at all while she was in his arms.

"Shouldn't we check in with the Pritchards, Mac? They must be more than ready for a break from Jason."

"I suppose you're right. But if they've all gone off exploring the island too, I think we should come straight back here."

"You don't want to be missing carnival now, man," Holly said in her best cabdriver imitation. "If everyone's deserted us, I think we should go in to Basseterre. This may be the only time in our lives we'll get to see the St. Kitts carnival."

"Holly," Mac muttered as they left the cabin, "has anyone ever told you that you have spoilsport tendencies?"

CHAPTER FIFTEEN

THE POUNDING, PRIMITIVE BEAT of distant music grew louder as the taxi rolled along Basseterre's main street. The driver glanced into his rearview mirror at Mac and Holly, then gestured at the square they'd just entered. "This be called the Circus. The parade be coming along two blocks over." He jerked the car to a halt. "Enjoy carnival, folks."

Mac took Holly's hand as they got out of the taxi. She squeezed his fingers affectionately, reminding him of everything she'd said last night and this morning, making him almost dare to believe she really did love him.

Lord! How he prayed she did. How he prayed she loved him enough to discard all those crazy notions she thought made sense. He wanted to spend the rest of his life loving Holly—being with her, sharing dreams with her, making love to her.

But if she really did love him, even half as much as he loved her, why didn't she tell him she'd decided to break off her engagement? She had to know how much he wanted to hear that. And she had to know that he'd love her forever.

He wanted to marry her. He wanted to ask her to marry him. But he was too frightened of what her answer would be. Too frightened that, deep down, she was still convinced she should marry her perfect David.

She was the one with a fiancé. She had to come to terms with the situation. If only she would say—

"Mac? Are we going?"

What? No. Damn. Merely wishful thinking. She wasn't asking if they were going to spend their lives together. She was merely asking if they were going to watch the parade.

"Yes. Of course. Guess there's no doubt about which direction, is there?"

Practically everyone in sight was heading into a narrow alleyway, following the distant music's lure as if the Pied Piper of St. Kitts were calling them.

Mac wrapped his arm around Holly's shoulder as they started off, reminding himself there were still a few days left on the cruise. They'd be sailing for San Juan tonight. They had tomorrow and January 2 there. Then a day in St. Thomas and then . . . well, he wouldn't think past then. But surely, if she really loved him, the next few days would be enough to make her realize—

"Look, Mac!" She smiled at him, and his heart melted. "Look at all the people up ahead. There's no room on that street for a parade to pass. We're never going to find Jason and the Pritchards."

"Well, if we don't, I'm sure they can cope without us until we're all back aboard ship."

They reached the end of the alley, pushed their way through the rear of the crowd and found a place to stand in front of one of the old stone structures lining the street.

Mac gazed along it. The music had grown louder, and half a block away onlookers were moving to either side, allowing a line of costumed people to snake among them.

"Here comes the parade, Holly."

"Oh, damn, Mac. I can't see a thing. Someday I'm going to start carrying a stepladder."

Mac glanced at the building behind them. "Here." He spanned her waist with his hands and lifted her up onto a ledge. "Just lean against my shoulders for support." He turned back toward the street. Holly obediently rested her hands on his shoulders, then leaned forward and wrapped her arms around his neck as the start of the parade reached them. His awareness of her breasts, their fullness against his shoulders, made it difficult to concentrate on the scene.

"Oh, Mac! Those costumes are fantastic. Look at the giant mice! And those silly dog outfits. People have spent months sewing. And St. Kitts must have cornered the market on sequins."

And Holly Russell must have cornered the market on sex appeal. The parade might as well not have existed. All Mac was aware of was her enticing perfume, her arms around his neck and her body pressing warmly against his.

"Look at that couple, Mac."

He forced his eyes into focus. The couple consisted of an extremely large man and a beautiful young woman. Both were dressed in bright green outfits and each carried a long stalk of sugarcane.

"Who do you suppose they are?"

A man standing beside Mac grinned up at Holly. "They be the king and queen of the cane. They be leading the people to the shore for food and drinks."

The music grew steadily louder as the parade passed. Eventually a tractor turned onto the street, pulling a flatbed loaded with eight enormous speakers.

The sound level leaped from loud to earsplitting. Mac could feel the thumping beat reverberating through his body. Holly was saying something into his ear but he couldn't make out a word.

He lifted her down from the ledge and, her hand firmly in his, joined the throng that was heading toward the shore. At the end of the street the waterfront was a mass of smiling humanity. Costumes mixed with street clothes; islanders mixed with tourists.

Mac and Holly were caught up in a writhing line of dancers. When they passed a makeshift bar set up on the beach, he dragged her out of the line and, hugging her tightly to him, made his way to the little wooden stand and ordered beer.

"Isn't this fantastic, Mac? I've never seen so many smiling faces in one place before. Wouldn't it be wonderful if life could be this happy all the time? For everyone?"

He bent and kissed her. Life *could* be this happy all the time. At least for them. All it would take would be a few words from Holly.

She laughed when their kiss ended. "What was that for?"

"Just for being you. And because I love you."

"I love you, too, Mac," she whispered.

A little voice inside his head cautioned him. This wasn't the right time or place. Maybe tonight, when they were back on the *Taurus*. What better time than New Year's Eve to talk about the future?

MAC KISSED Holly Happy New Year...a lover's kiss that made her want to cling to him forever. But then Sid was grabbing her and kissing her. And Kay pecked her cheek. And Jason was excitedly tugging at her hand.

She bent to kiss him as the band struck up "Auld Lang Syne," and then the five of them were joining hands and singing. Holly felt tears trickling down her face as she sang, "Should auld acquaintance be forgot..." This cruise wouldn't last forever. The next three days would pass in the blink of an eye. And then what? She simply didn't know. But forgetting Mac was unthinkable. Maybe the fact that she'd never be able to forget him meant she should...

If only she was certain of what they'd found together. If only she wasn't so afraid that it wouldn't stand the test of the real world.

Here on the pool deck, under the stars, celebrating New Year's Eve in the warm glow of champagne and colored deck lights, they were a million miles from day-to-day living.

She brushed away her tears as the song ended. Moments later the Pritchards appeared and wished everyone Happy New Year.

"Are you midnight-buffeting with us tonight, Jason?" Joe asked.

"Sure!"

Mac shook his head. "Haven't you two had enough of Jason?"

"No problem," Betty said, glancing from Mac to Holly, then back. "He can spend the night in our cabin again if you'd like," she offered quietly.

Holly felt herself blushing. She quickly shook her head when Mac looked at her, embarrassed by what

Betty was so clearly suggesting. Another night alone with Mac would be heaven. But facing her mother in the morning would be impossible.

"Well, then, we'll drop Jason off at your cabin after the buffet, Mac."

Jason waved goodbye and raced off with Kevin.

"Sid and I are just going to take a little walk," Kay offered. "See you later, Holly."

"Alone again," Mac murmured as the others left. "Would you like to dance?"

The band had begun playing a waltz. Mac folded her into his arms and slowly twirled her away from the center of the deck. She rested her cheek against his chest, listening to the rhythm of his heartbeat, breathing the faint aroma of his unique scent—a mixture of cologne and natural maleness. She loved the scent. She loved the man. If it were possible to make time stand still for eternity, she'd do so this very moment.

"Holly?"

"Mmmm?"

"If we stop dancing...if we just stand looking out over the water for a while...can I keep holding you like this?"

She answered him with a smile, and they stopped beside the railing. Mac shifted her a little in his arms so that they could both look out over the sea.

The dance music wafted across the deck, almost drowned by the sound of crashing waves below. Above, stars dotted the midnight sky and the moon hung like an enormous light, casting a pale swath across the water.

"Beautiful," Holly murmured. "I can't remember a more perfect New Year's Eve."

"They could all be perfect from now on, Holly...if we were together."

She didn't look up, didn't move a muscle, wanting to hear what else Mac might say yet afraid to.

"Holly...I want you with me every New Year's Eve for the rest of my life."

"Mac, I...oh, Mac, I don't know what's right from what's wrong anymore. I scarcely know up from down. My life was so settled on its course. And then you came along and you're the most unsettling man I've ever met. I just can't think straight."

"Holly, sometimes thinking straight isn't all it's cracked up to be. Sometimes you have to think with your heart instead of with your head. You know what I think?"

She shook her head against his chest.

"I think you should make a New Year's resolution about letting your heart have a little more say."

"Mac, I—"

"Three days, Holly. We only have three days left. Forget about your logical reasons for being engaged to David for those three days. Think with your heart for the rest of the time we have together. Think of what our future could be like. I love you, Holly."

Mac bent and kissed her, his lips banishing all logic, all reason, making her heart sing, making her absolutely certain that—right or wrong, up or down—three more days of loving Mac would mean the end to her engagement. No, that wasn't right. Her engagement was already over. It had ended the minute she'd decided to make love to Mac. But...what if she was making a mistake?

"GOOD MORNING, ladies and gentlemen. Happy New Year and welcome to San Juan. It is 7:15 a.m., the temperature is seventy-eight degrees and we have now been cleared for disembarkation. I hope you enjoy New Year's Day in Puerto Rico."

Holly stretched sleepily and smiled across the cabin at her mother. "Happy New Year again."

"Yes, Happy New Year again, dear. In fact, very Happy New Year. I think this is going to turn out to be an extra special one."

"Oh? Any secrets I should know?" Holly ordered her smile not to fade. If her mother had secrets, they undoubtedly related to Sid and they undoubtedly— A tapping on the door interrupted her thoughts. She flashed a silent question at Kay.

Her mother shrugged. "Who is it?" she called out.

"Special delivery for Holly Russell." The voice was muffled but definitely male.

Kay winked. "It's Mac."

A happy little bubbling inside Holly had already told her that.

"Just a second." She scrambled out of bed, grabbed her thin robe and peeked into the mirror on her way to the door. Ugh! She fluffed her hair with one hand and snapped the lock with the other. Then she pulled the door open . . . and blinked in disbelief.

"Surprise!"

She stared, making a conscious effort to start breathing once more. Then she blinked again. He was still there, grinning a giant grin.

"I knew you'd be surprised, Holly, but I never hoped for speechless."

"Why, David," Kay greeted him, her voice verging on a squeak. " 'Surprised' isn't the word for it. Come in. You've taken Holly so aback she's forgotten her manners.''

Come in. Right. Holly stepped away from the door, allowing David into the cabin.

He hugged her firmly, then held her by the shoulders and stared down at her. "Let me see you. You look great. A tan—and freckles on your nose again. You look every bit as healthy as you did after that trip to California.''

Holly was intensely aware of the smile she'd managed to plant on her face while David was talking. It was hurting her cheeks. But she couldn't make her lips move. Speech was out of the question.

"Well, well, David," Kay murmured, throwing on her robe and scurrying over to Holly's rescue. "Whatever are you doing in Puerto Rico? How did you manage this surprise? Here," she babbled on, shoving the door closed and grabbing David's arm. "Sit over here by the window and tell us all about it.''

Holly trailed dazedly after them and perched on the chair across from David. Kay hovered beside him.

He grinned at Holly again. "I desperately needed a break—the hospital was crazy over Christmas. So I checked your itinerary, then called one of those last-minute travel agencies.

"It had a three-day minipackage to San Juan and, considering this is the only port your boat spends two days in, it seemed to me that fate was taking a hand in our lives.''

"Fate," Holly repeated dully.

"Anyway, I got in yesterday afternoon and don't leave until late tomorrow—just a bit before you sail for St. Thomas.''

"You spent New Year's Eve in San Juan, David? Alone?" She eyed him guiltily, recalling her New Year's Eve with Mac.

"Yes, but I was tired anyway. So I got an early night and now we have today and tomorrow together."

"That's...that's wonderful, David. You don't usually do anything this impulsive."

He reached over and took her hand in his. "I was missing you, Holly. And I had the strangest feeling— I can't quite explain it, but I felt I had to see you."

Holly merely nodded; she hadn't the vaguest idea what to say.

"Well, David," Kay trilled, "if you'd just give us a few minutes to get dressed, you can spend the rest of the day seeing Holly."

"Sure. I wouldn't mind time to look around the ship. How about if I come back and collect you in half an hour?"

"Fine," Holly managed. "Half an hour would be good."

"Great." He bent and kissed her forehead, then was gone.

Holly stared at the closed door.

"Well?" Kay asked quietly.

"Well?" Holly repeated, turning. "I assume you're not asking about the state of my mental health at the moment. Oh, Mom, I'm supposed to be meeting Mac at eight o'clock!" She glanced at her watch. "That's half an hour from now, which somehow doesn't surprise me in the least. Oh, I knew I should have avoided Mac, Mom! I knew it from the first moment I saw him. I'm a total idiot! How could I have even thought...when I mean so much to David that... And what the hell am I going to do now?"

"Well, you obviously have to tell Mac about David being here."

"Yes! Obviously! I'll have to phone right now and explain. But I don't want to have to! Mac isn't going to take this calmly, Mom. What if he...how can this be happening to me?"

"Then," Kay continued, ignoring Holly's ranting, "I guess you'll have to decide whether or not you're going to tell David about Mac."

"Oh, I can't do that! David's come all this way because he loves me. I can't possibly tell him I've been...can I? I mean, I guess I'll have to tell him sometime. Or...or maybe I'll never tell him. I don't know. I don't even know how this is all going to end up. But certainly not here! Not now! I shouldn't, should I?"

"That, darling, is something you've got..." Kay paused, looking at her own watch. "Is something you've got twenty-seven minutes to think about." Kay pulled a dress out of the wardrobe and turned to the bureau. "Just let me find some underwear. Then I'll go and change in the bathroom so that you can talk to Mac privately."

"But, Mom, you aren't going to desert me, are you? You and Sid will spend the day with David and me, won't you?"

"I...I think you'd be better off spending some time alone with David. Besides, Sid and I have plans."

"But, Mother! At least have with us dinner tonight!"

"All right, Holly. If you really want company. But I guess that means a restaurant in San Juan, doesn't it? I don't imagine you want to bring David to dinner on the ship...even though there is that extra place at our table."

Holly moaned at the thought. "Oh, Mom, I want to be as far away from the *Taurus* as possible."

"IT CERTAINLY seems like a nice ship," David offered, taking Holly's hand as they headed up the stairs toward the Zeus Deck.

"Yes. Very nice."

"And your cabin's a good size."

"Yes. A good size." She tried to smile.

It didn't feel much like a smile from the inside, but David didn't seem to notice anything was wrong, so she concentrated on trying to banish all thoughts of Mac from her mind.

That proved impossible. There'd been at least forty million of them swirling around inside her brain since she'd hung up the phone.

Every moment that they'd talked she'd become more upset—and Mac had sounded more upset. But surely he hadn't *really* expected her to tell David what had been going on. Surely he hadn't. Because she simply couldn't. Not now. Not here.

She only hoped that, once she and David made it off the *Taurus*, Mac's words would stop ringing in her ears and she'd stop feeling as if she was about to burst into tears any second.

She realized David was speaking again and made an effort to listen.

"I've rented a car—thought we could drive up into the mountains and see some of the small villages instead of just San Juan. And there's a rain forest, El Yonque, that's supposed to be well worth the trip.

Or," he suggested, smiling down at her, "would you prefer to see my hotel room first?"

"I...oh, David, I have my...you know. I'm sorry. It's a bad time of month." She almost choked on the lie, but she couldn't go merrily to bed with David. She didn't want to. Not now. Not after Mac.

David squeezed her hand. "Don't worry about it. You'll be home soon. We can spend today seeing the island. But do you think anyone would mind if I had dinner on board the *Taurus* tonight? I'd pay for the meal, of course, but I'm curious about cruise-ship food."

"Oh, no! I mean, no, I don't think anyone would mind, but I assumed we'd eat in San Juan. I'm a little tired of Greek meals and I already invited my mother to have dinner with us in town. I said we'd call and let her know where. She's met a man I want you to meet, David. His name's Sid and he's an ex-cop from the Bronx and I'm really worried that they're serious about each other but, anyway, I thought we could all have dinner together in town. Could we? You aren't desperate to eat on the ship, are you?"

David gave her a strange look but shook his head. "No. I'm not desperate. Only curious. We can eat wherever you like," he added as they reached the Zeus Deck. "The dining room in my hotel's pretty good if we don't see anything that looks better."

"Thanks. I—" Her words froze in her mouth when she saw Mac standing beside the exit to the gangway. She forced one foot to keep moving in front of the other but she couldn't force her eyes away from him. And he didn't take his eyes off her.

"Morning, Holly," he said as they neared him. His gaze flickered to David's hand, closed over hers.

"Morning, Mac," she managed.

David stopped walking and stood looking at Mac, obviously expecting to be introduced.

"This is Mac McCloy, David. Mac, this is my fiancé, David Lawrence. Mac and his son are at the same dining table as Mom and me," she murmured as the two men shook hands.

David shot Mac a friendly smile. "We might have been having dinner together tonight, but Holly's determined to eat in San Juan rather than aboard ship."

"I see. Jason will miss your company, Holly."

She nodded, looking everywhere except at Mac. "Tell Jason I'll see him tomorrow night."

"Well, nice meeting you, Mac." David tucked Holly's hand even more securely in his own and started off again.

She followed blindly, mechanically answering his questions as they headed down the pier to where he'd parked his rental car. But it was a good hour before she felt even half human again.

By then they'd driven along the shimmering Atlantic coastline past Luquillo Beach. David claimed it was one of the world's most beautiful; it might have been one of the world's ugliest for all she'd noticed. And now they'd turned inland. The little car was climbing a road into the Luquillo Mountains, heading toward the rain forest.

David said something she didn't catch. "Don't you think so, Holly?"

"Ah...sorry. I was concentrating on the scenery. What were you saying?"

"Just that these villages we've been passing seem so primitive."

"Yes. It could be centuries ago, couldn't it? Except for the television antenna on every shack."

David chuckled. "At least there isn't a satellite dish in every yard. But, speaking of television, I saw a news segment the other day about a volunteer program called Med-Carib. North American specialists are coming to the various islands for a week or two to work in isolated clinics. And apparently cardiologists are in demand. How would the thought of my volunteering some time next winter strike you?"

"Sounds like a good idea." And a typical David idea. A fresh wave of guilt swept her. How could she possibly have betrayed him? Maybe he didn't make her almost die with passion the way Mac did, but David was one of the kindest men she'd ever met.

And he loved her so much—enough to come thousands of miles just so they could spend two days together.

He smiled over at her. "I'd bring my wife along, of course. You look terrific when you've gotten a little sun."

His wife. If she came south with David next winter they'd be a married couple.

Mac's image appeared in her mind's eye. She stared through the windshield, blinking back tears. How could she be so crazy about Mac when she knew, with every ounce of her common sense, that marrying David was the right thing for her to do?

The incline was growing steeper and the little car began to labor. Holly glanced anxiously at David. "Your Mercedes would be having an easier time on this grade," she offered.

"It sure would. Taking our chances with this little engine's more of an adventure, though."

"Right." She gazed straight ahead once more. She'd already had far more than enough *adventure* on this vacation. And the last thing she wanted was to be stranded on a road in the middle of the Luquillo Mountains.

She glanced out the passenger window and immediately revised her thought. Only inches away, the side of the road ended abruptly, with nothing beyond it but a sheer drop. Being stranded suddenly took a back seat to plunging off this mountain. Better to be stranded than dead.

As if the fates were tuned to her thoughts, the car began sputtering. A few hundred yards farther along it coughed ominously. Then, with no additional warning, the engine quit, and they coasted to a halt. David set the emergency brake, pulled the hood release and opened his door.

"What do you think's wrong, David?"

"I'll have a look, but don't get your hopes up. I haven't perfected my imitation of Joe Mechanic."

Holly opened her own door and, averting her eyes from the drop-off, joined David in front of the car. He began poking and prodding beneath the hood. She peered in, feeling totally useless. "I don't have the foggiest idea what you're doing, David."

"Unfortunately, neither do I."

Not the foggiest idea? But David always knew what he was doing. So how could they be suddenly trapped in the boonies of Puerto Rico?

And they'd be here for life. She just knew they would. They'd be up here, far enough away from San Juan that most people spoke only Spanish, and she'd spend the rest of her days walking through the Luquillo Mountains searching for someone who spoke

English and . . . and she was being utterly ridiculous. David knew enough Spanish to get them by.

She glanced at him once more, ordering herself to shape up. "What do we do now?"

"Well, I doubt that the AAA's likely to show up. But someone will come along. And, if we leave the hood up, they'll probably stop. Then we'll catch a ride to the nearest telephone and call the car rental place."

Of course. She silently thanked David for being such a calming presence.

Eventually, just when they'd started to wonder if the road was deserted except for them, they heard the sound of an approaching car.

A truck, Holly corrected herself as it rounded a curve and came into view . . . a pickup truck . . . an extremely dilapidated pickup truck.

It screeched to a halt behind their car. The driver grinned and, through his window, saluted them with a beer can. *"Buenos días. ¿La pena, señor?"*

"Sí," David replied. *"Perdón la molestia pero el automóvil no lo . . ."* He shrugged, glancing at Holly. "I don't know the right word."

She almost laughed. Most people wouldn't have known the other words, either. If she'd been with David in Santo Domingo, instead of with Mac, she wouldn't have spent hours in the police station, futilely trying to make herself understood. But if she'd been with David—if she'd been with the man she should have been with—she'd never have made love to Mac.

The driver got out of his truck, then reached back inside and propped his beer can on the dashboard. Once it was secure, he walked alongside the car and stood staring intently at its engine. Finally he shook his

head, glanced up and rattled off a monologue in
Spanish.

Holly inched back a little. It might not be noon yet,
but his breath told her that the beer on his dash wasn't
his first of the day.

"No problem," David said, grinning at her. "This
fellow says he'll take us to the next village. It's only a
mile or so along and we'll be able to phone San Juan
from there."

"But he's been drinking," she whispered.

"Well," David said quietly, "I certainly wouldn't
hire him as a chauffeur. But he seems sober enough
and we're not going far. Besides, we don't have a
whole lot of choice. Given the dearth of traffic we've
seen, we could be stuck here so long that you'd miss
your sailing tomorrow."

Her conscience gave a sharp, painful stab.

"We'll be fine, Holly. This guy could probably drive
the road blindfolded." David wrapped his arm protectively around her shoulders as they started toward
the truck. "If he's in worse shape than I think, I'll ask
him to stop and we'll get out. You know I'd never let
anything harm you."

No. He never had . . . and he never would. In all the
years she'd known him he'd never been anything but
wonderful to her. She was certain he'd keep on being
wonderful.

Whereas Mac . . . well, when she got right down to
the bottom line, no matter how desperately she believed she loved Mac, she barely knew him.

She'd been insane to think what she'd been thinking for the past couple of days. Hadn't she?

David lifted her up into the truck's cab and climbed
in after her. The Puerto Rican started his engine, then

pulled smoothly around their abandoned car and headed up the incline.

The man drove more carefully than she'd anticipated. And, of course, they'd reach the next village safely. And, of course, they'd get back to San Juan— no doubt in plenty of time for tonight's dinner with her mother and Sid.

Then, tomorrow evening, she'd be back on the *Taurus*. And so would Mac.

She glanced at David, wondering how she'd let herself get into such a mess, wondering what on earth she was going to do about it.

CHAPTER SIXTEEN

MAC SAT ALONE at the table, staring across the dining room to the doorway, willing Holly to walk through it. He hadn't talked to her for thirty-six hours...not since she'd waltzed off the ship yesterday morning... waltzed off the ship holding another man's hand.

And the one time he'd seen her since then had been from a distance—when he'd been on deck a few hours ago and David had brought her back to the *Taurus*. He'd brought her back and spent forever standing with her on the dock, kissing her goodbye.

Watching them kiss had almost killed him. He'd desperately wanted to intercept Holly on her way to her cabin—to find out where he stood. But he'd forced himself to stay on deck, telling himself to be calm, knowing he'd see her at dinner.

So where was she? His entire future was on the line, hanging in abeyance until he talked to her. So where the hell was she?

He spotted Kay...and Sid. But no Holly. Well, they didn't always arrive together. Holly would be along in a minute.

"I hope you and Jason weren't lonely without us last night," Kay said as Sid helped her with her chair.

"No. We were fine, thanks."

"And where's Jason tonight?"

"He ate at the early sitting. With the Pritchards."

Mac's gaze wandered back to the doorway. Where the hell was Holly?

"Pardon, Mac?"

"I..." Oh, God. She had him so crazy he was muttering. "I was just wondering where Holly is, Kay."

Sid cleared his throat with obvious discomfort and Mac's anxiety level leaped. What did Sid know?

"Holly was tired, Mac. She decided to eat in the cabin."

He felt his throat tightening. *Holly was tired.* Her time with David had tired her out.

Mac tried not to imagine how.

And tonight she'd decided to eat in her cabin. In other words, she'd decided *not* to eat with him. He stared across the table at Kay, willing her to stop fidgeting with her napkin so that he could catch her eye. She finished with the napkin and began a piece-by-piece examination of her cutlery.

"Kay?"

"Yes?"

He got the eye contact he'd wanted and immediately wished he hadn't. There was a clear message written in Kay's eyes. Holly had made a decision—in favor of David.

"Kay..." He didn't know what to say. The right words wouldn't come. Maybe there were no right words. But he had to say something. "Kay...what on earth should I do about Holly and me?"

Kay gave him an unhappy-looking little shrug. "Mac, I'm sorry, but I won't be put in the middle of this. I've known David for years. It's not as if he's some undesirable character who wouldn't be good to

Holly. He's a fine man. I'm not saying you aren't,'' she hurried on. ''I'm simply saying I'm not going to become involved. I'm not going to interfere.''

''Well I sure as hell am!'' Mac rose so quickly that his chair tipped back and smacked against the wall. He threw his napkin onto the table and stormed out of the dining room.

Holly had to listen to reason. She was right for him and he was right for her. She simply couldn't ruin both their lives for a ''fine man'' she didn't love.

He strode down the stairs and along the passageway, trying to think of what he should do when he reached Holly's cabin. He paused outside, afraid to knock. Finally he tapped on the door.

Silence.

''Holly? Holly, I know you're in there. We need to talk.''

After an eternity the lock clicked and she opened the door. Mac swallowed hard. She'd clearly been crying. Her eyes were swollen, her nose was red and her cheeks were stained from tears. And still she was the most desirable woman he'd ever seen.

''May I come in?''

''I'll come out, Mac. I . . . I could use some air.''

They walked in silence until they reached one of the upper-deck promenades. Gray twilight was fast vanishing into the black of night.

''Do you want to sit for a while, Holly?''

She nodded, sinking into the nearest lounge chair.

Mac sat on the one beside hers, wanting to talk with her but terrified of what she might say. ''I missed you, Holly,'' he finally offered. ''Yesterday . . . and today. I missed you like crazy.''

She shook her head, and the ring of fear surrounding his heart tightened.

"Don't, Mac. You're wrong about needing to talk. It won't help. It'll only make things worse. David coming to San Juan...well, it said a lot about what he feels for me. And it made me realize I've been behaving like a fool, Mac. I'm sorry."

"Holly, listen to me. I love you. I—"

"Mac, don't! I made a mistake. A foolish, foolish mistake. I'm sorry I did and I'm more sorry than I can say that it's hurt you. But it was a mistake, Mac. I'm engaged to David. You and I were a mistake."

"Holly..." He reached out to take her hands but she pulled back. He concentrated on breathing deeply for a moment, feeling his emotional grip slipping away, trying desperately to hold on to it. "Holly, we're no mistake. We're the furthest thing from a mistake I can imagine. I love you. And you love me."

"Mac, stop. Please?" A tear trickled down her cheek.

He managed to keep from reaching forward to brush it away. "Holly, I don't want to stop. I don't want us to stop. I feel as if we've been given a wonderful two-week microcosm of what our lives could be like. And we have a chance to make it last forever. But only if we don't let it end. Marry me, Holly?"

"Marry you?" She shook her head as if she didn't believe she'd heard correctly.

"Yes. Marry me. Holly, we've only got one day left on this cruise. The day after tomorrow we'll be in Barbados again. Then I'll be flying back to Denver and you'll be flying back to Winnipeg. Holly, I can't stand the thought of you being with David instead of with me. I can't stand the idea of life without you. I know all your arguments," he rushed on. "About not knowing me for long and this cruise not being reality and my not being an eldest son. And I know you've got yourself convinced that David is the logical choice and I'd be an emotional one. Maybe that's even true. But sometimes people have to go with their emotions, Holly. You can't possibly want what we've found with each other to die. It's just too great. Holly, being without you the past two days has been torture."

"Mac, don't do this! I'm going to marry David."

"And is that why you've been crying?" Mac asked softly. "What if you changed your mind and decided to marry me? Would that decision make you cry?"

"Mac...David is right for me for a hundred different reasons."

"There's only one reason that matters, Holly. Do you love him more than you do me? Can you honestly tell me that?"

She merely shook her head.

"Then, if you can't tell me that, tell me you'll marry me."

"No," she whispered.

"Why?"

"Because...because David's good. And I do love him, Mac. Just in a different way. And I know him so well that I'm certain we're compatible. Mac, with you and me...who knows? We overreact and rant and rave and—"

"And we love each other. We love each other wonderfully."

"Yes. Yes, we do. But it's a scary love, Mac. It's so much, so soon. Fireworks don't last. Poof. They're gone. And you're left with acrid smoke. Mac, I'm afraid that what we have would burn out."

"And with David there's nothing to burn out."

"Mac! That's not fair!"

He paused, hearing the anger in Holly's voice. He'd apparently overstepped some nebulous ground rule she'd established for this discussion. But how could he play by rules he didn't know?

"So...tell me." He tried to stop talking, aware how upset they both were, realizing he was on the verge of losing control. But the words pushed to escape. "Yesterday and today, Holly, when you and David made love. Did you feel anything like what you feel with me?"

"Mac! That's enough!"

"Damn it, Holly! Don't tell me what's enough! Don't I deserve to know? Maybe I've got this all wrong. Maybe I was just a little recreation for you. Is that it?"

"Mac," Holly whispered, "David and I didn't make love while he was here."

"Oh, Holly!" Mac couldn't imagine anything she might have said that could have made him feel better. "That's the truth, isn't it?" She didn't have to answer. He knew it was the truth.

She nodded slightly, not looking at him.

"Holly, doesn't that tell you something incredibly important? Doesn't that tell you that... Oh, hell! If they hadn't changed the laws I'd ask the ship's captain to marry us tonight!"

"Mac...no. Don't start thinking something that... Mac, that simply isn't going to happen."

Her words plunged him from feeling better to feeling awful again.

"I'm not going to marry someone because of fireworks, Mac. I did that once. And those fireworks were nothing compared to what I feel with you. But they didn't last. They fizzle into nothing. I made a mistake once. Not again. I'm . . . I'm going to marry David.''

Keep reasoning with her! a little voice shouted inside Mac's head. *Don't explode!* He took a deep breath and began to count to ten . . . but only made it to nine.

"Holly, you are the most stubborn, pigheaded woman—"

"No! Just stop! I don't want to argue anymore. When the cruise is over, I'm going back to Winnipeg and I'm going to marry David."

"You can't. I love you!"

"Maybe you do! But you've loved me on a Caribbean cruise for just a few days. David's loved me in the real world for a long, long time. I'm sure of him. And I'm sure he's the man I need."

"Whether he's the man you love or not? What the hell's the matter with you, Holly? I don't understand how an intelligent woman can be so idiotic!"

"I'm not being idiotic! I'm being sensible!"

"Sensible? Does a sensible woman expect guarantees in life? Because that's what you think you're getting with David. But you can't marry him simply because you're sure of him. There are no guarantees."

"David is completely and utterly devoted to me."

Ice. Her voice had turned to ice. How had she managed cold control when Mac was sizzling?

"Holly, you're settling for less than you should. If you marry David, you're settling for a life of peaceful boredom."

She glared at him. He sensed her icy veneer cracking an instant before she began shouting.

"And I should marry you? A man I can't even have a peaceful conversation with? You're yelling at me right now, damn it! One minute you tell me you love me and the next minute you yell at me. Do you think I'd marry a man who yells at me? Now that would really be idiotic!"

"Fine! Marry your damn doctor. I suppose he never yells. Big deal! There's no reasoning with you, is there, Holly? You're too damn stubborn to reason with. You're so damn stubborn you're going to spend your life being bored stupid."

"I'm not!"

"Oh, yes, you are! Whenever I think about you—if I do think about you, even though I'll try my damnedest not to—I'll be thinking about a bored woman."

Holly suddenly burst into tears, pushed herself up and raced away. Mac stared after her, hating himself more by the second, knowing he'd lost her.

KAY LEANED heavily onto her suitcase again, finally managing to snap the locks shut. "That's it. At last. If I'd realized how much I was going to buy in St. Thomas, I'd have brought along an empty case. Are you all packed, dear?"

Holly merely nodded, turning her gaze to the cabin window. The *Taurus* was nudging its way along one of Bridgetown's piers. In a couple of hours she'd be leaving for the airport... flying home... back to her real world that didn't include Mac McCloy.

"I'm sorry you wouldn't come shopping with us yesterday, Holly. You missed some wonderful bargains."

"I was better off staying in the cabin—probably saved a fortune. Maybe I've discovered the ultimate trick to consumer resistance." She tried smiling, but a stray tear trickled down her cheek. She hadn't thought there could be any left.

"And I suppose," Kay said softly, "not eating means you've discovered the ultimate trick to crash diets? Holly...dear, I don't know what to say. I'm sorry you're feeling so unhappy."

"It'll pass." Sure it would. In about a million years.

She glanced across at the phone. A hundred times she'd almost called Mac, not wanting them to part on such bad terms. But each time she'd reached for the receiver she'd stopped. Talking to him again might make her feel even worse—if worse was possible.

She should have called the Pritchards, too. But she couldn't bear the thought of trying to carry on a cheery conversation.

Someone knocked on the door. Her heart lurched. What if it was—

"It's me," Sid called from the passageway.

A surge of disappointment made Holly wonder whether she shouldn't call Mac after all. No. She was better off leaving bad enough alone.

"Sid's come to say goodbye," Kay murmured. "Dear, would you mind...?"

"Sure. Just give me a minute to wash my face and I'll disappear."

Holly darted into the bathroom and glanced at the mirror. A waif who looked as if she'd been crying forever gazed back at her. She couldn't recall ever having looked so ugly...or having felt so terrible.

From the other room she could hear her mother and Sid murmuring. It sounded like incredibly happy murmuring. They were undoubtedly talking about Kay's Valentine's trip to New York.

Holly's throat tightened and she swallowed back fresh tears. Things would never work out between those two. Why couldn't her mother see that? Kay was only thinking with her heart.

Whereas, when it had come to a choice between Mac and David, Holly had thought with her head. Sensibly. Rationally. She'd made the right decision.

But why did being right make her feel so wretched when being foolish clearly made her mother feel so wonderful?

No magic answer materialized.

Holly rubbed a cold, wet facecloth across her face, then opened the bathroom door and almost managed to smile at Sid. "Well, goodbye, Sid. I hope you have a safe flight home."

Sid grinned at her. "It's not goodbye, Holly. It's only *arrivederci*. We'll be seeing each other again—real soon."

"Well...great." Yeah. Great. She obviously hadn't been told about all of the upcoming get-togethers. After Valentine's Day in New York were there plans for Easter in Winnipeg?

"Well, Sid, I'll let you say goodbye to Mom. Let you say *arrivederci*, I mean." Holly pulled the cabin door closed behind herself and headed along the passageway and up the stairs. She might as well be miserable in the warmth outside. By tonight they'd be in forty below.

Good thing she was already as unhappy as she could possibly be. Otherwise, the thought of being back in that cold would be depressing.

She sat by the pool. It seemed lonely with no children playing in it ... children ... she felt awful about not saying goodbye to Jason. She should have screwed up her courage and called Mac's cabin.

No, she shouldn't have. Mac would have answered the phone and ... She vainly tried not to think about him, absently gazing at the pier below as passengers began disembarking.

"Holly?"

She jumped at the sound of Mac's voice, uncertain for an instant if it was real.

It was. He was standing beside her chair, looking absolutely, heartbreakingly, gorgeous.

"We're on our way, Holly. Jason wanted to say goodbye to you."

She forced her gaze from Mac to Jason. Instead of his usual grin, he was wearing a serious expression.

"I'm glad you found me, Jason. I was just thinking about you."

"I ... I wanted to give you my address, Holly. I was wondering if maybe you'd write me a letter. I've never gotten a letter from Canada."

"Sure. I'll write you one as soon as I get home—tell you exactly how cold it is in Winnipeg."

"Do you have a pen, Dad?"

Mac nodded.

"And some paper?"

"Do I look like a store, Jason? Poke your head into the bar and grab a napkin. You can write on that."

"Or I could use the back of one of your business cards, Dad. Then Holly'd have both our addresses. She might want to write you a letter, too. Right, Holly?"

"I ... I might, Jason."

Mac pulled a card from his wallet and passed it and a pen to his son.

"Thanks, Dad. I'm just going over there," he offered, edging away, his glance darting back and forth between Mac and Holly. "I need to use that table to write on."

Mac gave Holly an awkward-looking shrug. "Jason sure isn't going to win any prizes for subtlety. I'm sorry about this."

"It's all right, Mac. Is . . . is Jason flying all the way back to Denver with you?"

"Yeah. Connections to Maine were tricky and Margaret didn't want him arriving late at night. So he won't be heading east until tomorrow."

Holly nodded. Fine. She was doing just fine. She wasn't stuttering or stammering. And she was looking at Mac without crying. She was going to get through this in one piece.

She glanced across the deck at Jason. "He's really a great kid, Mac. I enjoyed spending time with—" Oh, hell! She shouldn't have tried to make any more conversation. She bit her lip, refusing to cry.

"Holly?" Mac quickly sat down beside her.

She shook her head, furious with herself. "I'm sorry, Mac. I'm so sorry about . . ."

"Holly, I understand. Listen to me for a minute. I meant everything I said to you. Everything except the bit about you being stubborn and idiotic, that is."

He smiled at her and she lost the battle with her tears.

"Holly," he whispered, brushing a few of them from her cheek, "if I thought there was anything I could do or say . . ."

"Mac, please don't."

"I know. You've made up your mind. But, Holly, if you ever change it...if you and David don't... Well, you'll have my card. My home number's on it. If you ever want to talk—or, better yet, if you want to see me—just call. You know, I've never been to Winnipeg. I'd love to visit it. In fact, if I got an invitation, I'd catch the first flight I could get."

"Oh, Mac—"

He pressed his fingers gently against her lips. It was all she could do not to kiss them, all she could do not to tell Mac she loved him.

"Don't say anything, Holly," he whispered. "Just remember what I said."

Jason was walking back across the deck. Holly quickly wiped at her face.

The boy stopped beside her chair and thrust Mac's card at her. "Here, Holly. You won't lose it, will you?"

"Of course not." Oh, damn! She couldn't talk for the lump in her throat and she couldn't see for the tears in her eyes. She sniffed loudly.

"Don't cry, Holly." Jason sounded as if he was about to start crying himself. "Maybe you could come and visit us sometime. Sometime when I'm in Denver. Huh?"

"Don't I get a goodbye hug, Jason?" she managed.

The boy threw him arms around her, and she held him tightly, not wanting to let him go. When she did, he and Mac would walk out of her life.

"Come on, son. We can't miss our plane."

Oh, Lord! Mac suddenly sounded as if he was about to cry, too. What a happy trio they made.

Jason pulled away. "You'll put my address some-place safe, won't you, Holly?"

She nodded, unable to look at either of them.

"Goodbye," Mac mumbled.

She simply kept nodding. Sid had said *arrivederci*. Mac had said goodbye.

THEIR TAXI BACKED out of Kay's driveway, its head-lights sweeping through the darkness that shrouded the snow-blanketed lawn.

Kay sighed quietly and turned her key in the front door's lock. "I guess you think I'm silly being so anxious about going into the house alone, Holly. And I know you must want to get home to your apart-ment."

"It's okay, Mom. I'm used to your Nervous Nellie routine. And I'm not in a rush."

"It's really too bad David had an emergency to-night," Kay murmured as they carted their luggage into the hall. "But at least the airline people gave you his message."

"Yes. We could have been waiting at the airport for him for hours."

Kay began her habitual postvacation inspection of the house, switching on lights as she went. Holly took off her coat and turned up the thermostat, uncertain whether she was more emotionally numb or physi-cally cold.

She was absently listening to Kay walking around upstairs, checking the bedrooms for boogeymen, when the phone rang. It stopped on the second ring and the footsteps overhead ceased.

Holly wandered into the dark living room and col-lapsed onto the couch, telling herself she'd feel better tomorrow. Of course she would. *Worse* wasn't an available option.

If she didn't hear from David tonight, she'd phone him in the morning. And she'd see him the first moment he had free. Yes. Seeing him would reassure her about her decision. She'd go to his office in the morning. And tomorrow was Friday, so then they'd have the weekend together.

She sat in the darkness, trying to think about David—instead, thinking about Mac—until Kay came downstairs and flicked the living room lights on. She was beaming.

"What's up?"

"Oh, Holly, that was Sid on the phone. And, dear...oh, Holly, Sid and I are going to get married. He said he was planning to ask me on Valentine's Day but he changed his mind. He said he couldn't..."

Holly stopped hearing. She knew Kay was still talking; her lips were moving. But Holly wasn't hearing. Her fears were coming true. Her mother was going to marry Sid Lambert. Holly mentally ordered her ears back to work.

"We thought April would be nice. How does that sound to you, dear? You'll be my matron of honor, won't you?"

"April. April's only three months away, Mom."

"Well, it'll be a small wedding here in the house. There won't be much to plan."

"Maybe not for the wedding, but what about planning everything else? Just for starters, where will you live?"

"Well...either here or there. We haven't decided yet. I'll see what I think of New York. And Sid will see what he thinks of Winnipeg. We'll work it out."

"But...oh, Mom, this has all happened so fast. And you and Sid are such different people."

"That's not always bad, Holly. Just think, if it hadn't been for Sid, I'd never have learned to play blackjack. And you know what? I like it."

"Oh, but, Mom, there must be hundreds of men who'd have more in common—"

"I don't want hundreds of men, Holly. I only want Sid."

"But—"

Kay sat down on the couch and patted Holly's hand. "Please don't start in on one of your logical lectures, dear. I'm happy when I'm with Sid and I know I'm going to be unhappy until I'm with him again. It's as simple as that. I could meet every one of your 'hundreds of men' and not feel the magic I feel with Sid. People can't choose who they're going to love, can they, dear? So be happy for me? Okay?"

"Oh, Mom." Holly hugged her mother for a moment. "I want to be happy for you. And I want you to be happy. I just don't want you to make a mistake."

"I'm not. Sid is someone special. I knew that the first moment I saw him. You know what I mean."

Holly nodded an understanding she didn't feel. Then an image popped into her mind that didn't make any sense. It was a naked pair of male legs and, in her imagination, her gaze was drifting curiously upward, slowing at the bare knees, noting a long surgical scar down the inside of one of them. And then the man dropped to his knees beside her and she was staring at someone special.

Mac. She could deny it all she wanted, but she'd known he was someone special the first moment she'd seen him.

What about David, though? She tried to remember first meeting David. She couldn't. He's always been around—her father's intern, then his colleague and then, after her father's death, her friend. And, finally, her fiancé. Their relation had gradually evolved because...because David was good and kind and they were compatible and she enjoyed his company.

But he wasn't the someone special Mac was. And suddenly she wanted someone special—wanted it desperately. She wanted to glow the way her mother was glowing right now. To hell with logical and rational and eldest sons and different countries and overreacting and ranting and raving. She wanted someone special and magic and tingles and fireworks.

She didn't want to look in a mirror and see a waif who'd been crying forever. She wanted to look in a mirror and see the same happiness on her face she was seeing on her mother's.

And Holly Russell was happiest when she was with Mac McCloy. And she was going to be unhappy until she was with him again. It was as simple as that. She wanted to marry Mac. She'd phone him. She stood up. She'd get her purse and find his card and call—

No. First she had to talk to David, had to explain. It would be a horrible conversation to get through, but they had to have it—and it had to be before she talked to anyone else about the situation. That was the least she owed David. Tomorrow morning she'd talk with him . . . and then she'd call Mac.

"You're going already, dear?"

"What?" Oh. She was standing. She looked back down at Kay. "Yes. I'll just phone for a cab. But, Mom, I really am happy for you. And I'll be thrilled to be your matron of honor. I'm happy about

Sid . . . and that you like blackjack. And you know
what I'm going to do?"

"What, dear?"

"I'm going to try skiing. I might like it."

CHAPTER SEVENTEEN

HOLLY TAPPED on the door of David's office, feeling like the she-devil of western Canada. The last thing in the world she wanted to do was hurt David. Well, almost the last thing . . . actually, it was the second last. The last thing in the world she wanted was to live her life without Mac.

"Come in."

She took a deep breath and opened the door.

"Holly. Hi. Here, let me take your coat."

She watched David get up from his desk and walk across the room. He looked . . . he looked upset . . . and she hadn't even started. She'd barely talked to him on the phone but something in her voice must have given her away because he was definitely edgy.

He tossed her coat onto a chair, then bent and gave her a brotherly kiss on the cheek. If Mac were here, instead of David, she'd be having the daylights kissed out of her by now.

"Sorry I couldn't pick you up last night, Holly."

"It's all right. We got home with no problems."

She gazed at David. He was looking more uncomfortable by the moment. Her face must be an open book.

"David—"

"Holly—"

They started and stopped at the same instant, then both laughed uneasy little laughs.

"Ladies first," David offered.

"No. No, don't go getting chauvinistic on me. Mine can wait." Besides, she'd forgotten every single word of her speech. She'd lain awake all night, trying to come up with words that would let David down as kindly as possible, but every line she'd thought of had vanished from her mind when she'd opened his office door.

"Well...here, let's sit on the couch, Holly."

She perched uneasily and waited for David to start speaking again.

He sat beside her, running his fingers through his hair. "Holly...when I came to San Juan..."

"Yes, David?"

"Remember I told you I had a strange feeling... that I couldn't quite explain it...but I felt I had to see you?"

She nodded, not actually remembering at all. David must have told her that while she was in her initial stages of shock over his arrival.

"Well, I think I can explain it now."

Oh, Lord! He was going to start in about how much he loved her. "David, wait. Maybe I should go first, after all."

"No. Now that I've gotten started I'd better finish. Holly, I love you."

She'd known that was where he was heading! She should have cut him off. He was going to make this scene even more difficult than it had to be.

"But the strange feeling I felt while you were gone was that I didn't miss you enough...didn't miss you quite the way I should."

What? What the hell was he talking about?

"And that was why I had to see you...why I didn't want to wait for you to get home. I had to see whether I was simply imagining something was wrong between us or I'd just been working too hard or... Is this making any sense, Holly? I do care about you so much. I really don't want to hurt you but—"

"Wait! Wait, David. You don't want to hurt me? Back up. I'm lost. Hurt me how?"

"Holly, what I'm trying to say is that I love you but...but I've got a sense that I don't love you enough...that when you're away from me I don't miss you as much as I should. I didn't talk to you about this in San Juan because I didn't want to spoil the last few days of your cruise. But, Holly, I don't think that—"

"That we should get married," she whispered in disbelief.

"That's...yes, that's it." David shrugged, looking absolutely miserable. "Holly, I'm sorry—"

"No! Don't be sorry. Oh, David, this is wonderful. David, I've been thinking the same thing. And I was so worried about hurting you. Oh, aren't we a fantastic pair?" She flung her arms around his neck and hugged him tightly—until she heard him whispering something about her choking him.

HOLLY SAT beside her phone, staring at Mac's card. M. McCloy & Associates, Architects.

Strange how until she'd looked at the card she hadn't realized Mac had his own company. Most men made a point of mentioning that sort of thing. But not Mac. On top of being wonderful, he was modest.

She focused on the numbers—business and residence. She didn't want to call his office...didn't want him to have to talk with anyone listening.

But it was only one o'clock. Only noon in Colorado. He might not be home for hours yet. But he might be there now. Maybe he wasn't working today. She wasn't due back at work until Monday. Probably he wasn't, either.

Maybe he'd put Jason onto his flight to Maine, then gone back home. Maybe he was sitting in his apartment right now—while she was wasting time fussing and fretting.

Okay. She'd try his home number. But what if he wasn't in? He probably had a machine and she didn't want to talk to a machine. She wanted to talk to Mac, to surprise him—not leave a dumb message. If she did that, she'd be in even worse agony, waiting for him to return her call.

All right. She'd try his apartment and, if a machine answered, she'd hang up.

She dialed a one...then three, zero, three...but then her hand began to shake and she couldn't make it dial Mac's number.

What if he'd changed his mind? What if the cold Colorado air had brought him to his senses and he'd realized he didn't really love her? What if—

"Please hang up," a female voice said from inside the receiver. "If you need assistance, dial the operator. This is a recording. Please hang up now."

Holly hung up, gave herself a stern lecture on being ridiculous, then tried again. This time she made it through all eleven numbers. She listened to the long silence. Then a phone began ringing... Mac's phone... one ring... two... three—

"Hello?"

Holly took a deep breath. "Mac, it's Holly."

"Holly?"

He'd paused before he'd said her name. Why had he paused?

"Holly! I... Holly, it's terrific to hear from you."

"Ah..." Now what the hell did she say? She should have thought up a wonderful opening line and written it down. That's what she should have done. Why hadn't she planned ahead? "Ah... did Jason get away all right?"

"Not yet. He's still here. His flight's in a couple of hours. Holly? Is everything fine with you?"

"Mac, that sort of depends. I'm not going to marry David. I mean, he isn't going to marry me. Well, we're both... neither of us is going to marry the other one, Mac."

"Oh, Holly, that's... are you upset? Should I say something sympathetic, or should I just say that's incredibly wonderful news?"

"Incredibly wonderful would sound good."

"Holly, you've just given me the most incredibly wonderful news I've ever heard."

Incredibly wonderful. The words ricocheted around inside her head and she breathed a huge sigh of relief. Everything was going to be incredible. Her future was going to be wonderful.

"Mac, I... I seem to recall you saying something about wanting to visit Winnipeg."

"Oh, Holly, more than anything."

"And . . . and didn't you mention something about catching the first flight you could get? I wonder if there's one leaving today? I mean, you'll be at the airport, anyway—with Jason. And we'd have the weekend."

She laughed nervously. She shouldn't have pushed! Dumb! But she wanted to see Mac so badly. Just as soon as she possibly could.

He was pausing again!

Holly's heart stopped beating.

"Well . . . Holly . . . I'm afraid it can't be the first flight. Something's come up."

Something had come up? What could possibly have come up? Mac had barely gotten home. There hadn't been time for anything to come up.

"What's happened, Mac?"

"It's . . . it's just a bit of bad timing, Holly. I can't really talk about it right now. I'll tell you about it . . . just not right now."

It? What was this *it* he didn't want to talk about? This *it* that had suddenly come up? This *it* that meant he wouldn't be coming to Winnipeg?

There was one very obvious answer to all those questions. The *it* was doubts . . . doubts about her.

Mac had woken up this morning in his own real world and realized he didn't love her after all. And here she was calling him like a love-struck teenager, making a total ass of herself.

She swallowed over the huge lump in her throat, praying her voice would sound somewhere close to normal. "Of course, Mac. I was only joking. You let me know when you might like to see Winnipeg. Actually, summer's a better time to visit, anyway."

"Holly, don't be absurd. I . . . give me a day . . . two at most. I just have to deal with something. Then I'll call you. As soon as I sort this thing out."

"No hurry, Mac. Call when you get a chance. My number's listed—the only Dr. H. Russell in the book. Bye now."

She almost got the receiver back into its cradle before bursting into tears.

HOLLY STARED blankly at the six o'clock news coverage of January's first storm. She might as well be watching a black-and-white set. All the screen showed was a background of the night, a foreground of heavily falling snow and the weatherman, broadcasting from the corner of Portage and Main. He'd started off in color but was becoming more solidly white by the moment.

He was wrapping up his segment, reminding Winnipeggers not to venture out unless absolutely necessary and predicting that schools and businesses would be closed tomorrow.

Closed? Of course . . . the storm had already dumped more than two feet of snow on the city. Even with every snowplow working through the night, most side streets would be impassable by morning.

But if she couldn't get out . . . She'd never looked forward to going back to work as much as she had during this weekend. How was she going to make it through another day of sitting hermitlike and miserable in her apartment?

Sunday at Six cut back to the studio—to an announcer who looked glad to be indoors. As he began speaking a screen split showed a snow-clogged airport runway.

"All scheduled flights out of Winnipeg International have been canceled for the duration of the storm and arrivals are being rerouted to Thunder Bay or Regina."

Holly flicked her remote to a different channel. Arrivals could be rerouted to Cuba for all the difference it would make to her. Mac wasn't on any of them.

He'd said to give him a day—two at the most. Then he'd call. That had been Friday. So Friday had been a day and Saturday had been two. And today was three. She glanced at her phone. Maybe the storm had . . .

No. Not a chance. She'd already checked the dial tone a million times. Mac simply wasn't calling.

Deep down she'd known he wouldn't. The instant he'd hesitated about coming to Winnipeg, she'd been overwhelmed by the terrible certainty she'd never see him again.

She hadn't wanted to face that prospect; the thought hurt too much. So she'd simply sat by the phone, trying to convince herself it would ring any minute. She'd done a poor job of convincing herself, though, and the weekend had been pure hell.

Eventually her tears had given way to an awful ache in her chest—a constant, physical reminder that she didn't want to live without Mac.

But with every passing hour it became more certain that she'd have to. If the problem had really just been something "coming up," he'd have called her back long before this.

A potato chip commercial appeared on the screen. Food. Junk food. The kind of food fat people ate when they were depressed. Maybe it actually helped. No. There was no *maybe* about it. Food altered people's moods. That was a scientific fact.

Holly pushed herself out of the chair and wandered into the kitchen, trying to remember the last time she'd eaten. Could it actually have been at breakfast on Friday?

She began foraging through her cupboards, suddenly ravenous but not seeing anything she wanted. Not chicken noodle soup or tuna or peanut butter or . . . there was a cheery red box . . . of fudge brownie mix . . . with chocolate chips included.

She glanced at the instructions. They went on about heating the oven and greasing a pan and blending in water and oil and an egg or two. She didn't think she was up to that. And what was this? "Cool at least two hours before cutting."

Oh, no. Another two hours of unfed misery and she might be suicidal.

She ripped the top off the box, pulled out the white pouch of mix and fingered it gingerly. Yes. There were little lumps of chocolate chips inside. She grabbed a bowl and spoon, headed back into the living room and flopped down in front of the television once more.

Carefully she tore the pouch open and poured its dry contents into the bowl. The first spoonful of crunchy, sweet powder sent a wonderful sugar jolt surging through her.

She ate a second spoonful, this time not gulping it down but savoring the chocolate chips as they melted in her mouth. Was it only her imagination or was she actually feeling a little less awful? Not great, by any means. She'd never feel great again. But *less awful* was an improvement.

Maybe it really was possible to eat away depression. Maybe the saying about people being fat but jolly had a basis in fact.

What if she just kept eating until she weighed two hundred pounds? How long would it take to double her weight? Would it be time enough to forget Mac McCloy?

The intercom buzzer sounded. Holly ate another spoonful of mix. The buzzer sounded again.

She set the bowl aside, headed across the room and pressed a button. "Yes?"

"It's the Pizza Hut. Sorry to be so long. The driving's ridiculous."

Holly stared at the intercom. One of her neighbors was waiting for that pizza and gradually starving. She'd better tell this fellow he'd buzzed the wrong apartment.

Instead, she glanced back at the bowl. If a few spoonfuls of brownie mix could make her feel less awful, what would an entire pizza do?

Holly pressed the button again, along with the foyer lock release. "It's apartment 612. To your left off the elevator."

She fetched her wallet, then waited by the door, almost able to taste melted cheese and pepperoni. If there were anchovies, she'd just have to—

The driver knocked and Holly peered through her peephole. The man looked like the abominable snowman; the hood of his ski jacket hid his face.

She opened the door. And then she felt her brain gearing down from third to first, her perceptual ability shifting to slow motion.

Her eyes saw that the man wasn't carrying a pizza. But the message took forever to reach her brain. And, by the time it had, her eyes were relaying another message... but her mind was having difficulty registering it... and she should be saying something but... but...

"You going to let me in, Holly? I'm practically frozen."

The sound of Mac's voice jolted her brain into overdrive. She screamed his name, threw her arms around his neck and realized that he actually was practically frozen.

At least his body felt practically frozen against hers. But his body was against hers! That was what mattered!

He grinned down at her. "Should I take it you're glad to see me?"

"Oh, Mac! Don't I get a kiss?"

"Ah... Holly, you have yucky-looking brown stuff all over your mouth."

"Oh!" She wiped her hand frantically across her lips. If Mac didn't kiss her within the next second, she'd die. "It's only brownie mix, Mac."

He bent and kissed her, his lips moist and cold against hers, the icy fabric of his jacket sending shivers through her... or was it Mac's kiss sending tingles through her? She didn't know. She only knew how incredibly fantastic she felt.

Mac pulled back a little. "That brownie mix is a nice touch. Not that I don't enjoy kissing you without it, but it adds a little zing."

"Oh, Mac. Come inside. You must be wearing six layers of clothes. I can't hug you properly."

"I made sure I dressed for the cold."

"Well, it isn't cold in my apartment."

"So," Mac asked, grinning again as she shut the door, "how many of these layers do you want me to take off?"

"I'll tell you when to stop." Sure she would. She wouldn't tell him to stop at all. "And while you're stripping, fill me in on how you got here when the airport's closed and why you didn't phone me back and what came up and...and...oh, Mac, I'm so glad you're here!"

Mac tossed his jacket onto a chair and took Holly's hands in his. They felt as cold as ice. She pressed them against the warmth of her face.

"Holly...we'd better talk for a minute."

She glanced anxiously at him, not liking the serious tone of his voice.

"Holly, we have to get those questions of yours answered before...."

His words trailed off. He led her to the couch and sat down, wrapping his arm around her shoulder and hugging her to him.

She snuggled against his chest feeling loved...but uneasy at the same time. What if the answers to her questions were horrible ones? She had to know.

"Start by telling me what came up, Mac."

"No. Let me start with how I got here. That's the easiest one to answer. My plane simply made it in before the airport shut down. The hard part of my trip was getting from the airport to your apartment. Taxis must be an endangered species in Winnipeg.''

''Only during storms, Mac. But what about the rest? What happened? What couldn't you tell me about over the phone?'' She held her breath, afraid to hear his reply.

''Holly, when you called I couldn't talk because Jason was in the room with me. And then, after I'd had time to think—after the surprise of hearing from you wore off—I realized what I had to say wasn't something I could lay on you long-distance.''

''Oh, but, Mac! When you didn't call me back I thought—''

Mac drew her even closer and kissed her cheek. His skin still felt cold against hers . . . cold and wonderful.

''Holly, I said I'd call in a day or two. Saturday was one day and today is two. And isn't my being here better than a phone call?''

''Yes! Oh, yes, Mac. I guess I just count days a little differently than you do.''

He laughed quietly. ''Sorry, Holly. I didn't mean to upset you. But if I'd phoned you back, you'd have weaseled every last detail out of me. And I have to see your face when I tell you this. I have to know what your gut reaction is.''

The ache in her chest—the one that had vanished when Mac arrived—was suddenly back. ''My reaction to what, Mac?''

''Well . . .'' He placed his hands on her shoulders and shifted his position so that he was looking directly at her face.

She wished she'd had acting lessons.

"Holly, I've spent the past two days in Maine—with Margaret."

With his wife? His ex-wife? He was thinking about getting back together with Margaret? That was definitely terrible news! But it was crazy! They'd been divorced for years. What had ever possessed him to—

"I phoned her on Friday morning, Holly—just to confirm which flight Jason would be on—and she dropped a bombshell. And then you called me not long after that and I...well, as I said, Jason was right there so I couldn't talk."

"Mac, what couldn't you talk about?" *For Pete's sake, get to the point!* she silently screamed.

He gazed at her intently. "Holly, Margaret's decided to marry Robert. Next month. And she wants me to take custody of Jason."

"And?"

"And ... well, that's it."

"What do you mean, 'that's it'? What's the problem you couldn't talk about?"

"I...I have to take him, Holly. I mean, I want to take him...I will be taking him. It's all arranged. But I didn't know how you'd feel about—"

"Me? You were worried that I'd object?"

"Well, I didn't know what you'd think about a ready-made, full-time son. I mean babies—yours and mine—are one thing but—"

"Mac, are you crazy? You thought I'd figure having Jason with us was a problem? Mac, I love kids. I particularly love your son. And, oh, Mac, I even more particularly love you."

"Only more particularly? What about *most*?"

"Most. Right. I most particularly love you more than anyone in the world."

"Then what," Mac whispered just before his lips met hers, "are we still doing in the living room?"

HOLLY'S CLOCK RADIO clicked on and the announcer's voice drifted into her bedroom midsentence.

"...not expected to taper off before tomorrow afternoon. Winnipeg schools will be closed today, along with most businesses. Public transit is limited to the downtown core and motorists are strongly advised not to attempt driving. Winnipeg International remains closed."

Holly turned a little in Mac's embrace. He was smiling sleepily at her.

"Guess you're stuck here for a while longer, Mac."

"What a pity. Imagine being stuck in bed with you." He kissed her—a long, lingering kiss that left her breathless. "This means," he murmured, finally ending the kiss and nuzzling her neck, "that we have the entire day to make love...and make plans."

"Plans?" Holly teased, curling a little of his chest hair around her finger.

He trapped her hand, stilling it. "You're supposed to be the logical one, so stop that. If we don't do the planning first, we may never get to it."

"I am," she said slowly, stroking Mac's hip with her free hand, "beginning to hate being logical."

He captured her other hand, drew it from beneath the blankets and kissed her fingertips. "We'll merely plan two things, Holly—make two decisions. Then you can have your way with me."

"Mmmm...deal. But only if you keep kissing my fingers while we plan. At least my fingers."

Mac gave her a sexy smile, which made her regret agreeing to even a moment's planning.

"First," he said, kissing her baby finger, "how soon can we get married?"

"Well... there's some requirement about blood tests... so we'll have to wait until the roads are cleared."

Her answer earned her a serious kiss on the mouth.

"And I think," she added when Mac's lips trailed to her ear, "we should wait until Jason can get a flight here."

"Good idea." Mac's kisses began inching down her throat.

She wriggled a little closer to him, hoping her suggestion about Jason coming for the wedding counted as decision number two.

"And second," Mac murmured, dashing her hopes, "where are we going to live?"

"Oh." That was a serious one. She tried to think, tried to ignore the way the downward progress of Mac's mouth was turning her body to liquid.

"I guess," he offered hesitantly between kisses, "you'd find moving away from Winnipeg, away from your mother, difficult."

"Well... actually... I'm not even sure she'll be living here for much longer."

He stopped nuzzling the swell of her breasts and looked up.

"She and Sid are getting married in April."

"Really?" Mac propped himself on one elbow and grinned. "Good for them. Or are you awfully upset about the prospect?"

"No. Not awfully. Almost not at all, in fact. I'm still a little concerned, but I realize... Oh, Mac, you should have seen how happy Mom looked when she told me.''

"That's great, Holly. So leaving Winnipeg wouldn't be out of the question, then?''

"Well, I might be willing to relocate.''

"As far away as Denver?''

"I'm not sure, Mac. I'd definitely go as far as the ends of the earth to be with you. Is Denver any farther away than that?''

She laughed at his relieved grin.

"Really, Mac, only children may be a bit difficult at times but I'd hardly expect you to give up your firm. And I can't imagine the associates of M. McCloy and Associates wanting to move to Winnipeg.

"Of course, I'll need a little time to make arrangements for my patients. But none of the children I'm seeing at the moment is extremely disturbed—none of them would have major problems adjusting to a new therapist.''

Mac gazed at her silently for a long moment.

"Something wrong, Mac?''

"Wrong? I can't think of anything even close to wrong. I guess I just didn't imagine our planning would be this easy.''

"Do you mean you thought it would take longer? And now you don't know what we'll do for the rest of the day?''

The smile that slowly spread across Mac's face established a new high on the 'sexy smile' scale'. "Holly, I know what we'll do for the rest of our lives. . .''

EPILOGUE

DAVID LAWRENCE SIPPED his champagne, feeling marginally self-conscious about being at Kay and Sid's wedding on his own. He glanced across Kay's living room at Holly. She was talking to her new husband, Mac.

Strange to think that just four months ago he'd been engaged to her. And now she and Mac seemed so incredibly happy together—gazing at each other with open adoration, touching at every opportunity—as if neither one could quite believe the other was real.

David continued watching Holly for another moment, feeling that same peculiar sense of sadness mixed with relief he'd felt when they'd broken up. And then he looked away.

Their breakup might not have devastated him, but watching Holly with Mac was making him more certain than ever that what had been missing from his relationship with Holly had been something missing from within him.

He seemed immune to the insane strain of romantic love that attacked other people. And, if he hadn't been struck down by thirty-four, he was awfully unlikely to ever...

He silently laughed at his musings. What sort of man would wish insanity on himself?

"Dr. Lawrence?"

He glanced down. Mac's son was grinning up at him.

"Yes, Jason?"

"Mr. Lambert asked me to be his messenger."

"He did. What's the message?"

"I'm supposed to tell everyone that his daughter, Christie—his *errant* daughter, Christie, he called her— is on her way from the airport. So the wedding's going to start soon."

"Good. Thanks for letting me know." David watched the boy move on to repeat his message. Holly had gotten a ready-made son. And Jason undoubtedly wouldn't remain an only child.

If love was actually giving David a permanent pass, not having children would be one of his major regrets. Damn, he'd like to have a son but—

Outside, a car squealed to a stop. Sid and Kay hurried to the front door. David casually wandered a little closer to the hallway, wondering why he was curious about Christie Lambert, telling himself it was simply because she'd be the only single woman under fifty at the wedding.

Seconds later a vision appeared in the doorway.

David blinked.

The vision was still there—firmly ensconced on Sid's arm. A vision in a pale yellow silk dress the precise color of her hair.

David stared in disbelief. This gorgeous creature must be Christie. Then his eyes met hers across the room and his heart began to do strange things...

*   *   *   *   *

But Christie and David need a book of their own. And Superromance will be delighted to give them one. Next month watch for Heartbeat, *a June 1990 Superromance by Dawn Stewardson.*

Harlequin Superromance®

A June title
not to be missed....

Superromance author Judith Duncan has created her
most powerfully emotional novel yet, a book about
love too strong to forget and hate too painful to
remember....

Risen from the ashes of her past like a phoenix,
Sydney Foster knew too well the price of wisdom,
especially that gained in the underbelly of the city.
She'd sworn she'd never go back, but in order to
embrace a future with the man she loved, she had to
return to the streets...and settle an old score.

Once in a long while, you read a book that affects you
so strongly, you're never the same again. Harlequin is
proud to present such a book, STREETS OF FIRE by
Judith Duncan (Superromance #407). Her book merits
Harlequin's AWARD OF EXCELLENCE for June 1990,
conferred each month to one specially selected title.

S407-1

HARLEQUIN
American Romance®

THE LOVES OF A CENTURY...

Join American Romance in a nostalgic look back at the Twentieth Century—at the lives and loves of American men and women from the turn-of-the-century to the dawn of the year 2000.

Journey through the decades from the dance halls of the 1900s to the discos of the seventies ... from Glenn Miller to the Beatles ... from Valentino to Newman ... from corset to miniskirt ... from beau to Significant Other.

Relive the moments ... recapture the memories.

Look for the CENTURY OF AMERICAN ROMANCE series starting next month in Harlequin American Romance. In one of the four American Romance titles appearing each month, for the next twelve months, we'll take you back to a decade of the Twentieth Century, where you'll relive the years and rekindle the romance of days gone by.

Don't miss a day of the CENTURY OF AMERICAN ROMANCE.

A CENTURY OF
AMERICAN ROMANCE
1900's

The women...the men...the passions...
the memories....

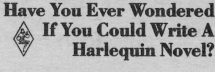

Have You Ever Wondered If You Could Write A Harlequin Novel?

Here's great news—Harlequin is offering a series of cassette tapes to help you do just that. Written by Harlequin editors, these tapes give practical advice on how to make your characters—and your story—come alive. There's a tape for each contemporary romance series Harlequin publishes.

Mail order only

All sales final

HARLEQUIN Temptation

This May, look for

Having Faith
BARBARA DELINSKY

*Faith Barry knew making love with Sawyer Bell
had been a big mistake. He was an old, dear friend,
and they were representing opposing clients in a
complicated divorce case. She wished they'd never
crossed that line between lovers and friends. But they
had. Now Faith faced a new dilemma—how to keep
the courtroom battle out of the bedroom....*

HAVING FAITH, Barbara Delinsky's nine-
teenth Temptation, is as fresh and exciting as
her first, an accomplishment that has earned
Barbara yet another Award of Excellence,
Harlequin's official recognition of its finest
authors. And Barbara *is* one of the finest.

**Don't miss HAVING FAITH (Temptation #297)
in May, only from Harlequin Temptation.**

T297-1

Indulge a Little
Give a Lot

A LITTLE SELF-INDULGENCE CAN DO
A WORLD OF GOOD!

Last fall readers indulged themselves with fine romance and free gifts during the Harlequin®/ Silhouette® "Indulge A Little—Give A Lot" promotion. For every specially marked book purchased, 5¢ was donated by Harlequin/ Silhouette to Big Brothers/Big Sisters Programs and Services in the United States and Canada. We are pleased to announce that your participation in this unique promotion resulted in a total contribution of *$100,000.*

*

Watch for details on Harlequin® and Silhouette®'s next exciting promotion in September.

INS